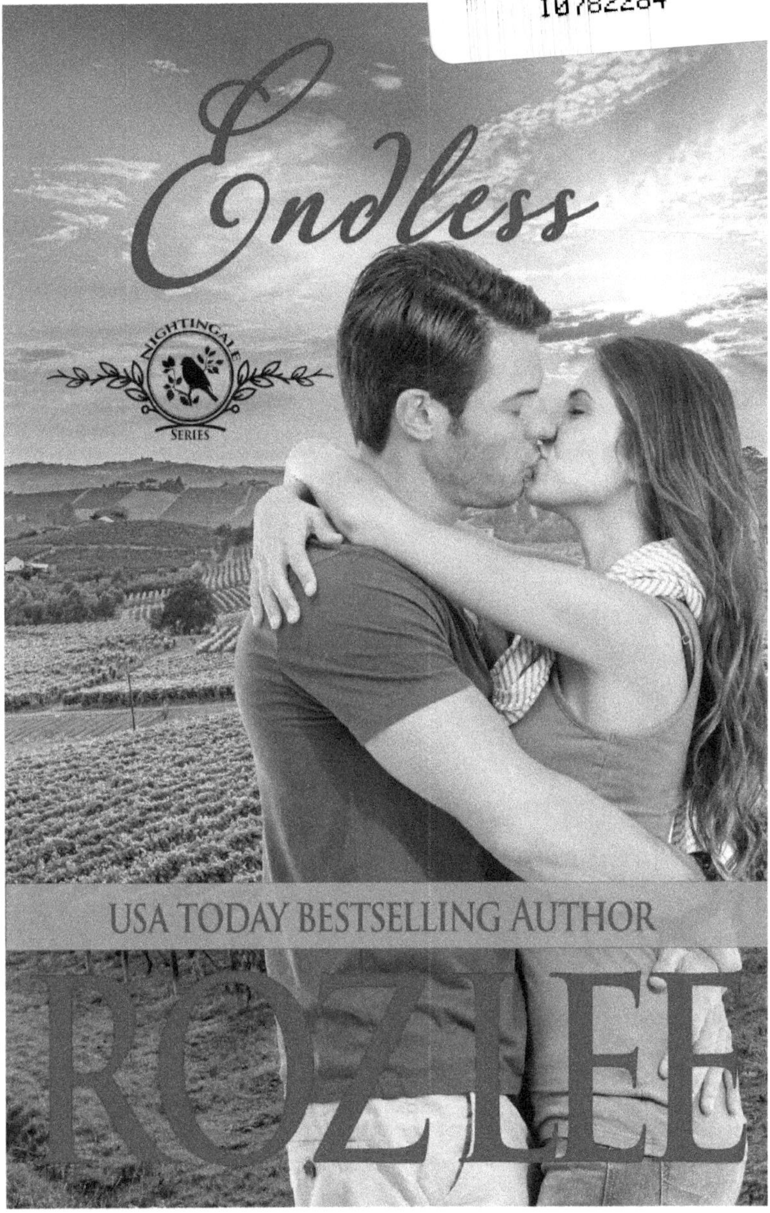
Endless
NIGHTINGALE
SERIES
USA TODAY BESTSELLING AUTHOR
ROZ LEE

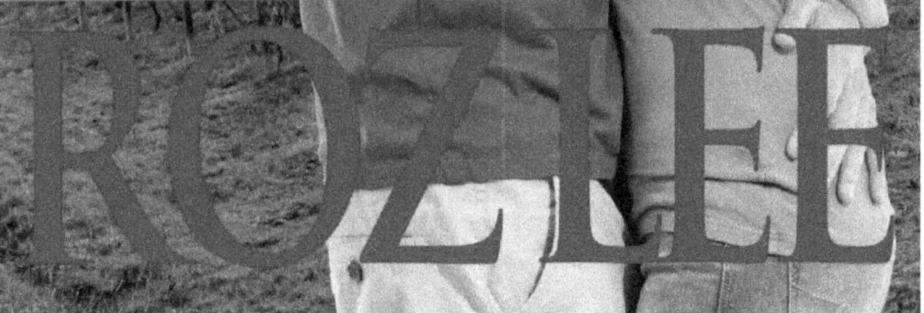

Endless

Roz Lee

ISBN: **978-1-966224-16-7**

DEDICATION

To the Ritter family and all the wonderful folks at Brook
Hollow Winery in Columbia, New Jersey.

.

ACKNOWLEDGMENTS

This book is a work of fiction. Characters, places, and events are all figments of my imagination, though some might be inspired by real persons, places, or things.

Many thanks to Paul, Debbie, and Jessica Ritter, who own and operate Brook Hollow Winery. Your kindness and friendship inspired this book series.

I admit to taking liberties with the television industry. Any errors in regard to the production of television programs are mine.

I invite you to have a glass of wine, sit back, and enjoy the story.

Roz Lee

INTERVIEW – IAN NIGHTINGALE

Host: "Welcome to *Love at First Sight*, Ian."

Ian: "Thanks, Steve."

Host: "The question of the day is, Why are you here? You're handsome. You're a member of the Nightingale family, well-known in the world of winemaking. You're a deputy sheriff, even though you don't need a job. By all accounts, you shouldn't have any trouble finding a date."

Awkward silence.

Ian: [Clears throat. Squirms on the high stool provided.] "I guess all of that is true. Not sure about the handsome part. You're right, though. I've never had trouble finding a date. But finding a date and finding the woman you want to spend the rest of your life with are two different things. I'm not here for a date. I'm here to find the love of my life."

Host: "What makes you think this is the way to do that?"

Ian: "The odds of one of these twelve women being the one I'm looking for are a lot less than the odds of stumbling across her, say…while doing a favor for someone. Wouldn't you agree?"

Host: "That's a rather specific example. Would you like to elaborate?"

Ian: "No."

CHAPTER ONE

"This is going to be a shitshow."

Ian adjusted the ridiculous pink necktie the wardrobe manager insisted would be perfect. He couldn't argue with Wade's assessment of the situation. "You don't have to sound so happy about it."

His brother clapped him on the shoulder. "You will never—I mean, *never*—live this down. What the hell were you thinking, bro?"

"Let's just say I wasn't thinking with my big brain when I agreed to do the show." He shrugged, trying in vain to get comfortable in the suit coat provided for him. Gray was not his color. He looked anemic, despite the stage makeup applied earlier.

"Women can do that to you," Wade agreed. He should know. Serenity had twisted him up in knots until he'd finally admitted he had feelings for her. He was engaged and happy as a pig in shit these days.

"Not women. Woman. Singular." There was only one woman he was interested in. Lexie Hanson. AKA the production manager of this shit show. A reality matchmaking show, *Love at First Sight,* had topped the ratings at home and abroad for the last four seasons. Maybe he was an idiot, but he'd endure a lifetime of teasing from his two older brothers if it meant spending the rest of his days with Lexie.

"I hope she's worth it, bro."

"She is." There was enough confidence behind his statement to earn an Emmy for best actor in a lead role. Maybe he'd missed his calling.

"Lookin' good, Deputy!" The sound of Lexie's voice sent his libido into overdrive. Damn, the woman had him enthralled.

"And that's my cue to get the hell out of here." Wade came in for a bro hug. "I've got shit to do. Nightingale's won't run itself."

"Tell Serenity hello for me."

"Will do."

Alone with Lexie, Ian scowled at his reflection in the mirror. "I look like Pee-wee Herman."

Stepping between him and the full-length mirror, Lexie flashed her megawatt smile at him. "You look hot, Deputy. The women are going to cream their panties when they see you."

He smiled for the first time since arriving on set. "What about you, Alexa?" Leaning in, he discreetly inhaled, taking in her scent—sunshine and wildflowers—a combination that set his libido on fire. Brushing his lips over the shell of her ear, he whispered, "Are you wet for me?"

Her hand on his chest felt like a brand as she pushed him away. "Down, tiger. I've got a dozen women waiting to meet you. They're all beautiful, accomplished, and ready for a relationship. All you have to do is pick one."

"Done. I pick you. You can call this charade off."

Lexie's sigh felt like his personal failure. "We've been over this, Deputy Romeo. You and me," she waved a finger between them, "will never be. You aren't my type."

"You don't know that."

"Trust me, Ian. I know." She smiled again, only this time it didn't meet her eyes. "Casting has done a great job coming up with potential wives for you. Promise me you'll give them a chance."

Ian clenched his jaw, grinding his molars almost to dust. What did a man have to do to break through Lexie's walls? "I will if you will."

"What?"

"I'll promise to give them a chance if you promise to give

me a chance."

"This is ridiculous. *You're* ridiculous. You don't know me at all, Ian."

"And you don't know me," he countered. "Yet you want me to spend the next three weeks getting to know a bunch of women I have zero interest in. I'd rather spend that time getting to know you."

That long-suffering sigh was going to be the death of him, especially when accompanied by a dramatic eye roll. "You signed a contract, Ian. You *are* the Charmed Bachelor, whether you want to be or not."

"Not. Definitely not."

"I have a contract that says otherwise, so suck it up, Deputy Romeo, and you might just find what you're looking for. Our casting crew does an awesome job. Five of the six couples we've matched are still together."

"They screwed up this time." Ian waved a hand toward the Nightingale Vineyard Events Center, where the dozen "contestants" awaited his arrival. "I told them who needed to be in the cast, and they ignored me."

"*I* ignored you, Ian. The final casting decisions are mine. I can't produce *and* be part of the cast. Besides, we've never let the bachelor have any input in the casting decisions."

"Lexie! Lexie! Where are you? Has anyone seen Lexie?" The disembodied voice snagged their attention.

"Get your shit together, Ian. You're due on set in ten minutes. I've got to go."

His gaze followed her perfect ass until she'd cleared the flaps of the tent designated as his dressing room. *Damn.* Every time he got a few minutes alone with Alexa, someone or something interrupted them. How was he supposed to convince her that he'd fallen in love with her at first sight if she only saw him as another pawn in her reality show empire?

"There you are!" The woman's voice that had interrupted them caught Ian's attention. Though she sounded relieved at having located Lexie, there was a hint of panic in her next words. "We've got a major problem." Uninterested in whatever problem might have cropped up, Ian picked up the book he'd brought with him to fill the empty hours between taping sessions. He had no idea what constituted a major problem on a show like this, but he hoped it meant a sizeable delay. The longer, the better, as far as he was concerned.

Absorbed in the excellent story, Ian forgot all about the chaos going on around him until a young man holding a clipboard and wearing a headset poked his head between the tent flaps. "Sorry for the delay. We're back on track now. This is your ten-minute warning."

His natural curiosity almost got the best of him, but then he remembered he wasn't a deputy sheriff here and swallowed the questions running through his brain. If the snafu involved him, someone would say so. Otherwise, it was none of his business.

Taking one last look in the mirror, Ian took a deep breath, then let it out slowly. *Patience.* He had three weeks to convince Alexa to give him a chance. "You've got this, Nightingale. She'll come around."

CHAPTER TWO

"She did what?" Lexie stared into the eyes of the casting director, hoping she'd misheard.

Joy Cox, casting director extraordinaire, grimaced and then repeated herself. "Bitsy Chambers eloped last night."

"Shit!" Clipboard clenched in one hand, the other pressed to the top of her head to keep it from exploding; Lexie paced away, stopped, then paced back. "Who do we have to replace her with, and how long will it take to get them on set?" Time was money. Moving this season's taping to New Jersey to accommodate Ian's work schedule had taken a big bite out of their budget, leaving them with a margin of zero for crap like this.

"That's just it." Joy swallowed hard. "We don't have anyone."

"No one? How is that possible?"

"No one else fit the profile we established as the perfect match for Ian. He's a tough one."

"How hard is it to find twelve women who want to marry a sinfully handsome, rich as Midas, successful, upstanding citizen?"

"He's a LEO."

"What does his zodiac sign have to do with his marriageability quotient?"

"LEO, as in Law Enforcement Officer," Joy clarified. "It's a hard limit for a lot of women."

This couldn't be happening. "What is wrong with these women?"

Joy shrugged. "We had to disclose it in the questionnaire. He has a dangerous job."

"There has to be someone else. All we need is one woman willing to overlook his Dudley Do-Right job."

"Well, there was one other possibility."

"Who is she? How soon can she be here?"

Joy screwed up her face like she had a severe case of constipation. "She's already here?"

"Is that a question or a statement?"

"Statement?"

"We don't have time for riddles, Joy. Is she local or not?"

"Maybe we should have this conversation in private?"

"Why is everything out of your mouth a question?"

"Because I like my job?"

The usually confident woman seemed to shrink before her eyes. Lexie glanced around. They'd attracted an audience. "Everyone! Get back to work!" The crowd scattered like cockroaches in the spotlight. She turned her attention to her casting director. "Who is this girl?"

"You?"

Lexie cocked her head to one side. Pointing a finger at herself, she asked, "Me? Me? Lexie Hanson?"

Joy nodded. "You."

At least it wasn't a question this time. "Have you lost your mind?"

"You're the only other person who met the profile. We usually cast at least fifteen women, but we could only find twelve. Plus, you, but you said you wouldn't do it."

"I won't." *I won't. Jesus, I can't.* His job didn't scare her, but she couldn't risk falling for the man. No matter how attracted she was to Ian Nightingale, she wasn't going to give up the job she'd worked so hard to get, in order to be with him. His life was here in New Jersey. Hers in California.

"Then we only have eleven."

"There has to be someone else."

Joy's head swiveled in the age-old sign of negativity.

"LEO's are a hard sell. No one wants to worry about their husband every time he leaves the house to go to work. Gun-toting men are out of favor these days."

"He's a good guy, not some gangster!"

Joy tried but failed to hide her smile.

"What?"

"You fit the profile perfectly, Lex. Out of all the women we surveyed, your compatibility score was highest."

"It was not."

"Was, too."

Lexie stared at the woman she considered a friend, letting her words sink in. "I can't cross the line, Joy. I'm the person behind the camera, not in front."

"It's your call, Lex, but from a budget standpoint, I don't see that you have any choice. We can shut down production long enough for us to find a replacement, or you join the cast. You don't have to fall in love with him. Just play the part. You can limit your on-camera interactions with him to the barest minimum. The audience will still see twelve women vying for his heart. They'll never know one of them is a member of the production crew. Besides, it would only be for one week, right? If you truly aren't suited, Ian won't give you a charm at the end of the first week, and you'll be back behind the camera."

She had a point. She'd just be another body on the screen. The camera mostly follows the bachelor around as he goes from girl to girl, talking and getting to know them. Occasionally making out. If she told Ian to avoid her as much as possible the first week, then he failed to give her a charm, basically voting her off the show… "That could work."

"Great! Problem solved. You go over to Wardrobe and see what they've got, and I'll speak with the camera operators and let them know to keep you out of the frame as much as possible."

"Wait a minute. What about the hidden cameras?" The sets were riddled with motion activated cameras meant to be unobtrusive and encourage the contestants to act naturally.

"We can't turn them off, but very little of that footage makes it on air anyway."

Lexie bobbed her head up and down. Joy was right. No one would believe how often women dressed to the nines wandered off to a corner to pick a wedgie out of their butt. Most of that footage wasn't suitable for airing. "Okay. Okay. This could work. Tell Ian to stay away from me, too. I'll hang back and let the other women be their pushy selves. No one will give me a thought. I'll be the camera-shy one no one remembers being on the show."

"That's it." Joy pushed her toward the wardrobe tent near the front of the event center. "Go put on something sexy, then head over to makeup. I'll take care of everything else."

What choice did she have? With eleven other women on set, it would be easy enough to stay under the radar. She'd be the shy one, not forcing her attention on the bachelor. The wallflower. Every season had one woman who refused to put herself out there to capture the bachelor's attention. Inevitably, that woman would be one of the first to go. Lexie hated how the show reminded her of a junior high dance, where only the brash girls danced with the cool guys. Everyone else stood around pretending they'd bought a new dress and slept with curlers in their hair just so they could sip warm lemonade and smile like they weren't crushed by their own insecurities.

Rafe, the head of the makeup department, tapped her on the forehead. "Quit scrunching up your face like that."

"Sorry." She attempted to relax her facial muscles. "Got a lot on my mind."

"I just bet you do. Ian Nightingale is one sexy hunk of a man. Too bad he isn't gay. I'd be all over him if he was." He brushed another layer of goop over her face. "You're one lucky woman, Lexie."

"Why do you say that?"

"Because he only has eyes for you." Rafe took a step back to admire his work. "Perfect. Not that you need any makeup, but you know what the lights do to bare skin. We couldn't have you looking like a ghost."

She knew all too well how harsh studio lighting could be. "Thanks for making me up, Rafe." Yanking the tissues out of the collar of her dress, she stood from the chair. "But you're wrong. Ian doesn't want me. He likes a challenge, and that's all I am to him. Mark my words. Once he realizes I'm part of the cast and he can have me, he'll toss me away at the first opportunity."

Rafe shook his head. "Oh, darling. You are delusional. That man is head over heels for you. Just you wait and see."

CHAPTER THREE

"She's doing what?" Ian focused on the woman's lips as he tried to make sense of her words.

"You heard me. One of the women eloped last night with her ex-boyfriend. We couldn't find a replacement, so Lexie will take her place. Just pretend she isn't there. She'll be introduced to you as Alexa. Once the introductions are done, spend time with as many of the other women as possible, but leave Lexie for last. Or don't speak to her at all. That would probably be best." Joy tapped her chin with her ever-present pencil. "The less footage of her available, the less chance any of it will end up in the final cut."

"What if I don't want to ignore her?"

"Then she'll probably cut you off at the knees as soon as the cameras shut off. Our budget is tight on this production, and a lengthy delay would put us in the red. Lexie has never busted a budget, and she's determined to maintain her winning record."

Ian had never been happier to be on a strict budget than he was right that moment. He'd have Lexie right where he wanted her for the next three weeks. No doubt she'd give him hell for keeping her on the show week after week, but a desperate man would take any advantage he could.

At Joy's insistence, he followed her from his tent to the

event center, where all the indoor scenes were to be shot. He'd seen the proposed layout that divided the space into several sound stages, but the reality of it was overwhelming. "Has Wade seen this?" he asked as they navigated miles of cables, aka trip hazards. Lighting standards and control panels created a maze he'd need a map to find his way out of.

"He has." She pointed out the set that would be used for individual interviews with the contestants—including him. "This is the smallest set. We've already taped interviews with the women, except for Lexie."

"What about my interview?" He'd been told to expect to answer questions as to his motivation for being there. Intrusive stuff like, "You're a good-looking guy with resources, why are you on TV looking for a wife?" Since the truth wouldn't work, he'd been trying to come up with a good answer for weeks and still had nothing.

"Don't worry about it. Someone will let you know when and where it will be."

Joy paused the tour in front of a larger set decorated to look like a modern but cozy private alcove with an overstuffed loveseat covered in white velvet. A plush rug would cushion bare feet—or knees. Lamps set on glass-topped tables would provide mood lighting. "You'll bring the women here for more intimate talks." If not for being open on two sides, he could see himself making out with Lexie there. "Come on. Times a-wasting. We'll start by taping the introductions to the other women. We'll work Lexie into the crowd when she's done with hair and makeup. She'll be the last one you meet." She used air quotes around the last word. "I know you're not an actor, but do your best to pretend you've never met her."

He didn't think that would be a problem. The woman took his breath away every time he saw her. In her presence, it was difficult to remember his own name sometimes. "Got it." He dodged a boom microphone. Joy was a head shorter than him and had the advantage of knowing where she was going. He almost ran her down when she abruptly stopped and turned to face him.

She pointed to a giant plywood wall braced with 2 x 4s. "This is the primary set. The group scenes will take place here. It's supposed to look like a Manhattan bachelor pad. The kind of place a rich dude like you would live in, so own it, Ian. Make yourself at home. You're the lord of the manor, so to speak." She waved him forward. "Come on. You'll have a couple of minutes before the first woman arrives at your penthouse party via the elevator."

"Elevator?"

"This is pretend, Ian."

They rounded the fake wall into another universe. How the hell had they built this inside the event center? The brightly lit set appeared massive. Spread out before him was an ultra-modern living space, complete with floor-to-ceiling windows that showcased the Manhattan skyline beyond a fake terrace. The furnishings were black, white, and gray with chrome accents. Scattered pillows, knickknacks, and the occasional potted plant added pops of primary colors to the otherwise bland backdrop. Suddenly, the gray suit and pink tie made sense. "Jesus. Who lives like this?"

"You do. For the next three weeks."

"I knew Hollywood was fake, but this is…crazy." And absolutely nothing like his current home. He was more of a brown leather, hand-me-down sofa sort of guy. He preferred comfort over appearance and had never met a potted plant he liked. His idea of décor was a television with an 86 inch screen and a reading lamp he'd found beside a dumpster while on patrol. He'd dusted it off and rewired it to be on the safe side. He could afford fancy furnishings like the ones they'd chosen for his fake penthouse, but this wasn't him.

Ignoring his criticism, his guide pointed to what appeared to be stainless steel elevator doors. "The women will arrive one at a time via the private elevator. You'll greet them with a glass of wine and a smile. They'll tell you something about themselves, then move away. Once they're all here, you'll go over and mingle, just like you would at any other cocktail party. Be yourself. Make small talk. Get to know them a little. None of this is scripted. Hidden microphones and cameras will capture everything. We'll edit the footage after the fact."

"Lexie will be last to arrive?"

"That's the plan for today. We'll edit her time on camera down to the barest minimum, but you don't have to worry about that. Treat her like all the others, and we'll be good."

Lexie wasn't like all the others, and he had no intention of treating her like she was. An hour ago, he'd dreaded the next three weeks. Now, he couldn't wait to get started. Scrap that. He couldn't wait to welcome Lexie to his Manhattan penthouse. "Let's get this show on the road."

Joy put two fingers between her lips. The ear-piercing whistle brought techs of every description scurrying out of the shadows. Enormous lights clicked on. A woman who looked vaguely familiar hustled onto the set. After positioning Ian where she wanted him, she barked out orders to the rest of the crew, reminding him where he'd seen her before. "You're Lexie's assistant. Right? I saw you at the Malibu house."

"Yeah. That's me. You were the asshole standing in the corner with the strawberries. Took balls to sneak on the set like that."

"It was for a good cause."

"I'd love to hear all about that, but can we save it for another time?" Her voice dripped with sarcasm. "With Lexie out, I'm in charge of herding the cats, and let me tell you, they don't follow directions."

"Got it. I'll just stand here and keep my mouth shut."

Her smile was almost as blinding as the lights trained on the set. "You'll do, Ian Nightingale."

"Thank you."

"I really hope you find your match." Then she was off, barking more orders. A few minutes later, a *ding* sounded, and the fake elevator doors opened to reveal a stunning blonde dressed to kill.

"Hello," she said, the elevator doors swooshing shut behind her. "I'm Haley. It's nice to meet you."

He'd have to be dead to miss her beauty, but as lovely as she was, he felt nothing when she raised up on tiptoe, wrapped her arms around his neck, and pressed her ample assets against his chest. Setting her back a step, he flashed her a genuine smile. "It's nice to meet you, Haley. Thanks for coming." He handed her a glass of Nightingale Chardonnay, sending her on her way.

And so it went. Eleven stunning women. Eleven glasses of Chardonnay. Eleven hugs. Zero sparks.

Before his trip to Malibu to locate Sean's missing woman, he would have jumped at the chance to date any of these women, but he'd come home a changed man. He'd met Lexie Hanson on the Malibu set of *Love at First Sight* and fallen head over heels in love with her. She, however, was fighting her attraction to him. Why, he didn't know, but he intended to find out.

"Last one," the production assistant called out.

Ian's heart raced. He wiped his sweaty palms on his trousers and tugged at the collar of his shirt. Christ, those lights were hot, and with his body temperature skyrocketing at the thought of seeing Lexie, he was sweating like the proverbial stuck pig.

Swoosh!

The fake doors parted, sucking all the oxygen from the room. Ian's lungs seized, and his mouth felt like it was stuffed with cotton. The most beautiful woman he'd ever laid eyes on stood before him. The red evening gown she'd chosen clung to every one of her generous curves like it had been painted onto her luscious body. A slit up one side revealed a long, toned leg and a slender foot encased in a bejeweled high-heeled sandal. Her gorgeous, thick mane of hair had been gathered into some sort of updo that left her neck exposed. Dangling earrings skimmed the tops of her bare shoulders and called attention to her wildly beating pulse. As she took the first step toward him, he shifted his focus to her face. *Gah!* The day he'd met her, she had worn no makeup—or at least none he could detect—and still, he'd thought her beyond beautiful. But now, done up like a fashion model, she was simply breathtaking. Her blue eyes sparkled like jewels under the bright lights, and her lips painted the same shade of red as her dress lit a match to his libido. Images of all the things he wanted to do to her, with her, flashed like a highlight reel through his blood-deprived brain.

"Cut!"

"What's wrong?" Lexie's lips moved, and words seemed to be coming from her mouth. "Ian." She snapped her fingers in front of his eyes. "Say something!"

"Someone get him some water. Cut the lights!"

CHAPTER FOUR

"Ian."

Concern. He heard it in the single syllable of his name. Forcing his gaze from Lexie's lips, he fell into her eyes. Twin pools of unease that snapped him out of his daze. "I'm fine. Just a little overheated." *Understatement of the century.* He was burning from the inside out. "I'm sorry." He grabbed the water bottle that suddenly appeared in front of him and drank half of it down in one long gulp. He couldn't take his eyes off Lexie. She was so far out of his league it wasn't even funny, but realizing his shortcomings did nothing to quell the desire ravaging his body. "Give me a minute, and I'll be alright." Raising the water bottle to his lips again, he closed his eyes and took a fortifying sip. Then another and another until nothing remained. He dropped his hand containing the empty container to his side but kept his eyes closed. *Shit.* His head was pounding, and his blood had pooled in his lower extremities. He recognized the cause of both. Dehydration for the headache. He should have thought to hydrate, but he hadn't expected the lights to be as hot as they were. Maybe he could blame dehydration for the reallocation of his blood supply, but it would be a lie.

"Ian."

Eyes still closed, he tried to alleviate Lexie's concern. "I'm okay." He tugged at his collar. "Give me a minute." He made the mistake of opening his eyes. The lights felt like spears jabbing into his skull. He swayed. Lexie caught him, steadying him with her hands against his chest.

"Whoa, there."

"I'm okay." He wasn't, but it felt like the right thing to say.

"You're not okay." Her arm came around his waist. "Turn the lights off! Now! And someone get him another water!" Lexie at her finest. Most of the lights clicked off, but not all of them. Several remained, including the one inside the fake elevator. Her dress shimmered in the indirect light, making her look like an angel. "Water! Where the hell's the water?" A pissed-off angel, but an angel, nonetheless.

Another water bottle was placed in his hand. He took a sip. That and the dimmed lights helped his headache. As long as Lexie was touching him, even in a non-sexual way, there wasn't anything to be done about his blood flow. It was what it was. "I'm good. Feeling better already."

"Everyone, take five." Lexie in charge. This was the woman he fell in love with that first day. Bossy. Demanding. A tiger when it came to taking care of the people she loved. She wasn't in love with him, but her concern for his health, or state of mind, at the moment was enough to give him hope. Wrapping both her arms around him, she walked him over to the ugly gray sofa vacated by the other contestants and guided him down to the cushion.

"Are you okay?"

Shit. Was he? He didn't know. "Yeah. Just had a moment there. You took my breath away." He smiled, trying to make a joke of what was, in reality, the absolute truth. "Maybe the lights had something to do with it. I don't know. For a second there, I couldn't get air in my lungs." He reached for her hand. It was the first skin-to-skin contact he'd had with her, and it felt more right than anything he'd ever done. He sucked in a deep breath and then let it out slowly. "Probably should have taken a break sooner. Hydrated better."

"I'll talk to my assistant about that. She should have known better, but then again, this set situation is different than what she's used to. It's not as open. Less natural airflow. I'll see what I can do about adjusting the air conditioning, too."

Nothing short of a nor'easter was going to reduce his body temperature around Lexie, but he'd let her do her job. "Thanks. I'm sure that will help. I'll try to remember to hydrate before taping sessions from now on."

"You do that." She patted his hand with her free one before removing her hand from his. "Sit here for a few minutes. I'm going to go see about the air conditioning and have a little chat with Emma."

He watched her perfect ass as she left the sound stage. Once she was out of sight, he closed his eyes and flopped back on the couch with a groan. His hand still tingled where he'd held hers. How in the world had he thought this was a good idea? What had sounded like three weeks of Heaven ahead of him now looked more like Hell. Pure torture. He thought he'd been okay with the other women. Nice. Polite. But there was only one woman he wanted to put his hands on, and she was off limits. Or was she?

"Hey." Wade's voice broke into his musings. "One of the crew said you'd freaked or something. I came to check on you."

Ian sat up. "I just got a little overheated. Can you show Lexie how to operate the air conditioning? The studio lights are hotter than the sun." He tugged on his sweat-soaked collar. "Especially in this get-up. The women get to wear barely there gowns, and I'm stuck in a suit. It's not fair."

Wade laughed. He clapped Ian on the shoulder, then stood. "I'll find Lexie and get the air conditioning situation under control. Maybe you should take your coat off for a few minutes."

"Once this thing comes off, it's not going back on." Ian stood. Taking in another deep breath helped with the headache, and talking to his brother helped alleviate the blood flow situation. "Besides, we only have to finish taping Lexie's intro, then we're done for the day. I think."

"You think wrong." Ian turned to see Lexie's assistant headed his way. What was her name again? Emily? Amy? No, those didn't sound right.

"What the hell else is there to do? I met them all."

"This is a cocktail party scene. You have to mingle. Talk. Take a few of them over to the alcove set if you want. The audience needs to see you making an effort to get to know the women as individuals. How else can you form an attachment to one of them?"

Wade scoffed, drawing Ian's attention and what's her name's ire. "I'm out of here. Again. Good luck with your dates, bro."

Ian shook his head at his brother's teasing. It was only going to get worse, of that he had no doubt.

"The ladies are on their way back. We'll finish up with Lexie, and then you can mingle for a while. You do know how to mingle, right?"

"Yeah. I've done it a time or two." *And hated every minute of it.* The din of women's voices coming toward the sound stage was enough to make Ian break out in a sweat—again. "Everybody's back. Lexie's in the elevator." Emma inhaled then blew out a breath. "Okay. Let's get this shot. Then you can mingle with the others for a while."

The lights were back on, and he was sweating like a pig again as he waited for the signal that the elevator doors were about to open. Ian steeled himself to see Alexa again. No other woman had ever affected him the way she did, and that was something he couldn't ignore. She was Delilah to his Samson. She stole his breath and made him weak in the knees, but at the same time, he felt an overwhelming need to take care of her. The woman worked too hard and gave too much of herself to the people she cared about. In that, she reminded him of his mother. There was another woman who didn't know when to stop. Self-care wasn't in either woman's vocabulary. His mother had his dad and her three sons to make sure she took time for herself, but Lexie had no one. According to Sean, who got it from his wife, who was Lexie's best friend, Lexie had lost her mother when she was just a kid, and her father had been distant ever since. According to Angellica, Lexie's dad had recently taken a job in Australia, leaving Lexie all alone. Ian sometimes hated how close the Nightingales were. His brothers were always up in each other's business, and his parents weren't much better. But given the alternative, maybe it wasn't so bad after all.

Ding!

Like Pavlov's dog, Ian's body immediately reacted to the ingrained stimulus. His blood rushed south, leaving him lightheaded again. Thankfully, the water he'd consumed during the break helped, and he remained on his feet. The doors opened on a *swoosh*, revealing the woman of his dreams. Any attempt at corralling his body's response to her would be futile. Aching to touch her, to claim her, he stepped forward, taking her hands in his as she exited the elevator.

Her fingers were cold, and her smile warm. "Hi. I'm Alexa, and I'm from Southern California. It's nice to meet you."

"The pleasure is all mine." Remembering his part in all this, he offered her a wineglass. "Join me in a drink?"

Alexa's fingers brushed his as she took the glass from his hand. "Thank you."

"That's good." The disembodied voice from off-stage was the equivalent of a bucket of cold water thrown on them. Lexie stepped back, putting too much distance between them. "Move on. Mingle. Time is money!"

Watching her step away from him caused him physical pain. "Where will you be?"

"Over there." She waved a hand in the general direction of the living room set. "Somewhere."

Ian took that to mean she planned on hiding behind a potted plant or something. He'd see about that. She could evade and resist all she wanted, but Ian was in hot pursuit, emphasis on the hot, and wouldn't stop until he had her in custody. His. For the rest of their lives.

Eager to put his plans into action, Ian played his part flawlessly. As he made his way over to the ladies awaiting their time with him, he monitored Lexie's movements. She remained on the periphery of the action, sometimes actually stepping out of the set so she wouldn't be in camera range. She was a slick one. Like a thief, she knew all the angles and how to avoid being captured. But everyone made mistakes, and he'd be there when she did.

In the meantime, he held up his end of the bargain. So it wouldn't seem like he hadn't given the woman with the dog a chance; he approached her first. "Hi, I'm Ian. I'm sorry, I don't recall your name."

"I'm Kelsey." She held the poodle up so they were cheek to cheek. "And this is Snookums." The ball of off-white fur squirmed in her hands. "Give me a kiss, baby girl."

Ian looked on with horror as Kelsey made kissy sounds at the dog, who wiggled even more before flicking its tongue out to lick at her owner's lips.

"Isn't she adorable?" She shoved the kiss-happy dog

toward Ian's face. "Your turn! Give Ian a kiss, Snookums!"

His first instinct was to reach for his TASER, but he quickly recalled he was out of uniform. No TASER. No gun. Not even a baton. Without a weapon in sight, he threw his hands up, blocking the canine just inches from his mouth. "No, thank you. I'm good. Don't want to mess up the makeup." He took a step back. "But she's a cutie." He didn't even choke on the lie.

Actually, now that he thought about it, the dog and the owner bore a remarkable resemblance to each other. Similar hair. Similar beady eyes. How had this woman made the cut? He'd seen the questionnaire all the women were asked to complete. In theory, every woman here should be reasonably compatible with him. For the life of him, he couldn't imagine what Kelsey and he could have in common.

Lowering the dog to rest on her hip, the woman did a Barbie hair flip and batted her fake eyelashes at him. "What do you do for a living, Kelsey?"

"I'm a ski instructor."

Ian nodded. *Okay.* He liked to ski. Had been on his high school and college teams. "That's a seasonal job, isn't it? What do you do the rest of the year?"

"Well," she stretched the word out as she twirled a lock of her bleached blonde hair with her free hand. "I tend bar at night, and I like to go to the beach as much as possible."

"Oh, you live down the shore, then?" He used the slang term New Jerseyites use to refer to the coastline.

Her brows knit in confusion. "No." Another long, drawn-out syllable. "Yes? I don't know what you mean by that, but I live in Fort Lauderdale most of the year. I have a condo with an ocean view. During ski season, I live in Aspen." She leaned in as if to confide something. Ian bent to hear her softly spoken words. "My parents have a chalet there."

Oh. *Well.* He dragged the word out in his mind. That explained a lot. "That's…convenient." She had *pampered heiress* written all over her.

"It is. I'd love to take you there sometime." A bejeweled fingernail flirted with his pink tie.

Ian took another step back. "I'm sure it's beautiful. If you'll excuse me." He held up his wineglass filled with sparkling water, downing the last of it in one gulp. "I need a refill."

Safely out of reach of the heiress and her poodle, Ian's gaze sought the one woman he wanted to talk to. As predicted, Lexie had found the only quiet corner on the set. Resting on the arm of an overstuffed chair, she occasionally took a sip from the glass of Nightingale Chardonnay he'd given her at their fake introduction. If he had to guess, those sips were fake as well. After each one, she'd sweep her tongue over her lips, grabbing the scant drops of wine clinging to her lips. To the casual observer, she appeared to be enjoying her own company. Ian wasn't a casual observer. He'd been trained to look deeper, and what he saw filled him with both admiration and need.

Lexie Hanson was a damn fine actor. By all appearances, she was simply resting in a quiet corner, but Ian saw right through her charade. Her practiced eye took in everything happening on the set. From the cliques forming among the women to the not-so-subtle scheming looks on some faces. He'd even caught a glimpse of her smirk when he dodged the kiss from Snookums. Lexie was shrewd. And totally in control of everything around her, even when she wasn't.

Mercifully, no one stopped him as he made his way to the bar cart, where he filled his glass to the rim, drained it, then filled it again. He really needed alcohol to get him through this, but with the bright lights and the confining suit, water was a better option. The game he was playing demanded his full attention if he hoped to win the ultimate prize.

Surrounded by a dozen women dressed to impress and eager to catch his eye, Ian fought the urge to call for backup. There'd be no backup. He was on his own. Mingle, Lexie had said. Get to know the women. He translated that decree to mean, pretend you give a damn. He'd never had trouble attracting female attention. Didn't need to have some casting director hunt up women for him. But here he was, acting the part of the wealthy bachelor looking for a wife. All because the production manager, Lexie Hanson, refused to go out with him unless he auditioned for the role. Three months later, Lexie said she'd be in New York for a couple of nights and invited him to join her for dinner. She'd brought a contract with her.

That dinner was the closest he'd come to a date with his now sister-in-law's best friend.

Rocking back on his heels, he sipped from the wine glass a

production assistant handed him when he walked in. Taping at the vineyard was all Serenity's idea. He had to admit, Wade's fiancée had negotiated well on behalf of his family business. Nightingale wines had an exclusivity clause in their contract with the production company which meant, at the very least, he wouldn't have to drink cut-rate swill while he pretended interest in a dozen random women. He got to work part-time at his regular job during the three-week taping. The extra money from the show would allow him to start construction on his dream house without touching his trust fund. He'd purchased a parcel of land last year and couldn't wait to move out of the condo he'd lived in since graduating from the police academy.

A commotion behind him on the set drew his attention.

The argument escalated quickly. He stepped between the women in time to prevent the raven-haired chick from slapping the blonde. "Whoa. Whoa there." He grabbed the slapper by the wrist. "I don't know what this is about, and I don't want to know. Cut it out or you're both out of here." He glanced toward the corner where Lexie's assistant had set up shop to watch and direct the camera shots to the action. Undoubtedly, the whole encounter had been recorded. It was just the kind of salacious stuff the publicity crew would use to drum up interest in the show. "These two need to go somewhere and calm down."

He turned them over to the handler, who escorted them off the set. He smiled inwardly. Brawls he could handle. Simpering women pretending to be interested in a relationship with him? Not so much. Call him crazy, but he'd rather break up bar fights than face the gang of females waiting for a scrap of his attention.

A bottle-blonde darted from the crowd to place a staying hand on his forearm. She batted her fake eyelashes at him. "That was awful." Her tomato-red, collagen-enhanced lips pouted. "But you handled it with such authority. I like a man who takes charge." Her lashes fanned the air. Her pout turned seductive. "If you know what I mean?"

Yes, he was afraid he knew exactly what she meant but wasn't sure *she* did. She struck him as the type to say whatever she thought her prey wanted to hear. He wished he had a set of handcuffs with him. She'd probably run screaming if he offered to cuff her to a chair for a little playtime. He gently removed her hand from his arm and put several inches between them. "Someone had to take charge…"

"Fawn," she supplied.

Ah, yes, Fawn. Age twenty-eight. Graduate of the Newark School of Cosmetology. Currently employed as a hairdresser. Divorced. *Twice.* Lexie knew how to pick 'em. "If you'll excuse me, Fawn, I was just on my way to speak with someone."

She muttered something as he strode away that sounded suspiciously like "asshole." If he was lucky, she'd withdraw from the competition and save him the trouble of having to eliminate her.

The next hour lasted an eternity. As he spoke with each contestant individually and in spontaneous clusters, he formed opinions on each of them. He couldn't see himself spending more than a few minutes with any of them.

INTERVIEW – KELSEY (CONTESTANT #2)

Host: "Welcome, Kelsey."

Kelsey: "Thank you, Steve. It's good to be here."

Host: "Who do you have there?"

Kelsey: "This is Snookums." Holds up poodle. "Isn't she adorable?"

Host: "Uh. Yes. Adorable. Uhm. Well, you met our bachelor, Ian Nightingale, tonight. What was your first impression?"

Kelsey: "Honestly?"

Host: "Of course."

Kelsey: "I didn't like him. Snookums didn't either."

Host: "Oh? Why not?"

Kelsey: Shrugs. "He's nothing like I thought he would be."

Host: "How so?"

Kelsey: "He has a job. Like a real job. I don't understand that. He's rich, right? Why would he want to work all the time? Especially in the kind of job where he has to wear an awful uniform and carry a gun." Shivers. "I mean, if it was a nice uniform, you know, like the kind the Marines wear, it might be different, but his is brown. Brown! Dirt is brown."

Host: "Ian puts his life on the line to help keep the citizens of his community safe. Surely the color of the uniform is of lesser consequence."

Kelsey: "Surely there are other people out there who need jobs who could do that? I don't see why it has to be him?"

Host: [Rolls eyes.] "Does that mean you aren't interested in receiving a charm from Ian at the end of the week?"

Kelsey:[Looks offended.] "I didn't say that. I want a charm! I deserve a charm! Snookums deserves a charm, don't you, precious baby?" [Holds dog up so it can lick her lips.] "Besides. We turned down an offer to spend the month on a yacht in Key West to be on this show. How would it look if we left after the first week?"

25

CHAPTER SIX

Lexie pretended to sip from her glass as she watched from her perch on the arm of a chair she'd had moved to the corner of the set. She'd checked the camera angles and verified this was out of range of all but one camera and that one would show only her back. It was the perfect place to observe the other contestants as they interacted with Ian.

She couldn't have chosen a better person for this season's bachelor. The man hailed from a wealthy, established family with a well-known history in the wine industry. He'd finished at the top of his class in high school, college, and the police academy. He dated, but not excessively, and every ex they could find said they'd parted friends. Ian Nightingale didn't flaunt his wealth. Working long shifts as a deputy sheriff in the remotest areas of New Jersey, he put his life on the line every day for a pittance compared to what he could make working for his family's wine business. On top of all that, he shared the same heart-stopping features as his two older brothers. And when he flashed his lopsided smile, women melted at his feet.

Watching him flirt with the other women was difficult, but watching every interaction was literally her job. She'd think watching her was *his* job if she didn't know better. She couldn't count the number of times she'd caught him watching her while the woman, or women, in front of him tried to engage him in conversation. Maybe it was the cop in him, or maybe he was a good listener because all the women, including the one with the poodle, vomited words at him while he stood there, looking like he was interested in everything they had to say. So far, not a single one had caught on that while he absorbed their stories, his attention was on someone else. Her. She'd have to speak with him about that. It had to stop before the other women picked up on it. The last thing she needed was to become embroiled in some kind of in-house drama with the real contestants. There'd be no way to remain in the background if that happened.

He'd been listening to the investment banker from Chicago go on about how she'd spent a summer in Italy learning all about wine production in order to better advise her clients who wanted to invest in the wine industry. Blah. Blah. Blah. All bullshit. The only wine investment she was interested in was Ian. The Nightingale name had brought out a few gold-diggers. Miss I studied grapes in Italy, was one of them.

Knowing the sound tech would pick up her comment, Lexie muttered under her breath. "Tell him to move on. One more, and then he needs to take one to the alcove for a private chat."

You never knew how a bachelor would perform under pressure. Some clammed up and had to be coaxed to take their next breath, much less make small talk with the women. Others never let the women get a word in edge wise. Ian seemed to have a talk show host's ingrained ability to put people at ease. *Probably something he learned in Interrogation 101: How to get the suspect to confess to everything from stealing from a friend's lunch box when they were six to murder, in under ten minutes.*

In her peripheral vision, she saw Emma out of camera range, twirling her index finger in the age-old motion meant to encourage forward progress. Ian dipped his chin, acknowledging the assistant producer's instructions. Lexie breathed a sigh of relief as Ian politely excused himself from the gold digger. Her relief was short-lived when his gaze landed on her. A moment later, he moved toward her.

No. She gave her head a little shake, hoping he'd pick up on her cues and turn away. Her heart picked up the pace as her mind swirled with possible scenarios. Maybe this was a good thing.

If she remained aloof, no one would question why he failed to give her a charm at the end of the week. But there was a fine line between aloof and rude. Blatant disinterest on her part would raise suspicion from the other contestants, who wouldn't miss a thing. This was a winner-take-all contest. With the affections of a man like Ian Nightingale at stake, knowledge of the enemy was power.

Then there were the viewers. If any of her interactions with Ian made it into the final cut for this or any other episode, her reaction to him could result in viewer backlash. Controversy could spike viewership, or it could tank it. She didn't want to be a part of any of it.

Don't do this. Don't do this. Talk to her, Ian. Please. That one's a criminal justice professor. Talk to her.

Her telepathic begging did nothing to sway Ian from his course. Resigned to playing her part, Lexie stood as he drew near. The smile she plastered on her face was so brittle it's a wonder it didn't flake off. "Hi." Maybe if she took charge of the conversation from the beginning, it wouldn't veer out of control. "Are you having a good time tonight?" It was the middle of the day, but Ian had to work tonight at his real job so they'd used some Hollywood magic to make it appear to be evening outside the fake windows.

He cocked his head to one side, his gaze delving beneath the façade. "I am, but it just got a lot better."

"Why is that?"

"Because I'm talking to you."

"That's a cheesy line, don't you think?" She wasn't too worried about what she said to him. Most of their encounter would be cut, anyway. "Do women fall for it?"

Ian shrugged. "Can't say. I've never used it before. It's never been true before." He sounded so damn sincere Lexie forgot for a moment that he was acting for the cameras. Before she could think of a witty comeback, he continued. "What are you doing over here in the corner? All by yourself?"

The truth—minus the feeling left out part—seemed like the best way to go. "Watching you work the room like a pro."

He did that head cock thing again. "You seem sad, Alexa. Want to talk about it?"

No. She absolutely didn't. Forcing her smile wider, she endeavored to give the editing staff something they could use. Something to explain her early exit from the show. "Truthfully? I was sitting here thinking it was a shame you weren't anything like I thought you would be."

Instead of being taken aback by her statement, Ian threw his head back and laughed. "Oh, boy. I knew it. You're the kind of woman who speaks her mind. Nothing fake about you. I like that."

Lexie's heart rate spiked. What the hell was he doing?

"Come on." Ian stuck his hand out in silent invitation. "Let's go somewhere more private so we can talk."

"No!" The editors were going to kill her for creating all this unusable content. "Go ask someone else."

All the mirth left Ian's face. "I don't want to ask anyone else, Alexa. Only you."

Those last two words, dripping with sincerity, brought her racing heart to a screeching halt. She took his outstretched hand, not to let him lead her away but to shake some sense into him. "What are you doing? This is not the way this is supposed to go."

"It's not? I thought I was here to find the love of my life. How am I supposed to do that if I don't follow my heart?"

Lexie ground her molars. "Your heart is leading you astray, Mr. Nightingale. Perhaps you should engage your brain in the decision."

The insult landed on deaf ears. He tugged her forward so there was barely an inch of space separating them. "Where's the fun in that, sweetheart? My heart is telling me you need to spend more time with me. Get to know me better before you write me off entirely."

With every eye in the place on her, she'd look like a real bitch if she turned him down. The editors would swoon at that kind of drama, and she'd find herself the unwitting center of attention in the first finished hour of taping. Not a place she wanted to be. Inwardly sighing, she looked the most exasperating man she'd ever met in the eye. "Maybe you're right, Ian. Let's go somewhere we can talk." Anyone with ears could hear the air quotes around the word *talk*. Let them think what they would. Only the two of them and the production staff would know their private conversation consisted of her ripping the star of the show a new one. Yanking Ian forward, Lexie grumbled to Emma as they passed by. The young assistant caught up with them at the darkened alcove set, where Lexie dropped her contestant persona and donned her woman-in-charge hat.

"Send the rest of the women to hair and makeup, then start the next round of individual interviews. Make sure to ask them about their first impression of Ian. That lawyer from Albany and the Paralegal from D.C. seem to be at odds with each other. See if you can fan that into a rivalry or bitch fight. Anything we can use to draw attention away from whatever this one," she pointed to Ian, "thinks he's doing with me."

Emma listened wide-eyed, then scurried off, leaving Lexie alone with Ian. To give the illusion of privacy on the alcove set, the lights, cameras, and microphones were all activated by motion sensors. As soon as they stepped foot on the set, it would come to life, recording their every word and action. When Ian turned to enter the set, Lexie yanked him back. "Oh, no you don't. You want a private conversation? You're going to get one." Barreling on, she didn't give him a chance to respond. "I don't know what you think you're doing, but it isn't going to work, Ian. So stop it. We're strapped for time on this production—because you insisted you wouldn't take leave from your job, so don't mess this up! Play by the rules, or I'll—"

"Or you'll what? Fire me? Good luck with that, sweetheart. The only reason I signed on to do this show in the first place was to be close to you. And I *am* playing by the rules. You're the one who put yourself in the cast. That makes you fair game." He snaked his free hand around her waist, drawing her up against his hard body. "You're the only one I want to spend time with. The only one I want to kiss."

"We can't do this." Her protest sounded weak even to her own ears. Her gaze locked on Ian's lips, drawing nearer and nearer. "Ian?" She wasn't sure what she was questioning. Could have been to see if he'd heard her. Could have been to find out why his lips hovered so close to hers but never connected.

His breath feathered over her lips. "What, Alexa? What do you want from me?"

Wasn't that the million-dollar question? "Ian." Not a question this time. A plea, maybe? Being in his arms felt good. Right. Like it was where she was meant to be. "I want…" *Everything.* "I…"

"Want me to tell you what *I* want?" His voice was a husky growl that made her lady parts tingle, and her knees grow weak. Swallowing hard, she squeaked out an affirmative reply.

Disentangling their hands, he cupped her jaw, tilting her face up so that with a dip of his chin, their gazes met and held. "I want to know everything there is to know about you. I want to spend endless days and nights mapping your curves, memorizing the way you taste on my lips, the sounds you make when I touch you in just the right way, the right place. I want you to give yourself to me. To let your pleasure be my pleasure. I want to hear my name on your lips when you come. Then I want to do it all again until there is no you and me, only us."

Lexie stared into his mesmerizing eyes. His words echoed in her mind, empty of everything that wasn't Ian Nightingale. "Think about what *you* want, Alexa. You know where to find me when you're ready."

INTERVIEW – ALEXA (CONTESTANT #12)

Host: "Welcome, Alexa."

Alexa: [Fake smile. Playing it up for the camera.] "Thank you. It's good to be here."

Host: "You had a chance to speak one-on-one with Ian at the cocktail party last night. What did you think of him?"

Alexa: "He's very nice."

Host: "That's all you've got to say?"

Alexa: [Taps finger on her chin.] "Yes, I believe that's all I've got to say."

Host: "But, you were the only woman Ian took to the alcove for a private conversation. Can you tell us anything about that?"

Alexa: "No."

Host: "No?"

Alexa: "No."

Host: "Did he indicate why he chose to take you to the alcove?"

Alexa: "Not that I recall."

Host: "Did you discuss anything in particular?"

Alexa: "We made small talk. Then he left."

Host: "He left?"

Alexa: "Yes. What part of that don't you understand?"

Host: "I get it. You don't want to discuss what went on between you two. Let's move on. Do you expect to receive a charm from Ian at the end of the first week?"

Alexa: "Absolutely not."

INTERVIEW – IAN NIGHTINGALE

Ian: "I thought we'd already done this."

Host: "That was your *before* interview. This is the first impression interview."

Ian: "First impression of what?"

Host: "Of the contestants. Now that you've met them all and had a chance to speak with them, we'd like to know what you think."

Ian: "They're a bunch of beautiful women. All with something about them that makes them unique."

Host: "Did anyone catch your eye?"

Ian. "I don't know what you mean. I just said they're all beautiful."

Host: Clears throat. "You only chose to have a private conversation with one."

Ian: "That's correct."

Host: "Why Alexa? And can you tell us what the two of you talked about?"

Ian: "Alexa because I wanted to hear her voice, and no, I can't tell you what we talked about. That's the definition of private."

Host: "You left immediately after speaking with her. The other women were disappointed. They were hoping to have more time to get to know you."

Ian: "Is there a question in there somewhere?"

Host: Refers to his cue cards. "In her interview, Alexa said she doesn't expect to receive a charm from you at the end of the week. This is a question. "Will you give Alexa a charm at the first-week ceremony?"

Ian: "Absolutely."

INTERVIEW – SYLVIA FROM ALBANY (CONTESTANT #3)

Host: "Are you having a good time, Sylvia?"

Sylvia: "I am. I think Ian is falling for me. He's so sexy in a suit. He should wear them more often."

Host: "At the welcome reception, you had an altercation with one of the other contestants. What was that about?"

Sylvia: "She thinks she has a chance with Ian. I told her that wasn't the case. He's worth millions, if not billions. She's nothing. A paralegal."

Host: "You're a lawyer?"

Sylvia: "Top of my class at Upstate University."

Host: "Did you say Upstart University?"

INTERVIEW – CHARMAINE FROM D.C. (CONTESTANT #7)

Host: "How are things at the B&B? Are you all getting along?"

Charmaine: "Sure. We're all friends."

Host: "It didn't look like you were friends with Sylvia the other night. What happened there?"

Charmaine: "You mean at the welcome reception? That was nothing. A silly misunderstanding. We cleared that up. We're besties now."

Host: "Oh? I'm not sure Sylvia would agree with you. Should we bring her in and ask her?"

Charmaine: "Okay. You got me. She's a bitch. Thinks Ian's going to choose her because she's smarter than the rest of us combined. It took her four tries to pass the Bar Exam. How smart is that?"

Host: "Do you expect to receive a charm from Ian at the end of the week?"

Charmaine: "We have so much in common. He'd be foolish to send me home."

INTERVIEW – KRISTINA FROM SEATTLE (CONTESTANT #5)

Host: "You had a long chat with Ian last night. Tell us about your first impression.

Kristina: Twirls a lock of her long brown hair around her index finger. "He's everything I thought he'd be. He's even more handsome in person and more intelligent than I thought he'd be."

Host: "Why were you surprised by his intelligence?"

Kristina: "Well, you know. He's a cop. They aren't the smartest people, which begs the question: Why would a man as rich and smart as Ian Nightingale take a job as a cop?"

Host: "Deputy Sheriff."

Kristina: [Brows knit in confusion.] "Same difference." [Shakes her head.] "I don't get it. He could work at Nightingale's. In an office."

Host: "The charm ceremony is in a few days. Do you expect to receive one?"

Kristina: "Why wouldn't I? We'd be perfect together."

CHAPTER SEVEN

As soon as Ian let her go, without so much as brushing his lips over hers, Lexie staggered to her rental car and fled to the only place she was guaranteed privacy. She tapped a nervous rhythm out on the dining table in the house she rented for the duration of the taping. "Come on, Jelly. Pick up!" Though her best friend was pregnant with triplets, with the three-hour time difference across the continent, Jelly should be awake. But then again, she was married to the middle Nightingale brother, Sean. They were probably together somewhere doing something Lexie didn't want to think about. To hear Jelly tell it, the pregnancy hormones made her horny, and her husband was more than happy to scratch her itch.

She was happy for her best friend, but she really needed to talk to her. This thing with Ian had gotten completely out of control, and she needed her best friend's advice on how to handle her brother-in-law.

"Lexie! How are things going in New Jersey?"

"Horrible. I'm in deep, Jelly. Ian…he…won't cooperate. He's making a mess of things."

"Wait. What do you mean he won't cooperate? He signed a contract. He has to play the part of the bachelor."

"Oh, he's playing the part, but he's made it clear there's only one woman he's interested in, and he cornered her today and said some…suggestive things to her." Lexie bit her lower lip, hoping her best friend wouldn't pick up on the things *she* hadn't said.

"What kind of suggestive things? Like sexual harassment things? He's a cop, for goodness sakes. He should know better."

"Are they sexual harassment if the person he said them to creamed her panties and had weak knees when he left without kissing her?"

Silence stretched over the three-thousand-mile gap.

"Jelly?"

"I'm here. Just processing."

More silence than Jelly came back on the line. "Are *you* the person Ian said those things to?"

Lexie dropped her forehead against the tabletop and groaned out her answer. "Yes. But nothing can happen between us."

"Why not? You'll tape for three weeks, and then his obligation to the network is done. Can't you both wait three weeks?"

"It's complicated."

A deep sigh preceded Jelly's reply. "Explain."

Jelly was going to make a great mom. The woman had ways of making people talk. So, Lexie talked. She told her friend how she'd become a contestant on the show and how Ian had agreed to vote her off at the first opportunity, but how he kept looking over at her even while he was engaged in conversation with one of the other women. "He made it clear he's going to continue pursuing me."

"But he didn't kiss you? Didn't touch you inappropriately?"

"No. He got me all hot and bothered, then just left me standing there."

"So, you wanted him to kiss you?"

"Yes. No! I don't know," she groaned. "What am I going to do?"

"What are your options?"

"Regarding the show? None. He's supposed to eliminate five women each week for the first two weeks. That'll leave two women the last week. If I leave, that'll throw the whole thing out of whack. And it's too late to find a replacement. We taped the opening segments today. We're on such a strict timeline here because we blew the budget moving the production to New Jersey so Ian wouldn't lose his job…" she paused to take a breath, "there's no time to spare. I'm stuck being the twelfth contestant until Ian comes to his senses and lets me go."

"Want me to ask Sean to talk to him? He would if I asked."

"No. Please don't do that. Besides, I don't think it would help. Ian's…" she searched for a word that didn't mean dominant or domineering and came up short. "He doesn't strike me as the type to take advice from his older brothers. He's a grown man. For heaven's sake, he carries a gun. Everywhere. He wanted to carry on the set, but the network lawyers shot that down. Pardon the pun." She'd seen photos of Ian in his uniform. He was absolutely drool-worthy. Women probably broke the speed limit around here all the time, hoping to be pulled over by Deputy Nightingale. She'd suggested they let him wear the uniform on set, but Ian's boss had said no to that.

"I could talk to him."

"And say what? Quit talking dirty to my best friend?"

"You'd want me to lie to him?"

Rather than deny how much she'd enjoyed the dirty little interlude, Lexie sighed into the phone. "If Sean is half as sexy as his younger brother, I can see how you fell so hard for him. I don't know where I'm going to find the strength to resist Ian, but I have to. For the sake of my job and my sanity."

"Would it be so bad to let this play out?"

"You mean act like a real contestant?"

"I barely know Ian, but maybe he's just playing with you. If you play along, maybe he'll back off."

"Or maybe he won't."

"Look, I've got to go. Sean went to the airport to pick up my dad. He decided to come see for himself that Sean didn't coerce me into marrying him."

They'd eloped shortly after finding out they were pregnant with triplets. Three boys if Sean's déjà vu moment was to be believed. "Have you told your dad about the triplets?"

"No." She could almost see Jelly's brows knit at the

admission. The woman was good at a lot of things, including making wine, but she'd never be able to stand up to her father. "I'm afraid to."

"Why? He likes Sean, and he loves you. You're his only child, and now you're going to give him three grandbabies at the same time. He's going to be ecstatic."

"I hope you're right. We plan to tell him at dinner tonight. Sean's even breaking out some of the new wine blends, hoping that will soften him up before we break the news."

Lexie laughed. "If anything will soften the old man up, that'll do it."

"They'll be here any minute. I've got to get dressed. I bought a new sundress that hides my bump pretty well."

A pang of jealousy stabbed Lexie's heart. Or was it longing? She wasn't really jealous of her best friend. It was more that her friend had found everything she didn't even know she was looking for when she fell in love with Sean Nightingale. Jelly and Sean made it look so easy. Love at first sight. If Lexie's show proved anything, it was that the first spark of love often fizzled out in the cold light of day. "Wear something tight. Shock the socks off your dad the second he walks through the door. Get it over with because if I know you, you'll worry yourself sick over his reaction. So, put it out there from the beginning. He'll be happy for you, Jelly. Especially once he sees how happy you are with Sean."

"You know me too well, Lex. And I know you, too. If you want Ian, let nothing get in your way. You've always gone for whatever you wanted, and you never fail when you put your mind to something."

"I'll think about it. Go. Get ready for dinner with dear old dad. Wear that purple knit. The one that looks like Merlot. It's fabulous on you and will show off your bump to perfection."

"Okay. You talked me into it, but only if you tell Ian you're interested."

"Deal," she lied. At least one of them would get their happy ever after.

CHAPTER EIGHT

"This is the worst idea ever." They'd been shuttling the women out to a stretch of road that once led to a fertilizer factory, all so Ian could pull them over for speeding. One at a time. "Whose idea was this anyway?" Lexie asked as her assistant handed over the fake license and registration she would give Ian when he pulled her over.

"It was your idea. You said seeing how the women reacted to being pulled over would be fun. So far, we've had three break down into tears. Two tried to bribe their way out of a ticket with money. Two others offered to trade sex for not being written up. One forgot it wasn't real and vowed to fight it in court. As soon as he handed her the fake ticket, she took off like her ass was on fire. Probably would have gotten another ticket if it had been for real."

"Must have been the lawyer."

"Yep. The rest of them flirted shamelessly with him but, otherwise, were gracious about being caught speeding. I tell you, if someone as hot as Ian pulled me over, I'd consider the ticket a fair price for the eye candy and pay up. No questions asked."

Lexie ignored the side commentary, though she couldn't exactly argue the point. Deputy Ian Nightingale was H.O.T. "How's our bachelor doing?"

"He says it's all in a day's work. Besides, he gets to sit in the patrol car with the air conditioning running most of the time. He's only out of the car for the five minutes it takes to write a pretend ticket, and then he's right back in his car."

"He's sticking to the script?" In order to simplify the process, they'd written an abbreviated version of what would transpire in an actual encounter. The main point of the activity was to emphasize Ian's job and to see how the women would react. The "speeding car" was tricked out with cameras, and Ian wore a body cam that would provide fabulous, authentic-looking footage for the editors.

"He does, but the conversations sometimes take off in a different direction. He's been good about letting them dig themselves in deep before he shuts them up with the ticket."

In order to get a genuine reaction from the women, they hadn't been told anything about today's exercise other than that Ian would pull them over for an imaginary motor vehicle violation. Ian's initial words were scripted, but after that, he was on his own. "I'm sure he's heard it all before."

"It's your turn." Emma opened the driver-side door and motioned Lexie inside. "Buckle up and remember to ease to the side of the road when he lights you up."

They'd borrowed an actual patrol car from the sheriff's department to add authenticity to the fake stops. It had all sounded like a good idea when she'd dreamed it up, but that was before she joined the cast. She hated seeing the blue lights flash in her rearview mirror. It had only happened twice before—once for failing to stop completely at a stop sign, and she'd been pulled over once for failing to use her turn signal. Both times had left her shaken. Not once, in either of those encounters, had she lusted after the officer ticketing her. "I'll do my best." Pulling the door closed, she dropped the faux paperwork in the passenger seat. Her assistant waved her off. "Here goes nothing," she mumbled as she accelerated down the closed road.

He should have pulled me over by now. She'd passed the spot where all the others had been pulled over, and still no sign of flashing blue lights in her rearview mirror. How much roadway had they closed down for this little charade? She couldn't recall the exact amount, but there was supposed to be a patrol car at the far end to divert traffic. Where was that?

A car passed her, in the opposite direction, and she instantly knew something was wrong. This production was going to be the death of her. It was one thing after another. Fuming at the time wasted, she watched for a place to turn around. As she passed a dirt track that intersected the road she was on at an angle that made it an undesirable place to turn around, a car screamed onto the road behind her. Siren blaring, blue lights flashing, the driver closed the distance between them until he was right on her bumper. Despite knowing this was staged, her heart raced. It was totally ridiculous to feel this way, but she couldn't help it. She'd always been a do-gooder. It was her nature to avoid trouble.

Gently reminding herself this wasn't real, she eased the car to the side of the road and cut the engine. It seemed like forever before Ian exited the cruiser. Not the sedan they'd used for all the previous encounters, but an SUV that filled her rearview mirror. Watching his approach in the side-view mirror, she couldn't help but admire the man. Not many men could make brown look good, but Ian rocked it. Or rather, his good looks and his confident mannerism made the color of the uniform irrelevant. When he was alongside her car, she rolled her window down. *Here goes.*

"Good afternoon, ma'am. Do you know why I pulled you over?"

"No, officer. Was I speeding?"

"It's deputy, and yes, I clocked you doing sixty. The speed limit on this stretch of road is forty-five."

"I'm sorry…deputy. I must have been distracted."

"I need to see your license and registration."

Lexie handed over the fake documents. Aware that Ian's body cam was recording her every move, she put her hands on the steering wheel and looked straight ahead while he examined the two items.

"Ma'am, I need you to step out of the vehicle."

"Wh…what?" This wasn't part of the script.

Hand on the butt of his weapon, Ian took a step back. "Please, exit the vehicle."

Perplexed, stunned at Ian's behavior, Lexie opened the car door and climbed out. The hot asphalt beneath her feet was no match for the white-hot anger brewing in her gut. "What's going on? This isn't part of the script."

"Turn around. Place your hands on the roof of the car and

spread your legs."

"You can't be serious? Ian, what's going on here?"

"Is this your car, ma'am?"

"No. It's a prop we borrowed from one of the locals to tape these scenes. You know that."

"Ma'am, this car has been reported stolen. The name on the registration is the same as the person who reported it stolen. Please, turn and place your hands on the roof of the vehicle."

"Serenity reported the car stolen? I don't believe it."

"Believe what you want, but you're under arrest for possession of a stolen vehicle. Now, turn around and assume the position."

"Ian, this is ridiculous. Let's get back to the script. All this can be edited out."

"Ma'am, I suggest you do as I say, or you'll be charged with resisting arrest in addition to the stolen vehicle charges."

Lexie searched his face for a crack in the veneer. His stern countenance proved impenetrable. This wasn't Ian, the reality show Bachelor. This was Deputy Sheriff Ian. And he was pissed. With one last pleading look that got her nowhere, Lexie turned and placed her hands on the roof of the car.

"Spread your legs."

She moved her left foot a few inches.

"More."

"Ian," she pleaded even as she complied. "Is this necessary?"

"Absolutely." He stepped in close behind her, and before she could take a full breath, his hands bracketed her wrists. His breath teased her ear. "Are you carrying any weapons, drugs, or other illegal items?"

"Of course not! Ian, let me go."

"I'm going to have to frisky you, ma'am."

Lexie opened her mouth to argue, but his hands slid down her bare arms to her shoulders, stealing the air from her lungs. When he palmed her breasts and pressed his groin against her bottom, she bit her bottom lip to keep from groaning out loud.

Ian growled in her ear, "I've been waiting to do this for ages. You're perfect, Alexa. So, damned perfect."

Holy, fuck. Knees weak, it was all Lexie could do to remain upright as Ian thoroughly searched her. Given their time constraints and maxed out production budget, she should call a stop to this, but for the life of her, she couldn't. All her previous anxiety about being pulled over melted under the heat of his hands on her body and the timbre of his voice as he drew her hands behind her back and cuffed her. "I promise you're safe with me." A promise she knew to be true. Ian wouldn't hurt her. So, whatever game this was, she'd go along with it. For now.

CHAPTER NINE

"Where are we going?" Sitting on the hard fiberglass rear seat of Ian's patrol vehicle was uncomfortable, to say the least. Having her hands cuffed—real cuffs, not the sexy kind—made relaxing impossible. They'd been driving down the dirt track where he'd been lying in wait for her for several minutes. "I've got to go over yesterday's edits and prep for tomorrow's charm ceremony. I don't have time for…whatever this is."

His gaze met hers in the rearview mirror. "We're almost there."

"Are the handcuffs really necessary?"

"You're a hard one to get to talk to. Not taking any chances."

She glanced out the window. Nothing but trees. If she were with anyone else, she'd be in a panic, but this was Ian. "Where would I go? On foot?"

"Still not taking any chances." He turned off the road onto another dirt track and then slowed to a stop. "How are you doing back there?"

"How do you think I'm doing? Take me back to the winery. I've got work to do."

"Not until we talk."

"I'm not talking to you while I'm in a cage."

"Fair enough." Ian shut the SUV off. In seconds, he opened her door, released her seatbelt, and helped her out of the vehicle.

"Aren't you going to take the cuffs off?"

"Not yet. I like having you at my mercy."

His steady gaze and stoic jaw told her he wasn't kidding. He really did like having her at his mercy. Her heart pounded, and her skin tingled as she imagined all the ways he could bring her to her knees. Desperately needing to diffuse the situation before she threw herself on his mercy, she wiggled her eyebrows. "Are you into kink, Ian?" To emphasize her point, she rattled her cuffs.

"If, by kink, you mean do I prefer to be in control in the bedroom, the answer is yes." He took a step toward her. She took a step back. "If you're asking if pain turns me on, the answer is no." Another step forward. Lexie retreated, her back hitting the side of the SUV. "Unless it heightens my partner's pleasure." Another step forward. He placed his hands on the vehicle on either side of her head, boxing her in. He leaned down so his face was on a level with hers. His gaze raked over her features, pausing eventually on her lips.

Her breath froze in her lungs, anticipating his kiss. Instead, he dipped his head, and his nose skimmed her jawline.

"You smell so fucking good, Lex. I want to eat you up." His lips fondling her earlobe sent a shiver down her spine. When his teeth nipped at the soft tissue, her long-neglected lady parts melted.

"Ian," she breathed.

"You like that? A little pain?" He bit her lobe again, then followed it up by sucking the sensitive flesh between his lips and flicking it with his tongue. A low moan escaped her as he continued to nuzzle her neck. Lips. Tongue. Teeth. Not vampire bites, but tiny little nips he immediately soothed with his tongue. "Imagine all the places on your body where a little pain would feel good."

She was having no trouble imagining his mouth working its way down her body. Her nipples were hard buds, anticipating his touch. She clenched her thighs together, imagining his mouth there. She'd never been a fan of oral sex, but Ian could probably change her mind.

"Has anyone ever spanked you, Lex?"

Unable to form coherent words, she shook her head. She'd never seen the appeal.

"Spanking can arouse, or it can be cathartic. It can also be a form of discipline."

She found her voice. "Punishment?"

"That, too." He dropped one hand to her ass, gave it a hard squeeze. "The first time I saw you, you were bossing people around out in Malibu. My hand itched to paddle your ass."

She shook her head. "No."

"No? Are you certain about that, Lex?" He squeezed her cheek again—a possessive squeeze that hurt in the best possible way.

"What do you want from me?"

"Everything, Lex. Every goddamn thing. But I'll start with owning your ass."

"What does that even mean?"

"It means I'm going to spank you."

She shook her head again. "No."

He worked his fingers beneath the waistband of her leggings. His big hand caressed the globe of her ass, the heat of him branding her. "Does that feel good, Lex?"

Fuck, yeah. "That's not the same as a spanking," she evaded.

"If I promise not to harm you, will you let me spank you?" He stroked her skin, then squeezed again. Her resolve slipped the tiniest bit.

Would it be so bad? She'd read romance novels with spanking scenes, but until she felt Ian's hand on her butt, she'd never thought there might be something to the kink. "I don't know."

"Let me put this another way." His hardened gaze met hers. "I'm going to spank you, Lex, and you're going to let me because we both want this."

"Ian…I…okay." Who was she kidding? The idea of baring her ass to him excited her, and it had been a long time since a man had made her feel that way. "Take the cuffs off."

"Not yet." Before she could protest, he yanked his hand out of her pants and grabbed her by the elbow. "Trust me, Lex, they'll enhance the experience."

She followed him to the edge of the small clearing to a large tree stump. He sat then pulled her down over his thighs. He held her secure with one arm while his free hand yanked at the waistband of her leggings until the sun beat down on her skin. Knowing Ian had an unfettered view of her ass was unexpectedly arousing but not arousing enough to overcome her trepidation. "I don't know…"

"Shh. No arguments. If you want me to stop at any time, say red. Otherwise, I'm going to spank you ten times. Count them in your head so you can gauge how much more you can take."

Ten times? The thought made her clench her cheeks.

Ian placed his hand on her lower back. "Keep your hands out of the way." He stroked a finger down her crack. "Relax. It will hurt worse if you clench."

The instant she unclenched, he landed the first blow and then followed it up by stroking the abused skin. "Ouch!"

"This isn't meant to be punishment, but since you can't keep your mouth shut, I'll add another one for every word that isn't red."

The second blow landed on the opposite cheek, followed by three more in quick succession, before he paused to soothe the sting away. "Fuck, I love seeing you like this. Trusting me with your body. You're doing great, Lex. Just a few more."

The heat of his palm felt so good, and she couldn't lie. Lying across his lap with her bottom exposed was kind of hot. The first five had initially hurt, but the pain had morphed into something else. Something that made her pussy throb and her nipples hard. Hearing his praise warmed her from the inside out.

He landed the next five, one after the other, so fast she almost lost count in her head. Her skin was on fire. She tried but couldn't stifle the whimper that pushed past her lips. Ian brushed his hand over her inflamed skin. "Shh. You've been such a good girl. Let me see how wet you are." One long finger parted her cheeks before slipping between her legs to stroke her swollen, oh-so-wet flesh.

"Gah." She squirmed, trying to get closer to his elusive digit. He skimmed her clit once, then withdrew, wiping her juices off on her bottom.

"Now that we know a little spanking makes you horny, it's time for your punishment."

Punishment?

Before she could formulate a response, his hand came down so hard it brought tears to her eyes. She tried to get up, but his arm banded around her waist pinned her in place. "Red! Red Ian! Red!" He immediately released her, helping her stand. Crap, that had hurt. Her legs trembled, and with her pants down to mid-thigh and her hands still cuffed behind her back, she felt exposed and vulnerable. Fighting tears, she demanded, "What was that for?"

"That was for talking when I told you to keep your mouth shut. I told you I was going to add one for punishment."

The tiniest of breezes brushed over her inflamed skin, making her all too aware of her sore bottom and the arousal pulsing between her legs. She choked back a sob. She'd never been into any of this—bondage—spanking—kinky stuff. But maybe she should have. She'd never been so turned on in her life. Not that she was going to tell Ian.

"Take the cuffs off. Now."

"Not until you admit the spanking turned you on."

She wouldn't admit it. Wouldn't give him the satisfaction. Not with her ass hanging out and still tingling from his touch. Not with her pussy throbbing, aching. "You're infuriating. Let me go!"

He brought his fingers to his nose and sniffed. "I can still smell your arousal on me. You don't have to admit you liked being spanked, Lex, because we both know it's true."

He stalked toward her; his movements measured. Calculated. Moving behind her, he placed a palm on her butt cheek, his touch instantly soothing, though she wouldn't admit that either. The man was way too cocky. Too sure of himself. "Don't touch me." The moan that escaped her lips made the words a lie. "I don't want you to touch me." There. That was better. Until he pressed his lips to her ear.

"Don't lie to me or to yourself, sweetheart." The hand on her ass squeezed then soothed with gentle strokes. "Every lie that comes out of your mouth from now on is worth two spanks. Not the kind that arouses you. The kind that brings tears to your eyes. Do you understand?"

Eyes closed tight; Lexie pressed her lips together into a thin line. God, he smelled good, and Lord, the things his touch did to her body. This…kink wasn't her. But once she'd gotten past the initial fear, her body reacted in the most unexpected way. She didn't believe him when he said she'd like it, but he'd been right. Used to controlling everything around her, she'd had no choice but to relinquish control to Ian. The initial shock and pain had quickly morphed into need, stoked to pleasure by his tender ministrations and probing fingers. Not that she was ready to admit any of that to him or to anyone else. She needed time to process her feelings.

His hot breath fanned her ear. "You are so stubborn, woman." A nip to her earlobe that sent a shiver down her spine. "So in control all the time. I bet you've never let yourself go. Let someone pleasure you unless it was your idea."

He wasn't wrong. In her experience, men couldn't find a clit without a trail guide and didn't know what to do with one when they finally found it. She'd grown accustomed to being both guide and instructor, but even her taking charge didn't always guarantee her pleasure. Somehow, she didn't think Ian needed any help.

His fingers delved between her legs, found her opening. "You're so wet. Ready. Needy. I could give you what you need right now, but you aren't ready for my kind of loving. Not yet."

When he withdrew his fingers, she almost cried out in frustration. Then he dropped to his knees behind her. Hands bracketing her hips, he pressed his lips to the meaty part of her ass in a passionate kiss she knew would leave a mark. She bit her lower lip to hold in her cries as her pussy flooded and her knees weakened. Needing to touch him, she flexed her fingers until they came in contact with his hair. Until that moment, she couldn't believe it was happening, but it was. Ian Nightingale was marking her. No one had ever marked her before. She never would have allowed it if they'd tried, but this was Ian. He'd spanked her, brought her to the brink of orgasm, then punished her for disobeying him. But this. This was more intimate than the spanking. More intimate than his fingers probing her secret places. This said, *you're mine* in a way she couldn't ignore but remained private. Only the two of them would know what he'd done to her. How he'd shifted the ground beneath her feet and made her want things she hadn't known existed.

She felt the loss of his possessive lips all the way to her toes. Her fingers itched to feel his hair again as he sat back on his heels. Still holding her by her hips, he brushed a thumb over the mark he'd made. "Beautiful. Your ass is still red from my hand, and now you wear my mark." With a sigh that sounded a lot like regret, he stood, bringing her panties and leggings up to cover her. "Got to get you back to work." Keys jingled, then he worked the locks on the cuffs, freeing her hands. Ending the scene. "You can ride in the front this time."

CHAPTER TEN

Lexie's hands trembled on the steering wheel as she navigated back to the winery. Ian's patrol SUV loomed large in her rearview mirror—an unnecessary reminder of what had just transpired between them. Her ass stung where he'd spanked her, and though the mark he'd left would fade, the feel of his mouth on her, claiming her, would live in her memory forever. Thinking about it brought a flush to her cheeks and tears to her eyes. His shenanigans had put them behind schedule, something that wouldn't go unnoticed. How she was going to explain her traffic stop taking three times as long as any other was yet to be seen. Thank God, most of it wasn't on camera. Ian had switched off his body cam after stuffing her into his vehicle. No one would know what he'd done to her. What she'd *let* him do to her. Things she couldn't stop thinking about.

Don't think about it. It's over. Focus on tonight's pool party. Once Ian sees all those beautiful women in bikinis, he'll forget all about me.

Lexie pulled up next to one of the equipment trailers and got out. "Sorry to be late." She gestured toward the car. "Get the camera equipment out ASAP and return the car to Serenity. I think you'll find her over at the tasting room." She took a few steps, then stopped. "Oh, and make sure it has a full tank of gas before you return it." It was the least they could do, since Serenity refused to accept payment for letting them use it all day. She was halfway to the production trailer when a familiar figure fell into step beside her.

"Whatever you want, Ian, I don't have time for it. And you don't either. The pool party starts in fifteen minutes."

"Won't take me long to change into swim trunks."

"They should be waiting for you in Wardrobe."

"Yeah, no. I saw what they'd picked out. No way I'm wearing that. I'll wear my own, thank you very much."

Lexie came to an abrupt halt. Hands on her hips, she stared him down. "You'll do as I say, Ian Nightingale. You signed a contract, remember?"

"I remember. Said contract did not specify that I had to wear any particular garments."

"You're right, but it did say you would participate fully in all planned activities. Wearing the wardrobe provided is implied as participation. Put the swimsuit on, Ian. Now." She pointed her arm toward the wardrobe tent. "Then get your ass over to your brother's house. We're losing daylight."

"Fuck, you're sexy when you get all bossy. Makes me want to do all kinds of things to you. For you."

"Ian," she warned, even as her body reacted to his words. He'd done more than enough to her body already. If he did anymore, she'd be a puddle of goo, and that wasn't her. She didn't go gooey over men, and she never let them tell her what to do. "If you like it when I'm bossy, then you're going to love this." She narrowed her eyes at him, and, using the voice that never failed to get results from her underlings, she growled, "Get your ass moving. Now!"

"Yes, ma'am. I'm going." He flashed her a crooked smile and slapped her butt as he headed toward the wardrobe tent. "See you at the pool!"

Lexie fought the urge to rub her sore bottom. He'd barely tapped her as he walked by, but the light touch made her skin tingle and sent a jolt of awareness to her pussy. It had been a long time since she'd been so attracted to a man, and none had ever touched her the way Ian had. None had ever made her question her sexual preferences like he did.

Stop! Stop thinking about it! She chastised herself as she climbed into the production trailer. She had work to do.

"I'll go over the edits after the pool party," she said as her phone rang. Glancing at the screen, she excused herself. Outside the trailer, she pressed the phone to her ear. "Emma. I'm on my way to Wardrobe right now. I'll need a ride to the pool in a few."

"No worries. Ian has a golf cart. He's waiting for you outside the wardrobe tent. Hurry up. The others have been here for a while, and some of them are pretty liquored up. Should be interesting."

"Wait!" Too late. Her assistant had ended the call. Lexie dropped her chin to her chest, and, closing her eyes, counted to ten. Nothing about this production was going right, and she seemed powerless to fix it. *Just twenty-four more hours until the charm ceremony. Ian won't give me a charm, and I can get back behind the camera where I belong.*

Lexie entered the wardrobe tent from the back. Since no encounter with Ian ever ended the way she thought it would, it was best to avoid him as much as possible. The wardrobe attendant spotted her and rushed forward with a few scraps of fabric in her hands. "There you are! Here," she shoved the tiny pile into Lexie's hands. "You can change in there." She pointed to a makeshift dressing room built into one corner of the commercial tent.

"What is this?" Lexie held the bundle out. It fit easily in one hand.

"A swimsuit. I know the color is odd, but they said you didn't want to stand out."

"It's…I'll look like I'm naked!" She shook her head and tried to force the woman to take the thing back. "No. I want a one-piece. Black." Black would make her look slimmer.

"Nothing like that here." The woman nodded to the bikini in Lexie's hand. "Should have gotten here earlier. That's the only one left. Good thing it's your size. Better get moving. That handsome bachelor is waiting out front for you." She walked over and held the curtain aside to reveal the bare-bones changing room.

Their budget was tight, but there wasn't room for one more swimsuit? On leaden feet, Lexie trudged inside the phone-booth-sized enclosure. The curtain dropped, sealing her inside. "I'll go tell the hunk you'll be right out."

"My underwear covers more," she said, studying her reflection in the mirror positioned outside the changing room.

"Maybe I should put them back on." The flesh-toned fabric did indeed make her look naked.

"Nonsense. You look spectacular! Not that anyone will notice you, with all the others wearing bright colors. You'll fade into the background." The woman stood off to the side, her seamstress eye going over the fit.

Lexie's phone rang. She didn't bother to pick it up. It had to be Emma calling to tell her to get her ass moving. My ass! Shit, she'd forgotten all about the mark Ian had put on her. Turning, she looked over her shoulder. The seat of the bikini bottom was nothing more than dental floss. Her pinkened ass cheeks stood out like beacons against her otherwise pale skin. And right in the center of her left cheek was a mouth-sized bruise. Disbelief warred with an emotion she wasn't prepared for—pride.

"Oh, hon, is that what I think it is?"

Lexie glared at the woman. "Get me a cover-up. A towel. A skirt. A shirt. Anything." Heart pounding, Lexie couldn't take her eyes off her reflection as she imagined Ian on his knees, his mouth pressed to her skin in a place only a handful of men had ever seen. None had ever staked their claim the way he had. Twisting, she placed her hand over the place his lips had been less than an hour ago.

"That's a doozy, hon. You've every right to be proud."

"What?" Lexie spun to face the woman. "I'm furious! He had no right."

The older woman raised an eyebrow as she held out a man's dress shirt. "Unless he held you down or tied you to the bed, I'd say you could have wiggled your ass out of reach. But you didn't, and he staked his claim. Did a good job of it, too. That's going to be there for a while."

Lexie snatched the shirt out of her hands. She jabbed her arms into the sleeves, all the while remembering the feel of Ian's hands on her hips as he kneeled behind her. Realization heated her face. She could have gotten away. *If I'd stepped out of his reach, he would have let me go.* But she hadn't moved. She'd stood stock still while he put his mark on her.

Her phone buzzed again, dragging her thoughts back to the present. A quick booty check in the mirror confirmed the shirttails dipped below her butt cheeks. The tightness in her shoulders eased. She'd have to be careful, but as long as she didn't take the shirt off or bend over, no one would see what Ian had done to her. Not that they'd know *he'd* put the mark there, but the optics were bad. She was supposed to be single, unattached. The hickey on her butt suggested otherwise. The other women would eat her alive. They were honest about their intentions, and she was anything but. They'd come here looking for a relationship with Ian while she had one she didn't want.

"Run along, sweetie. It's getting late, and I'm overdue for my break."

Lexie's phone rang again. She picked it up and accepted the call. "On my way. I'll hop out of the cart before we get in camera range so the women won't see me arriving with Ian."

"Okay. That'll work. I'll give them a heads-up that he's on his way." She clicked off just as Lexie plopped into the seat next to Ian.

CHAPTER ELEVEN

"Let's go. We're late." Lexie clutched the grab bar mounted to the dash in front of her. Painfully aware of Ian's naked torso almost shoulder-to-shoulder with her, she kept her gaze trained on the trail ahead. Ian expertly steered them through the maze of tents, trailers, and trucks until they were speeding through the vineyard toward his brother's house. They hit a bump that almost launched her out of the cart. Settled back on the seat, she glanced at her driver and instantly wished she hadn't. "What the hell are you wearing?"

Ian eased back on the accelerator as he faced her with a giant grin on his face. "This is what they had for me." He skimmed one hand down his naked torso, drawing her gaze past his washboard abs to an impressive red spandex-covered bulge. "Like it?"

"It's obscene!" Dear, God. Was that real? They couldn't show that on TV. Not without blurring it out.

He shifted slightly as he looked down at himself. "I prefer board shorts, but as hot as it is this afternoon, I have to admit, this banana hammock thing feels pretty good. I could get used to it." The cart came to an abrupt halt. "Are you okay?"

Unable to tear her gaze away from the outline of his cock

beneath the stretched fabric, she shook her head. "You can't wear that on camera."

"I wasn't going to, but you insisted I wear what wardrobe had for me. I had my doubts at first, but I've had time to get used to it." He jabbered on as she stared at his package hanging out there for everyone to see. "Had to put a towel down on the seat. My ass was sticking to the cushion."

That got her attention. She glanced up and met his gaze. "Please tell me that's not a thong."

"Banana Hammock. Sounds better than thong, don't you think?"

"You have something decent to wear at the house?" Ian had an apartment in town, but during the taping of the show, he'd temporarily moved into Wade and Serenity's guest room.

"My underwear would be better than this thing, but yeah, I have some board shorts."

"Let's go then. We're already running late, but stop at the house and get decent. I'll take the cart around to the pool. You can make your grand entrance from the back of the house like we originally planned."

Ian put the cart back into motion. The house was in sight when they heard the screams.

"What the hell?" Ian pushed the cart to its limit. They barreled onto the front lawn, sped around the corner of the house, and headed toward the pool, where chaos reigned.

"No. No. No." This couldn't be happening. Lexie's heart plummeted to her toes as she took in the scene. The bikini-clad contestants formed a tight clump on the pool deck. The human mass writhed like an amoeba under a microscope as the women at the center of the ruckus pushed and shoved each other, their angry voices rising above the melee. She made out enough words to know the confrontation had escalated to a dangerous level. "Stop!" She bolted from the cart. Where was security when you needed it?

Lexie dove into the melee, pushing and shoving her way through the outer ring of contestants, most of whom appeared to be observers, to the inner ring of contestants. Some were shouting at the combatants, others trying to pull them apart. Arms wide, she tried to isolate the fighting women from the rest. "Get back! Let me handle this."

"Bitch!"

"He's mine!"

"You wish!"

Fists flew. Fingernails scraped skin. Fingers pulled hair.

"Stop! Stop it right now!" Lexie's words fell on deaf ears as the two battled it out, apparently over which one Ian would choose. Gritting her teeth, Lexie attempted to wedge herself in between the women. Angry faces turned her way. Trying one last time to separate the women, Lexie extended her arms. Avoiding her touch, the combatants stepped back. Lexie watched in slow-motion horror as the two fell backward, their arms flailing for purchase. Hands grasped at anything to keep them from falling into the pool. Red enamel-tipped fingers grasped Lexie's shirt and held it, dragging her forward.

Under other circumstances, the cool water would have felt good, but these weren't other circumstances. Spitting and spewing, Lexie broke the surface. The other two women paddled to opposite sides of the pool, where more gracious contestants helped them climb out. Glares were exchanged, but the fight was over. Breathing a sigh of relief, Lexie stroked to the shallow end, then walked up the steps to where Ian waited, hands on his bare hips. Stalking past him to a stack of towels on a nearby table, she admonished, "Put some clothes on before another fight breaks out."

Ian followed her to the table. "Those two aren't staying, are they?" He nodded toward the far end of the pool, where the dripping women were each surrounded by their supporters.

"No. They're out of here." She dried her face and then wrapped the towel around her shoulders. "Go put on something decent while I deal with this. Your harem will be down to nine when you get back."

"Ten."

"What?"

"There were twelve. Now there are ten." Still not getting it, Lexie tilted her head and tried to shake the water from her ear. "You make ten, Lex, and you're the only one that counts."

Before she fully registered his words, he headed for the house, his firm ass hanging out for all to see.

"Good lord. That should be illegal." The curvy actress from Virginia sounded breathless.

Lexie glanced over her shoulder to see most of the women

had noticed their bachelor's departure. A few remained oblivious as they tended to the combatants.

"Did you see the front? Holy hell. The man's hung." This from a brunette Lexie couldn't place.

A scan farther afield revealed her assistant, Emma, half hidden behind the trunk of a giant shade tree. Lexie caught her eye and crooked a finger, beckoning her to come closer. "Where are the guys we hired for security?" she asked as soon as Emma was within hearing. Not caring to hear the answer, she barked out orders. "Find them. Have them escort those two back to the B&B. Remind them of the NDAs they signed, then put them on a plane back to where they came from."

"What about the pool party scene?"

Lexie sighed. "I'll take care of it. The remote cameras are on, aren't they?"

Emma nodded. "Yeah. They're on timers. You've got another hour before they shut off."

"That'll be enough." It had to be. They couldn't handle any more delays. "Get those two out of here. Ian will be back out here in a minute. I'll wrangle the others. Get this party started."

CHAPTER TWELVE

Ian laughed all the way to his room, where he changed into a pair of board shorts and a T-shirt. Maybe he should have jumped in to help Lexie defuse the situation, but wearing nothing but that ridiculous scrap of cloth, he figured, put him at a disadvantage. Then again, the two women who were fighting might have stopped fighting long enough to gawk at him. But he'd enjoyed the hell out of watching Lexie take charge of the situation. She was a ball-buster, for sure. She certainly had him by the balls. He'd do anything for her, including spend the afternoon playing nice with a bunch of cookie-cutter women at a pretend pool party. Lex would argue with him about the cookie-cutter comment, but it was true. Different hair color, different features, different jobs, and backgrounds, but all the same where it counted. They were looking for either a rich man or fame, or both. That's what made Lexie different. She wasn't looking for a quick way to the top or instant riches. She'd put herself through film school and then worked her way up from a gopher on a short-lived sitcom to a production manager on a hit reality show. Lexie was dedicated and driven to success. As he'd seen when she plunged headlong into the catfight earlier, there was no stopping her when she made her mind up.

Now, all he had to do was convince her to take a chance

on him.

He peeked out the window. Things were a lot calmer out there. The fighters had been hauled off, hopefully never to be seen again. Someone had turned on some tunes, and a few of the remaining women, drinks in hand, were swaying to the music. Ian searched for Lexie among the others, conversing in clusters near the bar. Not seeing her, he widened his search to include the oiled-up bodies sprawled on lounge chairs to take advantage of the ample sunshine. He wasn't dead, so he took a few seconds to appreciate all the feminine beauty gathered in one place—to impress him. Duly impressed but uninterested, he scanned the yard for the one woman who'd captured his attention.

He found her surrounded by her production crew beneath the sprawling oak that predated the house and all the outbuildings. Still wearing a towel around her shoulders, her hair a stringy, wet mess, she held a clipboard in her hand and commanded the attention of everyone around her. For the rest of his days, he'd treasure the memory of her walking out of that pool, water sluicing down her perfect body, the white shirt floating along behind her like a cloud. He didn't deserve her. He knew that. He also knew there wasn't a man on the planet who would love her the way he could.

If she'd let him, he'd treat her like the goddess she was. Others might try to hold her back, but there was no holding a woman like her back. All a man could do was be there for her. Be the person she turned to when the strain of being in charge became too much. Take the reins and give her a safe place to lay her burdens down, if only for a short time.

He'd given her a taste of that life earlier. He'd taken her mind off everything for a few minutes. On the ride back to her car, she'd been confused about what had happened, but her body had been like putty. Relaxed in a way he hadn't seen it before. That, more than anything, told him how much she needed his brand of love.

"How long are you going to hide out up here?"

Ian glanced over his shoulder. His soon-to-be sister-in-law, Serenity, stood in the doorway. He'd known her his entire life and had thought of her as a sister. How his oldest brother, Wade, saw her as anything more, he couldn't fathom, but his brother obviously saw something he didn't. "Just taking a minute to observe without being hit on."

Serenity's laughter echoed off the walls. "I never thought I'd see one of the infamous Nightingale brothers hiding out from a gaggle of admiring women. Beautiful, admiring women." She joined him at the window. "Which one has your attention? Don't tell me it was one they booted for fighting?"

"I like my women to have some spirit, but fighting over a man they've barely spoken to? No. I can do without that."

She studied the women around the pool. "I bet they all look great on camera, but is there any substance to any of them?"

"One. The rest are interchangeable."

Serenity turned her gaze on him. "Ah, so you do have your eye on one of them." Her smile broadened. "Which one? I promise I won't tell a soul."

Ian shook his head. "No way." She'd been a prankster all her life. God knew what she'd do if she knew he had a thing for Lexie. "Not telling you a thing."

"Does Wade know?"

Damnit. He moved away from the window so she wouldn't read the truth on his face. "I gotta go. The sooner I get this over with, the better." Grabbing his sunglasses off the dresser, he bolted for the stairs. Serenity's voice followed him.

"He knows, doesn't he?"

Shit. He hadn't specifically told Wade to keep his mouth shut. Probably wouldn't have done any good if he had. When Serenity wanted something, she could be tenacious.

As soon as he shut the backdoor behind him, one of the lounge chair women hopped up and crossed the lawn toward him. She must have been watching the door to have seen him before anyone else. Clever. Cunning. Whatever. Her efforts might gain her a few seconds alone with him, but that was it. Criminals were schemers. He doubted her criminal tendencies, but the last thing he needed to come home to was a woman who was always looking for an advantage. He dealt with enough of that crap on the job.

"Ian," the schemer called out. Her assets bounced and jiggled as she approached. "I'm so glad you came back out. Let me get you a glass of wine." She took him by the arm, pulling him forward. Then her hand slid down to his, and she intertwined her fingers with his, holding on tight.

What was her name? He vaguely recalled talking to her at

the reception for all the contestants. Heather? Hannah? Haley? Yeah, that sounded right. Haley from Las Vegas. Was she the kindergarten teacher? Didn't seem likely the way she'd been lying in wait for him, but ugliness was often hidden behind pretty wrapping. He had to admit that she was one of the more attractive women there. Almost a head shorter than him, her swimsuit emphasized her generous curves. She had a pleasant smile and a soft voice. Other than appreciation for her obvious attributes, he felt nothing for her.

Ian dug in his heels. "Look, Haley, I appreciate the attention, but I need to talk with the production staff first." He didn't. "No wine for me. I've got to work tonight." He tugged, trying to extricate his hand from hers. "Can I have my hand back?"

"I'll go with you." She changed direction toward the group gathered beneath the oak.

"No. I need to speak with them about what happened earlier." He peeled his hand out of her surprisingly firm grip. "You should go on. Have that glass of wine. I recommend Cabernet Franc. It's one of my favorites." It wasn't. "I'll be over in a few."

The smile she sent his way might fool the cameras, but there was nothing but pure malice behind it. If he'd been on the job, he would have taken a step back and silently assessed his defensive options. But he was on his brother's back lawn, and her swimsuit covered the bare minimum to be legal, which meant no hidden weapons. But if looks could kill… "Sure." She gave him a tiny wave. "I'll get a glass for both of us."

Shaking his head, he watched her walk away. Hadn't she heard a thing he said? He wasn't showing up for his shift with alcohol on his breath. When he was certain she wouldn't follow him, Ian cut a path to the patch of shade where Lexie and her crew had congregated. They were deep in conversation, but as if she sensed his presence, Lexie glanced over her shoulder. Her gaze met his, and he instantly recognized the stress hiding behind her beautiful eyes. "Hey." He placed his hand on the small of her back as he joined their tight huddle. "All good here?"

Emma spoke up. "We were just discussing the charm ceremony for tomorrow."

"What about it?"

"You were supposed to eliminate five tomorrow, then five next week. We booted the two who were fighting, so that made the charm ceremonies uneven. We're trying to decide if we leave it that way, three tomorrow, then five next week, or if we even it up. Eliminate four each week."

"Do I have a say in this?" He shifted his hand, sneaking underneath the towel draped over Lexie's shoulders to stroke the very spot where he'd marked her.

"No." Lexie sounded firm in that decision. She didn't move away from his touch. He counted that as a win and continued to stroke her soft skin.

Ian tried again. "If anyone is wondering, I have no problem eliminating four tomorrow." The sooner they were all gone, the better, as far as he was concerned.

Lexie lasted longer than he thought she would. Another win in his column. When she stepped forward and whirled around to face him, Ian dropped his hand to his side.

"No one asked you, Ian. We're losing daylight. Go over there and party with the contestants. Have a drink. Dance. Talk. Use the time to figure out which *three* women you want to send home." He didn't miss the emphasis she'd put on the word three. She'd decided, and her decision was final. "And don't forget. I'm one of the three."

Ian stared into her determined eyes and tried not to smirk. "Yes, ma'am." He gave her a mock salute, and then, his hand still tingling from the feel of her skin, he strolled off to party with the masses. Haley from Las Vegas met him at the edge of the pool deck with a glass of wine. There was nothing he detested more than a woman who didn't listen.

INTERVIEW – IAN NIGHTINGALE

Host: "You had a busy day yesterday."
Ian: "Yes, I did."
Host: "Most of the traffic stops went well. Did any of the women talk their way out of a ticket?"
Ian: "One."
Host: "Care to elaborate?"
Ian: "No."

INTERVIEW – ALEXA (CONTESTANT #12)

Host: "Word is you are the only contestant who didn't receive a traffic ticket yesterday."

Alexa: [Shrugs]

Host: "Everyone is curious. What did you say to convince Ian to let you go with only a warning?"

Alexa: "Nothing."

Host: "Nothing you're willing to admit?"

Alexa: "Just nothing. I don't have time for this." [Gets up. Walks off.]

CHAPTER THIRTEEN

"Lexie."

"Huh?" She'd thought Ian in board shorts wouldn't be as distracting, but she'd been wrong. The way the garment hung low on his hips drew attention south and emphasized his confident gait. She wasn't the only one who noticed. One-by-one, the women lounging by the pool headed in his direction. *Like bees to pollen.* No doubt Ian could pollinate the lot of them. Why that idea made her seethe with anger, she didn't know. He wasn't hers. Never would be. He could spread his pollen wherever he liked. It was none of her business. Forcing her attention back to her assistant, she asked, "What?"

"I asked if you're sure about your decision."

"What decision?"

"To only eliminate three this week."

Oh. That decision. She'd made the declaration just to remind Ian who was in charge of this shitshow. The smirk on his face when he acquiesced indicated he knew exactly what she was doing, and it amused him. The domineering ass. It made sense to eliminate four each week, but having one less contestant next week would mean making adjustments to all the activities they had planned. The changes would put additional strain on their budget.

"I'm sure. We've had enough disruption. No need making more work for next week."

"Okay, boss lady. I'll let everyone know."

"Thanks, Emma. Can you keep an eye on this?" She nodded toward the pool party. "I need to change clothes and fix my hair."

"You aren't going to join the party?"

"Not on your life. We need to put the fight behind us. If I go over there, questions will be asked, and I don't want the focus to be on me. Ian needs to spend time with the real contestants. If you get a chance, remind him to be thinking about who, besides me, he's going to eliminate tomorrow."

"Will do." Emma hurried off to join the rest of the production crew, who'd taken their places off-camera.

Lexie gripped the towel tight around her shoulders and, without a second glance at the pool, made a beeline for the golf cart she'd abandoned earlier. She'd just settled in the driver's seat when a woman darted across the lawn toward her.

"Can I hitch a ride with you?" Blonde and beautiful enough to be a contestant on the show, she wore white shorts and a burgundy Nightingale polo shirt. "You are going over to the winery, aren't you?" Not waiting for an answer, the newcomer plopped into the front passenger seat. She turned a megawatt smile Lexie's way. "I'm Serenity Granger, and you must be Lexie Hanson. I'm the marketing director for Nightingale's and Wade's fiancée."

Wow. Most of what she knew about Serenity Granger came from the lawyers who'd negotiated the contracts for taping the show at the winery. They'd described her as sharp and a force to be reckoned with. Meeting her for the first time, Lexie wasn't sure about the former, but agreed with the latter. "Lexie Hanson, at your service. Nice to meet you, Ms. Granger. I'm going to the wardrobe tent, but I can drop you anywhere you want to go."

"It's nice to meet you, too. Would you mind if I tag along to wardrobe? This is our first taping at Nightingales. I'd love to learn more about the inner workings of a production like this."

Putting the cart in motion, Lexie made a U-turn and headed back the way they'd come. "Hoping to host more productions?"

"Absolutely! *Love at First Sight* will bring us international exposure, and you're paying us for the privilege of taping here. If that isn't a solid win, I don't know what is."

Lexie agreed with the lawyers. A sharp mind resided inside Serenity's blonde head. "I'd be happy to show you around. Answer any questions you have." According to her sources, Ian had known this woman most of his life. Maybe she could ask a few questions about their bachelor—find out something they could use to spice up the show.

"That would be wonderful, but you must be busy. I don't want to take you away from your work."

"Let's start with wardrobe. You can look around while I change into my street clothes."

After introducing Serenity to the wardrobe coordinator, Lexie ducked into the changing room, emerging a few minutes later, wearing the same clothes she'd had on that morning for the traffic stop scene. She'd briefly considered selecting something different to wear, but like everything else, the wardrobe choices had been pared down to stay within their tight budget. She'd put on her own clothes as soon as she returned to her rented house. Meeting up with the two women who'd moved on to the makeup tent, Lexie asked, "Ready to go?"

"I think so. This is fascinating." She thanked her tour guide. "Where to next?"

They went through the event center, where Lexie explained how the remote cameras and microphones worked. Afterward, they toured the outdoor set where the charm ceremonies would take place. In Lexie's opinion, the gazebo with the million-dollar overview of the vineyard was the big money shot that would wow the audience. Despite the extra expense involved in moving production three thousand miles away, the views here, so different from their usual beach venue, would hook viewers.

"Building the event center and gazebo was Wade's idea," Serenity offered. "Took some doing to convince the rest of the family, but he persisted, and look at this." She swept her arms wide. "It's magnificent."

"I agree. It's a beautiful setting." They took a minute to enjoy the view before heading to the editing trailer sitting in the event center's parking lot.

"This is where all the raw footage is cut and spliced into a sequence that tells the story we want the viewers to see." Opening the door, they were met with a blast of ice-cold air. "The computers give off a lot of heat, so the guys keep it cold in here," Lexie explained.

Serenity crossed her arms over her middle as they advanced into the trailer lined with monitors and consoles filled with blinking lights and switches. "This is crazy."

"Yeah, it kind of is," Lexie agreed. A flash of color on one of the monitors grabbed her attention. It took a few seconds for her brain to decipher what she was seeing. Once it registered in her brain, she cried out, "What are you doing? Delete that! Right now!"

The editing tech looked over his shoulder and then back at the screen. "No can do. This stays in."

"What is it?" Serenity stepped closer to look over Lexie's shoulder. "Oh. Is that…?"

Lexie lived in earthquake country, but never in her life had she wished the earth would open up and swallow her whole—until that moment. There, for all to see, in the best color technology could produce, was a close-up of her ass right before she fell into the pool. The mark Ian had put there earlier stood out in stark relief against her pink skin.

"It's an ass with a hickey," the tech helpfully supplied. "Best footage we got all day."

"But," Serenity turned her gaze on Lexie. "Isn't that…"

"Come on." She hustled Serenity to the door. Over her shoulder, she admonished the tech, "Delete that. Now."

CHAPTER FOURTEEN

Outside, Lexie covered her face with her hands and silently willed the last twelve hours to go away. She needed a do-over in the worst way. "I'm sorry. They're the best techs in the industry, but they can be…"

"Asses?" Serenity laughed. "Pardon the pun."

"Yeah. That."

"Speaking of asses…that was yours, right?"

"How did you know that?"

"I was upstairs when I heard the commotion, so I peeked out the window. Saw you and Ian rush up. You were the only one of the three who went in face-first."

Lexie groaned.

"I also heard your traffic stop took a lot longer than anyone else's. I wonder who put that hickey on you?"

Serenity wasn't even trying to be subtle. She knew exactly who had done the deed. The woman wasn't just sharp. *Nothing* got past her. "It…" What could she say about the time she'd spent with Ian? "Oh, hell. I'd say it's not what you think, but it's probably exactly what you're thinking."

"I'm thinking you mean a lot to Ian. He's always been the most serious one of the Nightingale boys. I can't tell you how many times he tattled on me, Wade, and Sean. He was a little shit growing up, but I probably owe him my life."

"How's that?"

"Wade had talked me into jumping off the barn roof. Ian went and told on his brother. Their mom put a stop to it before I could break my neck."

"You were going to jump?"

"Of course I was. I was just a kid, but would have done anything to get Wade's attention. I didn't know it then, but looking back on my childhood, I think Wade and I were meant to be together from the beginning."

"That's sweet."

Serenity shrugged. "It is what it is. How did you meet Ian? He said something about being blackmailed into auditioning for the show?"

"I could use a drink. Know where we can get one?"

"Come on, girlfriend. I've got this."

Lexie followed Serenity through the back door of the tasting room. "Wait here. I'll be right back." True to her word, she returned shortly with a bottle and two wine glasses bearing the Nightingale logo. Back out they went, past a children's playground to a wide lawn that sloped gently toward the vineyard. Serenity tossed a couple of bar towels on the ground. "So we don't get grass stains on our butts," she said as she bent to spread them out. Lexie followed suit, and soon they were sitting side by side, sipping some of Nightingale Winery's finest.

"You were going to tell me how you and Ian met," Serenity prompted.

"No, I wasn't, but I'll give you something." She took a sip, savoring the excellent blend. "I'm sure you know Sean asked Ian to help him locate Angellica?"

"Ian mentioned it."

"Angellica was with me and still shell-shocked from finding out she was pregnant, probably with multiples. She didn't want to see anyone, but Ian was persistent. I kind of wanted to see how desperate he was to talk to her, so I made a deal with him. I'd let him see her so he could report back to Sean that she was okay. In return for my kindness, he'd have to audition for the show. One—I didn't think he'd agree, and two—I figured once he spoke to her, he'd forget all about the audition."

"But he agreed, then he returned to audition?"

"Yep. I probably shouldn't have forwarded the audition tape to the casting department, but again, I didn't think it would go anywhere. Sure, on paper, he's exactly the kind of bachelor they look for, but in reality, he's completely different from anyone we've had before."

"I've been a fan of your show for years, and I agree Ian isn't your usual bachelor. I'll also tell you this—he never would have agreed to be on the show if he didn't have a very good reason."

"You think he's really looking to settle down?"

Serenity gave her a pointed look. "I think he's found the woman he wants to settle down with."

"You can't mean me." Lexie shook her head. "No. I mean, I'm not a real contestant. I'm just filling in, evening out the numbers."

Serenity raised one eyebrow in silent challenge. "If Ian didn't put that mark on your butt, then who did?"

Lexie downed an unladylike gulp of wine. Serenity was every bit as sharp as she'd been told. The woman had put two and two together and came up with five. She'd see through any lie Lexie could spin in a heartbeat. She reached for the half-empty bottle and refilled her glass before speaking. "You can't tell anybody."

"I promise."

"Not even your husband."

"Wade and Ian are very close. If he doesn't know already, he will soon."

Lexie took another giant swig from her glass. At this rate, she wouldn't be able to drive herself home. "Guys don't talk about that kind of stuff. Do they?"

"The Nightingale brothers are thick as thieves. Who did Sean call when his girl went missing?"

"Ian."

"Who did Sean call first when he found out about the triplets?"

"Ian?"

"Wade, but Ian and Wade were having breakfast together at the time." At Lexie's curious expression, Serenity continued. "When Ian works the overnight shift, he and Wade have a standing breakfast date at Dott's Diner. Everyone knows it, including Sean. That's why he called when he did. He knew they'd be together."

Lexie groaned. "Ian…he's…he makes me…feel." She raised her glass to her lips, then thinking better of it, set it on the ground. "He stresses me out, but then he looks at me, and it's like he really sees me, you know?" She hesitated, wondering how her next words would be received.

"What's really bothering you?"

"This morning…at the traffic stop. Ian handcuffed me and spanked me."

"Oh?" Serenity refilled her glass and took a sip. "How did you feel about that?"

"I was furious. We're on a tight schedule, and we don't have time for extra shit."

"You won't convince me he spanked you without your permission. All the Nightingale men are domineering, but they'd never disrespect a woman."

"You're right. I gave him permission."

"And?"

"And, I liked it. Never thought I would like something like that, but it was erotic."

"How did you get the mark on your butt? That doesn't look like it's from a spanking."

"That came…after. I was still cuffed and trying to get my leggings up. Ian…offered to help. Next thing I know, he's sucking on my ass. I thought I was going to melt into a puddle right there. No one's ever done that to me before."

"Claimed you?"

"Yeah." She picked up her glass and drained it.

"What are you going to do?"

"Nothing. After the charm ceremony tomorrow, I'll be back behind the camera, and our interaction will be at a minimum. One of the other women will attract his attention, and that will be the end of it."

Serenity raised her very expressive eyebrow. "Girlfriend, if you believe that, then you don't know the Nightingales at all."

INTERVIEW – ALEXA (CONTESTANT #12)

Host: "That was some pool party, don't you think?"

Alexa: "I don't want to talk about it."

Host: "It's all anyone can talk about. You tried to break up a fight between two other contestants, and the three of you ended up in the pool."

Alexa: "I was just trying to keep anyone from getting hurt."

Host: "Commendable of you, but that's not the biggest story to come out of the incident." [gestures to a close-up photo of her ass right before she hit the water.] "Care to comment on that?" [points to a clearly visible bite mark]

Alexa: "No." [walks off set]

CHAPTER FIFTEEN

Ian sat across from his brother at Dott's Diner. Both held a heavy white porcelain cup filled with steaming coffee in their hands. "Thanks for coming to meet me on my lunch break." It was nearly midnight and the place would be closing soon. Few people were out, but they'd still chosen a booth at the back, far away from the windows facing the street. Ever since a gunman had mistaken their father for Wade and shot him on the sidewalk in front of the bank, his oldest brother had become more cautious. They'd caught the former bank president, who blamed Wade for exposing his dirty dealings, but Ian couldn't fault his brother for taking precautions. He'd seen plenty of senseless violence. A person couldn't be too careful. Especially when they were worth millions. Or was it billions now? He didn't pay much attention to the family business; he just checked the balance on his own trust every so often to make sure it was still there. It was. He was a wealthy man by any standard and got more so with every bottle of Nightingale wine sold.

"Not a problem, but couldn't this have waited until our usual breakfast meeting?" He sipped at the hot liquid.

"No. It couldn't."

Wade frowned. "Okay." He lifted his mug. "What's up?"

Squaring his shoulders, Ian scrubbed a hand over his face and then blew out a breath. Talking about this with his brother wasn't easy, but he had to talk to somebody, or he'd explode. "I'm in love."

Wade set his mug down so hard hot liquid sloshed over the rim onto his hand. "Fuck!" He grabbed a wad of napkins from the table dispenser and mopped up the mess with one hand while he soothed his blistered skin with his mouth.

"Don't do that."

"What?" Wade tossed the sopping napkins to the side. He examined his abused skin.

"That. Don't put your hand in your mouth." Okay. So that might have been a strange thing to say. Wade's raised eyebrows confirmed it. "Just don't. Okay? It reminds me of something." Wade studied him so long he felt like a bug pinned to a board.

"Has your mouth been somewhere it shouldn't have been?"

Ian wanted nothing more than to knock the knowing smirk off his brother's face, but he had asked him to come, and it was near midnight and the man had a beautiful woman in bed waiting for him. Wade was doing him a huge favor. "Maybe. It's not what you think." Because he knew exactly what his brother was thinking. Ian planned to go *there*, but not yet. "It hasn't been *there*, but close." *Christ.* This was harder to talk about than he imagined it would be. "I love her, but I may have pushed a little too hard. I'm not sure she's ready for…me." Wade knew more about Ian's dominant tendencies than anyone else, so he hoped he wouldn't have to spell it out for him.

"Is this about where you put your mouth or something else? It's late, and you are not the person I want to be talking about sex with at this hour."

Ian scrubbed at his face again. "I shouldn't have called you. I'll figure this out on my own. Go home to your fiancée."

Wade shook his head. "No. I'm here. Talk to me."

"I spanked Lexie today."

Wade's eyebrows rose nearly to his hairline. He slowly nodded. "Okay. Not what I expected you to say." He sipped from the mug cradled in both hands. Setting it on the table, he fixed his gaze on Ian. "How did she take it?"

"Not well at first, but she liked it. She's not used to

relinquishing control. I may have forced the issue a little."

"Do I want to know what you mean by that?"

Ian explained about the fake traffic stops and how he'd pulled strings so Lexie would be the last one of the day. "She reacted just the way I thought she would, so I handcuffed her and took her out to my property."

"That's kidnapping, bro."

Ian shrugged. "Maybe. Technically, yes, it is."

"I'm going to ask again. Why am I here? Is she going to press charges against you for kidnapping and sexual assault? Do I need to find you a lawyer?"

Ian reared back. "No! For Christ's sake, Wade. She was pissed at first, but after the first few taps, she relaxed into it. I'm just afraid I showed her too much, too soon. She'd make a great sub. The strong ones are always the hardest to convince."

"If you say so, bro." Wade took another sip of his coffee. "Damn. It's cold." He shoved the mug to the side. "Probably don't need to be drinking it this late, anyway." Stretching his arm across the back of the booth, he tapped the fingers of his other hand on the Formica tabletop. Dott's Diner was stuck somewhere in the 60s, décor wise, but the food was good. "I won't pretend to understand your lifestyle, but being honest with her is the prudent way to go. Tell her. Hell, take her to that club you belong to. Let her see for herself. She might surprise you."

"She's been one surprise after another since the day we met. She's hell on wheels on set, and it suits her. And she's a caretaker. You should have seen how protective she was of Angellica. She's a mama bear when it comes to the people she cares about, but I have to wonder who takes care of her?"

"Does she want to be taken care of?"

"Absolutely not." Ian smiled, knowing his assessment of her nature was true. "But she practically melted for me today. She could have used her safeword, but she didn't. She was curious and turned on."

Wade held his hand up like a stop sign. "I'm going to use my safeword here."

"What's your safeword?"

"Enough. I've heard enough. More than enough. Don't say another word about what the two of you did today. I don't want to hear it."

"Sorry. Let's just say she wasn't turned off by what we did. Confused, maybe, since I think the idea of submission has never occurred to her before."

"Stop. Please, for the love of God, stop."

Ian burst out laughing. It wasn't often he got the upper hand with his oldest brother. "What? You've known about my preferences since that time you caught me in the wine cellar with…what was her name? I was thirteen, as I recall."

"And you had what's her name tied spread-eagle to the worktable, sipping her wine. Yes, I remember, baby brother." He took a sip of his cold coffee and grimaced. "I wish I didn't, but you don't forget something like that."

"Amber. Her name was Amber." Ian gazed out the window at the dark sidewalk. "She taught me a lot about myself, and I'll forever be grateful for that, but that was a long time ago, and I've grown up. It's not all about me and my needs now."

"You think Lexie needs you?"

Ian nodded. "I do. I wasn't sure, but after today, I am."

Wade nudged the toe of his sneaker against Ian's booted foot. Ian looked up, meeting his brother's wizened gaze. "Then don't let her get away."

"I won't."

INTERVIEW – IAN NIGHTINGALE

Host: "That was some pool party."

Ian: "I guess you could say that."

Host: "How does it feel to have women fighting over you?"

Ian: "I'm a law enforcement officer. Physical altercations are never the way to solve problems."

Host: "To clarify, two women got into an argument over which one of them you would choose. If they were still here now, what would you tell them?"

Ian: "They should have asked me. I would have told them the truth."

Host: "What truth is that?"

Ian: "That I wasn't interested in either one of them." [stands] "This interview is over."

CHAPTER SIXTEEN

"Is all this necessary?" Lexie dutifully kept her eyes closed as Rafe worked what he called his magic on her left eyelid. "I'm only going to be on camera for a few seconds."

"You want to go unnoticed, right? Well, if you go out there looking like death warmed over, I guarantee you everyone will notice." He switched to the right lid. "But if you look as magnificent as the other contestants, you'll blend right in."

"That's a load of horse crap, and you know it."

"Maybe it is, but my name is the one in the credits for makeup. No way am I letting you go out there with visible bags under your eyes. You should have come to me yesterday. I would have made that mark on your ass disappear."

"We aren't talking about that."

"Hon, that's all *anyone* is talking about. Those in the know think the sexy Deputy Nightingale put it there."

"Why would they think that?"

"I don't know. Could be because the two of you disappeared during your traffic stop. Or it could be that you both arrived late to the pool party—in the same golf cart."

"There are explanations for both."

"Sweetheart, I'd love to hear them, but you're done here."

He yanked away the cape he'd draped around her to protect her evening gown, then spun the chair so she faced the mirror. "Go forth and dazzle!"

Lexie stared at her reflection in the light-rimmed mirror. Her hair was swept back from her face into an elaborate updo that exposed her neck. If she hadn't just spent half an hour having her makeup done, she'd swear she wasn't wearing any at all. Her skin looked fresh and well-rested, though she was anything but. The long hours and stress had taken a toll on her. "You're a miracle worker, Rafe."

"It helps to have a beautiful canvas to work with."

Lexie blushed at the compliment. "You're too kind."

Their gazes met in the mirror. "I can see what Ian sees in you. If I wasn't gay, I'd mark your ass myself."

"He…"

"Don't even try to deny it, sexy Lexie. We all know who put that mark on you. Deputy Nightingale is a smart man. You're the whole package, hon, and he knows he can't do any better than you." Before she could issue another denial, he urged her out of the chair and sent her on her way.

The gazebo looked like something out of a fairy tale. Sheer fabric softened the hard lines and angles of the wooden structure. Giant bouquets of pink and white flowers, along with white candles flickering inside glass hurricane lamps, added a touch of elegance. Discreet lighting kept the shadows at bay. It was beautiful, but nothing could compare with the dazzling sunset that provided a stunning backdrop.

Lexie filed in with the other nine contestants, taking her place in the back row where it would be easy to edit her out of the footage. Of course, she'd have to appear heartbroken when she was one of the three not receiving a charm, but that couldn't be helped. The audience had to believe her appearance on the show was legitimate.

Even though the outcome of the charm ceremony was predetermined for her, butterflies swarmed in her stomach. She'd been too busy getting dressed for the ceremony to bother with the list Ian had prepared of the seven women who would receive a charm. She'd passed that duty on to Emma so that each name that was called was as much a surprise to her as it was to the chosen woman. Lexie tried to be happy for them, but her smile was as fake as the dazzling image she presented in her designer gown and professional makeup.

What would it be like to see Ian smile at her and offer her a charm for the bracelet on her wrist? She wouldn't get a charm tonight, but her body still bore his mark. Remembering the feel of his mouth on her made her pussy throb with need. Clenching her thighs together to ease the ache, she tried to focus on the proceedings. Ian was stunning in his custom tux. The set decorators and lighting crew had done a fantastic job. Mother nature lent a helping hand with a sunset worthy of a painting. The footage was going to be some of the best ever and would make excellent promo clips.

She was so wrapped up in her own head she was startled when the woman to her right elbowed her in the ribs. "What?"

"You're up." Hand on Lexie's back, she shoved her forward. "Go," she hissed. "You lucky bitch."

They'll have to edit that out, she thought, even as the women in the front row parted to let her pass. It was their movement that made her look up. Ian was looking straight at her, a gentle smile on his face drawing her forward. One foot in front of the other, she shook her head as she closed the distance between them. *No. No. This isn't what we agreed on.* But there he was, the last charm resting on his open palm. His smile was just for her as she stopped in front of him.

"Alexa, I've enjoyed getting to know you this week. I'd like the opportunity to show you who I am. Will you accept this charm as a token of my affection?" He thrust his hand forward, the spotlighted charm gleaming.

Her heart pounded as she searched his eyes, looking for the joke that surely must be there, but found only compassion and sincerity. *Why is he doing this to me?* They'd had an agreement. She'd fill the twelfth spot for the first week, then she'd be gone. Back behind the camera, where she belonged. The other women were going to be pissed. Her bosses were going to be pissed. *She* was pissed.

"Alexa? Please? I want you to stay. Will you accept the charm?"

He voiced the plea so softly she wasn't sure the mics could pick it up, but she couldn't bring herself to care as his words washed over her. He'd gone off script the first time, saying he wanted to show her who he was, then again, telling her he wanted her to stay and repeating the question.

Lexie glanced down at the coveted charm. She'd chosen the tokens herself, a gold heart inscribed with his name on the front and Week 1 on the back. They were never meant for her; she had never wanted one, but she wanted this one. Catching her lower lip with her teeth, she thought of all the reasons she shouldn't accept it. "I shouldn't." Her voice was barely a whisper. "But I'm going to, anyway."

She wasn't Cinderella, and Ian wasn't Prince Charming, but watching him fix the alligator clasp onto the thin chain encircling her wrist reminded her of the scene in the story where the prince places the glass slipper on Cinderella. Ian's hands shook. Her arm shook. It took three tries, but once the charm was safely attached, Ian bent and whispered in her ear. "Thank you." Then his lips brushed her cheek—a feather touch that stole her breath and caused her heart to trip all over itself. Damn, the man didn't need to carry a gun. He was lethal all on his own.

Lexie made it back to her spot with the other contestants. The three going home shot daggers at her with their eyes while the ones remaining for another week pretended she wasn't there. Ian's last-minute switcheroo hadn't won her any friends. She'd give them some time to cool off, and then she'd attempt to explain the situation in the morning. They were all scheduled to attend a group date with Ian at Dott's Diner for breakfast. She'd carve out a few minutes to talk to them before Ian arrived. Then, like before, she'd stay as far away from the cameras as possible. Everything would be okay. Or not.

INTERVIEW- RILEY FROM TEXAS (CONTESTANT #10)

Host: "You're one of the final seven, but you haven't spent much one-on-one time with Ian. How do you feel about that?"

Riley: "I'd be worried, but have you seen the way he looks at me? He's totally into me."

Host: "Are you into him?"

Riley: "He's everything, you know? The whole package."

Host: "Only two women will receive charms at this week's ceremony. Will you be one of them?"

Riley: "Oh, yes. I'm certain I'm going to make it to the final week."

CHAPTER SEVENTEEN

Lexie stood aside as the contestants poured out of the stretch limo double parked in front of Dott's Diner. The mayor had arranged to have a section of Main Street closed off long enough for them to tape the arrival scene, and Dott had closed her doors to all but a few regulars so the place would look like business as usual, plus a bunch of disgruntled women on a group date with the town's most eligible bachelor. The women filed in past the checkout counter with the ancient cash register and red Formica top, past the booths filled with locals pretending to mind their own business, to an arrangement of tables set aside for them. No one was told where Ian would sit, so they played a cutthroat game of musical chairs, minus the music, until there were only two empty seats available. One for her. One for Ian. Miraculously, no one sustained injuries in the process, and no one had to be arrested. Lexie counted it as a win.

Approaching the table, Lexie assessed her audience. They must have stayed up late last night, as no amount of makeup could hide the bags under their eyes. *Probably trash-talking me.* Only the former Miss Possum Fest had her game face on. Not a hair out of place, a Mona Lisa smile carved into her flawless face. She was a quiet one, but determination showed in her startlingly blue eyes.

Lexie wondered if the others noticed or if they were too wrapped up in their own drama to see the beauty queen for the threat she was.

From the looks Lexie received as she stood at the head of the table, she wondered if she should ask Dott to use plastic flatware, just as a precaution. *I should have talked to them last night.* She signaled the camera operators to cut. The last thing she needed was footage of this conversation coming back to bite her in the ass. There'd been enough ass biting already.

Squaring her shoulders, she took a deep breath and let it out. "Ladies," she raised her voice to be heard over the grumbling assembly. "Good morning. Congratulations on receiving a charm last night. Ian has seen something in each of you and, by giving you a charm, has expressed his interest in getting to know you better."

"What does he see in you?"

Lexie snapped her gaze to the left side of the table where the question had come from, but no one had the guts to meet her gaze.

"Yeah. You were supposed to be gone. Why are you still here?" This from the right side of the table. Heads bobbed all around, silently agreeing with the criminal justice professor from Seattle, who at least owned her thoughts. Lexie met her gaze head-on.

"That's a valid question, Kristina. As you all know, I stepped in at the last minute to replace a contestant who didn't show up for taping on day one. I've tried my best to remain on the perimeter, to not call attention to myself. And yes, Ian agreed at the beginning that I would fill the space for the first week only, and then I'd be gone after the first charm ceremony. I'm as frustrated as you are over the situation. I still have my job to do behind the camera, so being part of the cast has added hours to my day. As to why Ian gave me a charm, you'd have to ask him."

"Why did you accept it?"

Good question, and one she'd asked herself countless times since she'd let him clasp the charm onto her bracelet. "Believe me, I thought about turning it down, but that would have caused more drama that couldn't be edited out without revealing that I'd never intended to stay beyond the first week. As it is, we can edit the footage of me receiving the charm down to the barest minimum, placing the attention on all of you, as it should be."

"So, you aren't really a contestant?"

Lexie cut her gaze to the beauty queen and shrugged. "Let's just say I never intended to be. However, minimizing my appearance in the cast for one week was doable, but doing so for the second week when the cast is smaller, and the interactions with Ian become more personal wouldn't go unnoticed. I've worked on this show since the beginning and know our audience. They get emotionally invested in the cast members, especially during the second week. I promise you I'll try my best to fade into the background. I won't seek Ian's attention, but as the production manager, I have no choice but to interact with him off-camera. I hope you all understand the position I'm in here and know that I'm doing all I can to maintain the authenticity and integrity of the show."

Lexie's gaze swept the table. She'd won a few over, but not all. "Okay. Now that we've got that cleared up, Ian will be here shortly. He's been on duty all night and is stopping in at the end of his shift to spend some time with you. You've got an hour with him, then he's going home to get some sleep."

Signaling the camera operators to power up, she took one of the two remaining seats at the table, earning dirty looks from the women on either side of her. Clearly, they'd expected Ian to take the spot, and she'd thwarted their plans. The two women flanking the other open seat preened at their luck.

As previously arranged, Dott and her servers brought out platters mounded high with traditional breakfast foods and placed them down the center of the table, family style. Coffee mugs were filled. Carafes of juice were brought out for the women to serve themselves. Lexie stabbed a pancake with her fork. "Dig in, everyone. Ian will be here shortly." She filled her plate with bacon and home fries and topped it off with one of the cinnamon rolls she'd heard Dott was famous for. All her meals since arriving in Riverside had been eaten on the fly and she wasn't going to pass up the opportunity to eat sitting down. And she, for sure, wasn't going to worry about calories or looking like a hog in front of the model-perfect women surrounding her. *You do you,* she thought as she savored her first bite of cinnamon roll. Lordy, the rumors had been right. She'd never tasted anything more delicious. Smothered with a sugary glaze, the roll beneath was light as air, probably because of copious amounts of real butter she refused to think about as the heavenly spice burst on her tongue. She might have groaned but couldn't be sure, as she took another giant bite.

"Glad to see someone is enjoying themselves."

Lexie froze. Her mouth full, she raised her gaze to the source of the comment and almost choked. Ian stood on the opposite side of the table looking tired, maybe a bit rumpled in his uniform, but still sexy as hell. Hastily chewing and swallowing, she washed the sugary lumps down with a swig of orange juice. "What?" she croaked out.

His smile dazzled as he reached across the woman in front of him and snagged a cinnamon roll off the platter in the center of the table. "Best part of working the night shift is knowing one of these, hot and delicious, will be waiting for me in the morning." He took a giant bite. Closing his eyes as he chewed, he groaned out his pleasure at the decadent treat. Lexie squirmed in her seat, remembering the way he'd made that sound when his lips had been on her ass. Heat rushed to her face. She reached for her juice glass and downed half of it in a feeble attempt to cool her libido.

Oblivious to their exchange, or perhaps simply ignoring it, the other women at the table came alive like unseen marionettes pulled their invisible strings. Smiles appeared. Voices called out, hoping to snare Ian's attention. But when Lexie dared to look up again, his gaze met hers and held until, certain they were remembering the same moment in time, she forced her gaze away.

"Ian. We saved you a place."

"Thank you."

In her peripheral view, she watched as he settled into the last seat at the table. He finished the roll and then filled his plate with generous helpings of everything else. Women chattered at him as he ate with gusto.

Grateful his attention wasn't on her, Lexie returned her attention to the first good meal she'd had in over a week.

CHAPTER EIGHTEEN

Lexie looked good enough to eat. Yeah, Ian was sleep-deprived and frankly so exhausted he could hardly keep his eyes open. That had been the case until he dragged himself into the diner and saw her. His rational brain told him the other women were there, but his other brain homed in on the one woman he couldn't get out of his mind. Before he knew it, he was standing there watching her enjoy a mouthful of cinnamon roll. The tasty pastries were the reason he'd added another mile to his daily run and extra reps on every piece of gym equipment in his home workout room, so he could relate to the ecstatic expression on her face. The problem was twofold. Make that three-fold.

First, he wanted to be the one to put that look on her face and cause those sexy moans to issue from her throat.

Second, he loved Dott's cinnamon buns, but now that he'd tasted Lexie, he'd gladly give up the sweet treat if he could put his lips on her after every shift. She was equally addictive, but with way fewer calories.

Third, he'd make a snack of her right there, right then, if it weren't for the gaggle of women surrounding her. Since he couldn't have her, he took another giant bite of his cinnamon roll. Eyes closed, he chewed, enjoying the second-best thing he'd ever tasted.

"Ian. We saved you a place."

Shit. He forced his attention away from Lexie. He'd been so focused on her that he'd ignored the other women. "Thanks." Taking the empty seat, he loaded his plate with generous helpings from the platters in the center of the table. He'd been running on fumes for days now, barely taking time to eat and sleep. He finished off the pastry and then went to work on the rest of the plate, concentrating on the protein first. Women chatted at him and around him. He pretended to be interested, but heard little of what they said. It was a good thing he wasn't on duty, and this wasn't a crime scene. He'd be hard-pressed to repeat anything he'd heard. Tired as he was, he recalled the reason he'd asked for this event in the first place. Sitting back to enjoy Dott's excellent coffee, he scanned the table, taking in the details he'd missed earlier.

He loved Dott's Diner. Fine dining, it wasn't, but the food was damn good, and you could always count on the locals to make sure you didn't eat alone. Wade met him here once a week for breakfast. The other five days, yes, the department was understaffed, so he worked six days a week, he either sat at the counter where Dott or one of her employees would keep him company, or he'd join one of the regulars at their table. Riverside was that kind of town. The woman for him would have to fit in at a place like Dott's. He also couldn't abide a woman who viewed food as the enemy. Food was fuel for the body, and by food, he didn't mean lettuce leaves and vitamin pills. His woman didn't have to have a sommelier's pallet, but he expected her to enjoy food.

His gaze stopped on Lexie, who was whole-heartedly enjoying the full plate in front of her. The only things he didn't see on her plate were biscuits and sausage gravy. He wondered if she hadn't seen it on the table or if it wasn't something she liked. Making a mental note to ask her the next time he saw her, he continued his perusal. Most of the women had something on their plates: a few bites of fruit from the fresh selection Dott had put out or a slice of toast. One had dared put some of Dott's homemade jelly on her half slice. The Possum Fest Queen was nibbling on a slice of bacon, her plate as clean as it was when it was placed on the table. A few others pretended to eat. Like on a sitcom. They'd fork up a bite, bring it halfway to their lips, then get distracted, on purpose, it seemed, and down the fork would go. The food never made it to their mouth, much less past their lips. Christ. How did they stay alive? Was it that important to them to be rail thin that they'd miss out on life's simple pleasures?

Then there was the one who kept glancing around the diner, her expression telegraphing what she thought of the place. You wouldn't find any white tablecloths or linen napkins here. Plain flatware that might have been new when Ian's parents were kids. Paper napkins in cheap holders sat on every Formica-topped table, along with plastic squeeze bottles of ketchup and mustard. No one would come by and offer fresh ground pepper for your meal. If you wanted seasoning, it was in shaker bottles next to the napkins. For this special event, there wasn't a laminated menu in sight.

Ian could afford to eat anywhere in the world. He could borrow the company jet and have dinner in Italy if he wanted to, but he preferred Dott's. Anybody who didn't understand that about him wasn't the person he was meant to be with. Without conscious thought, he watched Lexie again. She'd finished everything on her plate and now, like him, sat back enjoying a cup of coffee. As if she sensed his gaze on her, she turned and looked his way. Their gazes met, and something inside him shifted. Not a little jolt. A tsunami-sized shift. Yeah, he wanted her with an ache that went bone deep, but he could see taking her to a fancy restaurant. Maybe even borrowing the jet to take her some place special. Unlike most of the women here, she'd protest that it was too much. That she'd be just as happy going out to Dott's for the meatloaf special, followed by a movie at the single-screen theater down the street where they could neck in the balcony.
Ian laughed out loud, drawing the attention of everyone in the place. Scooting his chair back, he stood, adjusting his duty belt. Maybe it was the lack of sleep or the two cinnamon rolls he'd had, but he knew exactly who he would take on the one-on-one dates this week. Better yet, he knew where they would go. For the first time since he'd agreed to do the show, he saw a bit of fun in his future.

INTERVIEW – IAN NIGHTINGALE

Host: "How did the group date at the diner go?"

Ian: "The food was good. Great, actually."

Host: "I'm sure it was." [clears throat] "Did you gain any insight into the women hoping to become your wife?"

Ian: "Is that what they're here for?"

Host: "Why else would they be here?"

Ian: [shrugs] "I can think of a number of reasons that have nothing to do with me."

Host: "That's rather cynical, don't you think?"

Ian: "I stay alive by observing and assessing behavior."

Host: "I don't think the women would appreciate your approach to dating them."

Ian: "What approach is that?"

Host: "You just admitted you judge them the same way you would a criminal."

Ian: "I assess and judge everyone. Like I said, it's how I stay alive."

Host: "At the end of this week, you'll have to eliminate five women. Do you think that's going to be difficult to do?"

Ian: "No."

Host: "Just, no?"

Ian: "Just no."

INTERVIEW – RILEY FROM TEXAS (CONTESTANT #11)

Host: "What did you think of Dott's Diner?
Riley: [wrinkles nose] "It reminded me of home."
Host: "Where is home?"
Riley: "Frognot, Texas." [twirls a lock of bleached blonde hair] "I won Possum Fest Queen two years in a row."
Host: "That sounds like a great honor."
Riley: "Every girl in Frognot wants to be Possum Fest Queen. It can launch your career."
Host: "What kind of career do you have in mind?"
Riley: "I want to be rich."
Host: "Uh. Okay. I wasn't aware that wealth was a career path on its own."
Riley: "Of course it is. Why do you think I'm here? I'm going to marry Ian and live happily ever after."
Host: "Because you'll be rich?"
Riley: "Exactly."

CHAPTER NINETEEN

"Where are we going?"

Ian glanced at the woman seated beside him in the back of the limo. He'd agreed to do one-on-one dates with three of the remaining contestants this week. This was the first one, and he had a special day planned for her. "We're going to one of my favorite places."

"Then I know I'm going to like it."

We'll see about that. "My friend, Chris, owns the place. It's been in his family for four generations."

"We're here," he said as the car drove through an impressive gate and then along a gravel drive lined with tall evergreens, some of which were dead or dying due to an infestation of bark beetles a few years back. "Chris is going to take us on a tour."

She leaned closer to the window, taking in the scenery. Other than the dying trees, this part of the farm looked impressive. He smiled to himself, anticipating her reaction to the working part of the property.

"This is so…grand."

In its own way, it was. Five hundred acres with frontage on the main road. Chris and his family had turned down multiple offers on the property over the years. He'd done a great job navigating the changing landscape of family farming to keep the place viable and out of the hands of unscrupulous developers. Where once they'd relied on consumer crops to fill their coffers, they now profited from…

"Goats! You brought me to a goat farm?" The look of horror on her face was priceless.

Ian flashed her a smile that didn't come anywhere near his eyes. "Watch what you say next," he warned. "One of my best friends owns this place, and he makes a damn good living at it."

"But…I thought we were going someplace special."

He narrowed his eyes. It was a look that put most miscreants in their place. "It is special. It's special to me and it's special to the family who lives and makes a living here." He'd thought a former Possum Fest Queen would appreciate goats.

"It's a goat farm, Ian."

"And my family are farmers. We just happen to grow wine grapes. There's nothing glamorous about what we do. It's hard work, and every crop is subject to any number of factors we have no control over."

"But *you* aren't a farmer."

"I am when I need to be. I save my vacation time and use it all during harvest season. It's grueling work, but it's also satisfying work."

"You don't take vacations?"

"You mean the kind where you go sit on a beach somewhere?"

"That, and travel. See other parts of the world?"

"No." But he would if he had the right partner to share it with. Seeing his friend approaching the limo, Ian opened the door. "Come on. This place is fascinating."

It was all he could do to keep a straight face for the next hour as Chris led them around the barns and various goat pens as he explained how they'd shifted their focus from tilling the land to raising goats in order to remain afloat in the modern economy. His date for the day couldn't keep the disgust off her face or the muck off her designer shoes. He'd cautioned her to dress casual. It wasn't his fault his definition of the word and hers were different. Finally, feeling sorry for her, he decided to end her misery. "This is all fascinating, Chris, but aside from selling goat's milk to high-end grocers, bakeries, and restaurants, do you have other revenue streams?"

"Actually, we do." He waved them to a souped-up all-terrain vehicle with room for four. "Let me show you."

Instead of taking the well-groomed roads, Chris took them across pastures where herds of goats leisurely grazed. The trip was scenic and rough. His date looked like she was going to throw up more than once, but heck, she deserved it for the judgmental attitude she'd had since spying the first goat.

"What's that?" she said as the modern building came into view.

"That's our production facility." Chris swung the ATV onto a paved road. "I think you'll like this part of the tour."

Ian wasn't holding his breath on that one. It was an impressive business, though. Thanks to a segment they'd landed on a major morning news show, their business had grown exponentially since its inception.

They came around to the front of the building. The Possum Fest Queen gasped when the logo became visible.

"This…really?" She glanced at Chris, disbelief and admiration transforming her features. "This is one of the premier brands on the market."

Chris shrugged. "We do okay."

His friend was a master of understatement. They'd grown from a kiosk on the side of the road to a multi-million-dollar business in a few short years. All thanks to Chris's vision and his sister's experimentation with goat's milk products.

As soon as the vehicle stopped, the snobby woman bounded out. "Can I see? Is this where you make the products?"

"Yes, you can go inside. Most of our products are made in a larger building in town, but my sister, Miranda, still hand makes the soaps and a few other products here."

She was like a kid in a candy store, taking in the soap-making process with wide eyes as Miranda showed her around. Afterward, Chris's sister presented her with a gift basket filled with their signature products. Ian thanked his friends profusely before ushering her to the limo that had pulled into the parking area in front of the building.

"Ian?"

"What?"

"Thanks for taking me there. I'm sorry I behaved so poorly. I hope Chris can forgive me. I learned so much today."

Maybe there was hope for this one after all. "Don't worry about it. He's used to people judging him for being a goat farmer. He'd tell you he's laughing all the way to the bank."

"Can I tell you a secret?"

His danger radar went on high alert, but he was curious what kind of secret she wanted to confess. "Sure." She leaned in and whispered in his ear. He drew back and saw the dreamy-eyed smile on her face. "Really?"

Nodding, she bit her bottom lip, her shy gaze convincing him of her sincerity.

"Huh. Who would've thought?" He smiled all the way back to the B&B where he said goodbye to her with a promise to pass her secret on to the appropriate person.

INTERVIEW – IAN NIGHTINGALE

Host: "Did you have a good time today at the goat farm?"
Ian: "Absolutely."
Host: "The footage suggests your date didn't enjoy it."
Ian: [shrugs] "I think she came around."
Host: "Care to tell us what she whispered in your ear that had you smiling all the way back to town?"
Ian: "No."

CHAPTER TWENTY

One-on-one date number two, in all fairness to his date, required some special equipment. So, on the way out of town, they stopped by Tricia Heyford's shoe store, a few doors down from Dott's Diner.

"Hey, Ian." Tricia greeted them at the door. "Thanks for thinking of us for your hiking needs."

"Hiking?" The stricken look on his date's face reminded him of a cartoon character. Exaggerated much?

The store owner flashed a brilliant, if not indulgent, smile on the city girl. "We've got just what you need. Come over here and take a look."

Ian stood back while the camera operator caught every moment of the selection process. When Wendy from Chicago sat down to try on the first pair of hiking boots she'd probably ever seen, he joined her. "Proper footwear is essential for hiking," he explained. "You need a good sole to prevent slipping and protect your foot from sharp rocks and other trail hazards. The high top provides ankle support and protection against snake bites."

"There are snakes?"

"And bears, but it's rare to see them along the trail."

"Bears?"

Ian delighted in watching the blood drain from her face. "No worries. I brought my rifle. I won't let anything happen to you." He'd thought she couldn't get any paler, but he'd been wrong. *Damn.* He swallowed the laughter bubbling inside him. These city girls were fun to mess with.

"Maybe we could do something else today?"

"Like what?"

"I don't know. Go into the city? See a show? I bet we could get tickets for a matinee."

"Trust me, there's not a show on Broadway that can compare with the view from Mt. Tammany."

"We're hiking up a mountain?"

"It's a small one." Steep, but small as mountains went. He wasn't lying about the view, though. "You'll be fine."

"I don't know. I've never been hiking before."

"Hiking is just walking on trails. And if these guys can do it carrying all those cameras and sound equipment, you can surely do it." He'd verified the crew didn't have a problem hiking a mountain before committing to the outing. Thankfully, they'd been excited about the trip or he would have called it off.

He stood, offering his hand to help his date up. "Come on. We don't want to miss the sunset."

Why anyone would prefer city streets to hiking a forest trail, he didn't know, but his date hadn't given up on convincing him to change his mind. As he shouldered the backpack he took from the trunk of the limo, he shook his head. "What's the tallest building in Chicago?"

"The Willis Tower."

"Is that the one that used to be called the Sears Tower?" Wendy shrugged. "I think so."

"Have you been to the top of the Willis Tower?"

"Yes. The view is beautiful."

He pointed to the top of the mountain looming over them. "This is my version of a skyscraper, and personally, I prefer the view from up here."

She worried her bottom lip with her teeth. "Is there an elevator?"

Ian ground his molars. "No. But the hike will make you appreciate the view that much more." After handing her a walking stick he'd made himself out of a fallen branch, he took off on his favorite trail. She'd either follow or have to sit and wait for him to come back since the limo had left as soon as he'd unpacked the trunk.

"Hey! Wait for me!"

He slowed but didn't stop. She eventually caught up. She was out of breath, and a glance told him they'd have to make frequent stops on the way to the top. "There's a place to rest up ahead."

"That's good," she wheezed as she brushed a stray hair out of her face. "How much further?"

"To the rest stop or to the top?"

"Both?"

"We'll rest around the next turn. Best not think about the top. Concentrate on small goals, like getting around the next bend." *Without collapsing* went unsaid. When they reached the turnout, he dropped his pack at his feet and settled on a fallen log in the shade. "Have you eaten today?" he asked as she joined him on the log. He passed her a water bottle.

She took a long swig. "I ate. Why?"

"What did you have for lunch?"

"Uhm. A salad."

"Big salad? Little salad?"

She made a circle with her hands, her fingers touching to indicate the size of the bowl. Ian dug in his pack and handed over a power bar. "Here. Eat this. I don't want to have to call in a rescue helicopter when you collapse on the trail."

"Thanks, but I'm good. I don't need that many calories."

He shoved the bar under her nose. "I promise you'll work off every one of these calories before we get to the top. Now eat."

What was with these women? What did they have against food? As his stick-thin companion reluctantly downed the protein bar, his mind wandered to Lexie and her lush figure. She wasn't fat, not by a long shot, but she did have curves. Beautiful, womanly curves that made his fingers itch and his mouth water. It had been days since he'd touched her, and his patience with the production was wearing thin. When he signed on for this, he'd envisioned more time spent with Lexie. Instead, he'd given up hours when he should be sleeping to drag an emaciated woman up a mountain she didn't want to climb just to teach her a lesson. A lesson he was sure she didn't want to learn. "Idiot," he mumbled.

"Did you say something?" She wadded up the empty wrapper and tossed it on the ground.

"Are you kidding me?" He glared at her. "Pick that up."

"Seriously? What am I supposed to do with it? There aren't any trash cans up here. They should put some up here."

He had planned on packing the trash back down himself, but her diva attitude infuriated him. "Put it in your pocket. You can put it in the trash when we get back to the parking lot."

She bent to pick it up. "I don't know what you're so bent out of shape about. It's one little wrapper."

"Thousands of people use this trail every year. If every one of them dropped one little wrapper, we'd be hiking through a trash dump instead of a pristine forest. Do you like trash dumps? I don't." He snatched the water bottle from her hands, stashed it in his pack, then took off up the trail, not caring if she followed or not.

The sun had started its descent by the time they reached the summit. Ian breathed a sigh of relief while his hiking companion just struggled to breathe. "Not used to fresh air?"

Bent at the waist, her hands braced on her thighs, she wheezed out, "You're trying to kill me. Why?"

Hands braced on his hips, Ian stood tall, taking in the magnificent view spread out before him. Ignoring her accusations, he filled his lungs with untainted air and then slowly let it out. "Tell me this isn't a view to die for."

Minutes passed until, at last, the wheezing stopped, and he felt her presence behind him and slightly to his left.

"It's beautiful."

Ian noted the awe in her voice. *Finally.* He glanced over his shoulder at her. "Come here. Let me show you something." A few cautious steps forward brought her to his side. He pointed to where the river below wound out of sight. "Nightingale's is right over there, just beyond the curve of the river. My family has lived there for over two hundred years."

"You're connected to the land."

"It's in my blood."

"I can see why."

"It's not the view from the Willis Tower."

"No. It's not. This is stunning, Ian. Thank you for bringing me up here."

Satisfaction hummed through his veins. He'd hoped to show this city girl what she was missing. Mission accomplished. He had one more goal. "Hungry?"

"Starved. Is there a five-star restaurant around here someplace?" She looked around as if a swanky building might be hidden among the trees.

"Ha. Ha." Ian swung his pack off his shoulders. "You won't find anything like that here, but I brought dinner." He sat down on a large, flat outcropping of rock. "Care to join me? We can have dinner and watch the sunset."

She joined him on the rock. "How are we going to get down after dark?"

"Let me worry about that." He set out two plastic wine glasses and then uncorked a bottle of Nightingale wine. After pouring, he produced two foil-wrapped pouches from his pack. "Dott's famous chicken salad wraps." He reached back in and brought out a bag of potato chips. "Voila! Dinner is served."

He expected an argument from her, but for the second time since they'd arrived at the summit, she surprised him. She snatched a sandwich and unwrapped it. "Thank God! I'm starving."

Ian smiled and bit into his own sandwich. *My work here is done.* They ate and enjoyed the spectacular sunset in silence. When the last rays of light dimmed, Ian brought out two headlamps and a large flashlight. He packed up their trash, then led his date to a short, easy trail that ended at the parking lot where their limo waited for them.

"Why didn't we take that trail to get to the top?" she asked.

Ian shrugged. "Didn't want to."

INTERVIEW – WENDY FROM CHICAGO (CONTESTANT #8)

Host: "Earlier this week, Ian took you on a hike. Can you tell us about that?

Wendy: "It was hot and exhausting."

Host: "Did the two of you talk about anything in particular while you were on the trail?"

Wendy: "Who could talk? It was all I could do to breathe."

Host: "Did you have a good time?"

Wendy: "No. Like I said, it was hot, and there were bugs. I had to wear hiking boots. I don't think my feet will ever recover."

Host: "The charm ceremony is just a few hours away. If Ian offers you a charm, will you accept it?"

Wendy: "Oh, he'll offer me a charm, and you bet your sweet bippy I'll accept. We're meant to be together."

CHAPTER TWENTY-ONE

This was his final one-on-one this week, and after the first full eight hours of sleep he'd had in days, he was ready to take her on. She'd argued and texted him relentlessly, begging him to reconsider, but that wasn't going to happen. He wanted to spend time with Lexie, and he needed her to understand his life on a visceral level.

As expected, she stepped out of the house she'd rented from Wade, wearing a scowl on her face. "I hate you, Ian Nightingale."

"No, you don't." He helped her into the passenger seat of his patrol SUV.

"You aren't going to cuff me and stuff me in the back this time?"

"I can if you want me to." He winked at her as he buckled her in.

"You don't have to do that. I'm not a child."

"Believe me, sweetheart. I've noticed." Couldn't get her out of his head. She'd been on his mind 24/7 since the day they'd taped the traffic stop. Buckling her in had been nothing more than a covert way to fill his lungs with her scent. Maybe not the wisest idea since it made his head spin. How he was going to survive the next eight hours sitting next to her, he didn't know.

"Ready?" he asked as he buckled himself into the driver's

seat.

"As I'll ever be." The frustration in her voice made him feel like a jackass.

He paused, his finger hovering over the start button. "If you really don't want to ride along tonight, you don't have to. I promise I won't put you in danger." He'd hand her off to the camera crew following in another car if he even thought responding to a call would put her in harm's way.

"It's not that. I trust you, Ian."

"Then why the attitude?"

"You should be with one of the other women. Doing something fun. Getting to know them. One of them could be the woman of your dreams, but you haven't given them a chance."

He pressed the starter, and the engine roared to life. After reporting his location to the dispatcher, he drove away from the house. "I've found the woman of my dreams, and she's right here. I know all I need to know about her, but she's kept me at arm's length, so tonight is about showing her who I am."

"I know who you are, Ian." She crossed her arms and stared straight ahead.

Damn, her pout was cute. His hands itched to spank her bottom for being a brat, but he was more interested in hearing what she thought of him. At least then he'd know where he stood. "Who am I, Lexie?"

"You're the most annoying man on the planet. You're stubborn and domineering, and you don't take no for an answer."

"You forgot intelligent, decisive, and loyal." He tapped his index finger on the steering wheel. "And let's not forget filthy rich and sexy."

"You got the filthy part right."

He raised an eyebrow and dared a glance her way. Her shoulders weren't up around her ears anymore. He counted that as a win. "Are you talking about the traffic stop?"

"I'm talking about you spanking me. Touching me."

The last two words were barely a whisper, but there was nothing wrong with his hearing. They registered loud and clear. "You mean *marking you*." Not a question. She was as easy to read as a first-grade primer.

"I mean, putting your hands, your fingers, your mouth, in places they don't belong."

"If I wasn't on duty right now, I'd take you back to that same spot and do a reenactment. I think you need to be reminded how much you liked the way I touched you."

"Ian, stop. It doesn't matter if I liked it or not. It can't happen again."

"That's where you're wrong, sweetheart. You're a control freak…"

"I am not!"

He held a hand up to stall her protest. "At work. You're a control freak *at work*."

"I'm the one in charge. Being a control freak comes with the job."

"It does, but you don't know how to turn it off when you aren't on set. You're letting it wring the pleasure out of your life, Lex. You need a partner strong enough to fight you for control. Someone you trust to keep you safe when you finally let go."

"I don't lose control."

"You did the other day. You could have stopped me. You had that choice, but you didn't. Admit it, Lex. It felt good to submit to me."

"Submit? I didn't submit. You had me in handcuffs, Ian. I had no choice."

"One word, Lex. That's all you had to say, and I would have stopped."

"You left marks on me. It was embarrassing."

"I never intended for anyone to see that but you. I hoped you'd let *me* see it again, but knowing you would see it and remember how good it felt to be free, to accept the pleasure I gave you, was enough for me. I'm sorry others saw it, but I'm not sorry I marked you."

"Look who's being a control freak now."

"Never said I wasn't, but I know how to let go. Give me a chance, and I'll prove it to you, Lex. I'll give you the handcuffs, and you can do anything you want to me."

"Anything? What if I wanted to cut off your dick?"

"You wouldn't do that."

"How do you know?"

"Because you want me to fuck you as bad as I want to do it."

CHAPTER TWENTY-TWO

"You're an arrogant pri…oh! Did you see that?" There'd been a car ahead of them for a while, its taillights disappearing around curves in the road only to reappear on the straightaways. Lexie found it comforting in the total darkness to know they weren't alone out there. She watched in horror as the tiny specks of light suddenly veered to the right and then spun, one over the other, multiple times before disappearing completely.

"Dispatch. Unit R one-five responding to a single vehicle accident." He spouted off the name of the road and the nearest mile marker. "Send the works." Ian pressed a button on the dash. Blue lights lit up the night as they sped toward the scene of the accident.

Tires squealed on the asphalt as they came to a stop, angled across the road so their headlights illuminated the crash site. Ian threw open his door and jumped out. "Stay here," he admonished before racing away.

Trembling, Lexie released her seatbelt and scooted to the edge of her seat in time to see Ian practically sliding down the steep drop-off. At the bottom, the car they'd been trailing lay upside down, the passenger side wedged against a tree. Movement outside her window caught her attention. She'd forgotten all about the camera crew following them. They'd been far back, only there in case something happened the cameras inside the patrol car couldn't capture. Lexie rolled the window down to speak with them but was cut off by the sound tech's voice.

"Holy shit! What's he doing?" Lexie's gaze followed his outstretched arm. The back windows of the wrecked car glowed orange. "Ian! Get out of there! The car's on fire!"

"No!" Lexie opened her door and spilled out onto the asphalt, still hot from the sunny day. "Ian!" Either he couldn't hear her, or he was ignoring her because he crouched at the driver's side door to peer through the broken window. "What's he doing?" she cried.

"I'm going to help." The audio tech, Pete, she thought his name was, dropped the boom mic he'd just deployed. Before she could stop him, he was sliding on his butt down the embankment toward the burning car.

Hands in tight fists pressed against her lips to hold back her screams, Lexie's heart pounded as abject fear gripped her as Ian crawled inside the car. It seemed like a lifetime before he wiggled his way out, pulling the driver through the window with him. Pete ran to assist, and the two of them hauled the injured man away from the wreckage.

Sirens sounded in the distance. Help was on the way. Lexie breathed a sigh of relief, but it was short-lived as Ian returned to the vehicle, presumably to search for additional victims. "Please don't let there be anyone else inside," she prayed. In her heart, she knew if there was anyone still in the vehicle, Ian wouldn't hesitate to attempt a rescue.

Seconds became hours as his torso disappeared inside the vehicle. Emergency vehicles filled the roadway. Firefighters, EMTs, and more deputies than she could count blocked her view as they swarmed down the steep embankment. *Oh, God. Ian!* What would she do if he was injured? Or, Heaven forbid, killed? Her heart lurched, and she choked back tears as the truth broke through the walls she'd put up. Ever since the day she and Ian had walked on the beach together in Malibu, she'd fought her attraction to the man. She'd known then that he was loyal and trustworthy and completely different from the men she knew in Los Angeles. They dated her because they wanted something from her. A job on the show, or a night in her bed. None of them saw *her*. None of them looked beyond the surface to see the real Lexie Hanson. But Ian had. He'd proven it the day he'd turned her over his knee and spanked her. For a few short minutes, he'd wrested control from her hands and freed her to just feel. To accept pleasure. Even though she hadn't known it, it was exactly what she'd needed. *Be safe, Ian. I need you.*

What had been a faint glow now lit up the sky. Firefighters sprayed foam from handheld fire extinguishers as others unrolled and hooked hoses to the tanker truck to spray down the vegetation and stop the spread of the fire to the surrounding area. All around her, radios squawked, and men shouted orders. Controlled chaos. She was about to climb up on the hood of Ian's SUV so she could look for him when the wall of men in front of her parted, and Ian climbed the last few feet to the shoulder of the road. His face, arms, and hands were covered in soot. His uniform was torn in a couple of places and bore the signs of the battle he'd fought. Soot. Blood. Her brain froze at the sight of the blood. Lexie rushed forward. "Ian!"

His gaze met hers, and his eyebrows knit. "I told you to stay in the car." A small smile replaced the frown. "Damn, stubborn woman."

"Deputy Nightingale." An EMT rushed to his side. "Come over here. Let me look you over."

"I'm fine," he protested. "The blood's not mine."

Lexie followed him to the back of an ambulance, where the paramedic verified that most of the blood on his uniform wasn't Ian's. He cleaned a couple of scratches and bandaged a small cut on Ian's hand.

"That was a brave thing you did, Deputy." He handed Ian a wet towel for his face. "You saved that man's life."

Ian swiped at his soot-covered face. "How is he?"

"I haven't seen him myself, but word is he'll recover. He's got a couple of broken bones and some contusions. Probably a concussion, too, but we won't know that for a while. He woke up long enough to say he swerved to avoid hitting a deer that ran in front of him and nearly killed himself instead."

"I guess he's lucky we weren't far behind. We saw him go off the road and called for help. Out here, no telling how long it would have been before someone came along. By then, it would have been too late."

Lexie'd been allowing the EMT room to work, but now that they were chatting, she went to stand next to Ian. Placing a hand on his arm that hadn't needed any bandages, she tried to contain her anger. "You could have died, and all because a stupid deer ran into the road?"

"I wasn't going to die, Lex. But I also wasn't going to let someone else die if I could save him." He smiled at her. "I admit, I should have taken my fire extinguisher with me. That was my mistake. Won't happen again." He snaked his injured arm around her waist and dragged her onto his lap. When she was settled, he raised an eyebrow at her. "I told you to stay in the car."

"I did, but I couldn't see, so I got out."

"What if the gas tank on the car had blown up? You could have been hurt."

"But I wasn't."

"Doesn't mean you're off the hook." He wrapped his free hand around her nape, pulled her head down, and whispered in her ear. "Prepare to be punished for disobeying me, sweetheart."

Visions of him spanking her filled her head and made her squirm in his lap. He pulled her to him again. "I know what you're thinking, but you're wrong. This time, you won't enjoy the spanking."

INTERVIEW – ALEXA (CONTESTANT #12)

Host: "We heard there was some excitement during your one-on-one date with Ian. Care to tell us about it?"

Alexa: "The date was a ride-along in his patrol car. Long story short, Ian rescued a victim from a burning vehicle."

Host: "That must have been exciting."

Alexa: "It was terrifying. Ian could have been hurt or killed."

Host: "News reports are calling him a hero."

Alexa: "He's most definitely a hero."

INTERVIEW – IAN NIGHTINGALE

Host: "How did your date go with Alexa?"
Ian: "You know how it went, Steve."
Host: "They're calling you a hero."
Ian: "I was just doing my job."
Host: "What actually happened that night?"
Ian: "Watch the video." [leaves the interview booth]

CHAPTER TWENTY-THREE

Ian crawled into bed. His entire body ached like he'd been the one to roll his car off a twenty-foot embankment. When he'd peered over the side of the road and saw the car upside down, he hadn't stopped to think. Focused entirely on getting the driver out of the vehicle, he hadn't noticed the smoke rising from the backseat. If he had, it wouldn't have changed anything. He'd committed to rescuing the driver, and nothing would have stopped him. He was paying for it now.

He blamed his actions on adrenaline and some innate compulsion to help people. His brother's called it Boy Scout Syndrome. It wasn't inaccurate. He'd been a Boy Scout and even earned Eagle Scout status for protecting a Bald Eagle nesting site on the Nightingale property and erecting an observation deck where people could see the pair of nesting birds without disturbing them.

Lying in bed, the evening played on an endless loop in his tired brain. Everything had been going well with Lexie until the car in front of them had vanished from the road. Here, one second. Gone the next. Knowing the stretch of road well, there was only one place it could have gone. He'd tried multiple times to get the county to put guide rails up on that section, but it was never in the budget. Someone could have died there tonight. Hell, he could have died if the fire crews hadn't arrived as quickly as they did. But guide rails were a subject for another day.

He had more pressing problems. Namely, one Alexa Hanson. The woman was driving him insane. He never should have taken her on a ride along, but if there was any future for them, he wanted her to see what his job entailed. He'd expected a boring night issuing speeding tickets and patrolling the back roads looking for drunk drivers. *Hey, look at me, Lex. Keeping the driving public safe.* Instead, it had turned into, "Hey, Lex, watch me risk my fool life to pull an unconscious person out of a burning car." Then he'd gone all Dom on her for getting out of the car when he'd told her to stay put.

It was the adrenaline talking. After checking the vehicle to make sure no one else was inside, he'd glanced up at the road, and among the flashing red and blue lights, he'd spotted her. An angel watching over him. He'd felt her anguish. Felt her fear. Felt her unspoken prayer. He was halfway up the hill when it hit him. *I told her to stay in the car.*

Damn stubborn woman. What if the gas tank had exploded? What if a drunk driver barreled into her on the side of the road? It happened all the time. They'd see the flashing lights and misjudge the distance or be drawn to them like moths to a flame. Who knew what caused drunks to crash into obvious obstacles? He could have lost her before he ever had her.

And that alone was enough to keep him awake when he should be sleeping.

She disobeyed me. Closing his eyes, he willed his heart to take it down a notch. He'd promised to punish her, and he would, but not until he'd sorted through the mix of emotions churning in his gut.

He was furious with her for getting out of the car and putting herself in danger.

He was furious with himself for taking her on the ride-along in the first place.

Hated that she'd had to see the extreme side of his job.

Hated the fear he'd seen in her eyes. Fear he'd put there because he was the kind of man who would risk his life to save someone else's.

Hated that he'd promised to punish her when what he'd

really wanted to do was fuck her senseless in the back of the ambulance.

Hated that he couldn't claim her the way he wanted to.

Hated that when the taping was over, she'd go back to her life in California, and she'd take his heart with her.

Hated that he'd fallen in love with a woman he couldn't have.

"This is absurd." Ian and Wade stood in the shade of the event center building, watching the crew from the show dump grapes into plastic kiddie pools. "Everyone knows we don't stomp grapes anymore, and if we did, we wouldn't do it in a plastic swimming pool from the dollar store."

"It's not even harvest season," Wade added. "They had these flown in from South America."

Ian rolled his eyes. "I can't believe I let you and Serenity talk me into doing this show."

"Don't blame us. You could have said no, but as I recall, you had your own reasons for signing the contract." Wade nodded, directing Ian's attention to the woman arriving in a golf cart.

"She's it for me, Wade, but honestly, even if she had feelings for me, I don't see how it can work out for us. I'm not leaving Riverside, and her life is in Los Angeles."

"I've already lost one brother to California. I don't want to lose another, but we'd all understand if that's what it takes for you to be happy. On the other hand, are you sure she wouldn't relocate?"

"What's here for her?" Ian admired Lexie's ass as she walked along, issuing instructions and checking off things on her clipboard.

"You?"

"I'm not sure I'm enough for a woman like her. She's worked hard to get where she is in her career. I don't see her giving that up for anything or anyone."

"You've worked hard, too, and you've got a real shot at becoming sheriff at the next election. Would you give that up to follow her to California?"

Ian turned the question over and over in his brain before answering. "I don't know. I would if I knew without a doubt, she felt the same way about me as I do her. But that's not a fair question. I don't need a job. I can sit on my ass for the rest of my life and never run out of money."

"She wouldn't need a job either if she were married to you. Besides, what you do is important. Can you say the same about what she does?"

Wade made a good point but he was saved from admitting it when the woman they were discussing joined them in the shade. Her smile lit up the dark corners of his heart.

"This is going to be epic," she said.

"Easy for you to say. You get to stand on the sidelines and watch." He glanced her way. "Why is that, again?"

"This event is for the women you haven't spent any time with this week. They deserve to get to know you, and you should get to know them, too. How can you make an informed decision if you don't spend time with all the contestants?"

"I hate it when you call them contestants like I'm a prize to be won."

"Aren't you?"

"No."

"Look, Ian." She placed a hand on his forearm, beckoning him to look at her. When she had his full attention, she continued, "They signed on to this with good intentions. They're all looking for a good man to spend the rest of their life with. A hero. Let them have their moment with you."

Ian clenched his jaw so tight he could hear his molars grinding. "I'm not a hero."

"I saw it with my own eyes. You are a hero."

Her gaze had gone all soft, and her voice husky. They still had crates of grapes to unload. He could take her inside the event center, to the storage room at the back, and fuck that hero nonsense out of her. "You wouldn't say that if you could read my mind right now."

"What are you thinking, Ian Nightingale?"

"Trust me. You don't want to know." He shifted his gaze back to the developing scene. "Tell me about this. I've never stomped grapes before."

"It will be you and four women. Each of the women will have their own tub of grapes. It will be up to you to move around and engage with each woman. I expect it'll take about an hour to get enough footage of you interacting with the con…women. After that, we'll spend another half hour or so doing close-ups of all of you stomping the grapes. After that, you can clean up. We have a wash station set up around the corner."

"This is ridiculous. I'm going to have purple feet for a week."

"It'll make good TV."

He turned and leaned one shoulder against the side wall of the event center. Her beauty nearly took his breath away, but what really got to him was the way she hugged that clipboard to her chest like it contained the nuclear codes instead of a list of absurd tasks. "Is this what you really want to do with your life, Lex? Does this make you happy?"

"What are you talking about? I love my job."

"Do you really? Because it looks like it stresses you out."

"There's a lot riding on this, Ian. Not everyone can be independently wealthy and have zero cares in the world."

"You think I don't have any cares?"

"I'm sorry. I didn't mean it to come out that way. You put your life on the line every day for the people in your community. I get that, but…"

"But, what?"

"But you can quit anytime you want. I don't have that luxury, and the people working on this show don't either. If I screw this up, the network will look for someone else to do the job, and then where will I be?"

"Where *would* you be?" He crossed his arms over his chest and studied her expressions. "If you weren't riding herd over people stomping grapes in a kiddie pool, what would you be doing?"

She cocked her head to one side. "I'd be looking for another job."

"What kind of job?"

"The kind that pays the bills."

"If money wasn't an object. What would you do?"

"This is ridiculous."

"No." He nodded toward the lawn. "Stomping grapes in plastic wading pools is ridiculous. This," he waved a finger between them, "is a serious conversation."

She took a long time to answer, but when she did, her words stunned him.

CHAPTER TWENTY-FOUR

"I'd make true crime documentaries about cold cases." She hadn't admitted that to anyone before. Not even Angellica, and she shared everything else with her best friend.

Ian shoved off the building and uncrossed his arms. "That's pretty specific. Why cold cases?"

Lexie shrugged, hoping to appear nonchalant. "I've always been a true crime junkie, and cold cases are interesting." His assessing gaze unnerved her. She'd said too much. Revealed too much. Time to change the subject. "Your dates will be here in a few minutes. Put your game face on, Deputy Nightingale."

She felt his gaze on her as she toured the set, checking things off on her to-do list. What was it about Ian Nightingale that made her do stupid things?

Glancing over her shoulder, their gazes met for the briefest moment before he looked away. She followed his gaze to see a black SUV pulling into the parking lot. One of the production assistants waved the vehicle over to the edge of the asphalt parking lot, where cameras were set to record the arrival of Ian's grape stomping dates.

One by one, the women exited the car. As instructed, they preened for the cameras and smiled their biggest smiles. Hand-selected as possible mates for Ian; physically, they could be sisters. The man had been specific about what he liked and didn't like. Joy and her casting/matchmaking department had done a fantastic job meeting all his expectations. It was up to her to convince him to choose one.

"You think one of them has a chance?"

Lexie glanced at her assistant, who'd ridden along in the front passenger seat of the limo that delivered the contestants. "I hope so."

"Did you talk with Ian about the charm ceremony tomorrow?"

"Not yet."

"He can't give you a charm. That would royally screw things up."

"I know. Boy, do I know." She was on the verge of a panic attack just thinking about it. "I'll talk to him before he leaves today. He'll see reason."

"He'd better."

"On another subject, how are things at the B&B?" They'd had some problems with all the contestants living under the same roof. She'd thought the incident at the pool party would have been enough to put them on their best behavior, but that wasn't the case. There'd been more than one verbal altercation and a near fisticuff one evening. "Are the women getting along?"

"I wouldn't say they're getting along, but they aren't trying to kill each other."

"That's progress, I guess." She didn't want to have to boot anyone else off the set if she didn't have to. Discord among the contestants didn't look good for the show or for her ability to keep everyone in line.

"Looks like everyone is all set." Emma waved the contestants forward. "Let's get this show on the road."

"Okay, everyone! Look lively! Get those feet moving!" Emma worked it, trying to get the women engaged in the process. Harper, an actress from Virginia, jumped right in and seemed to be having fun stomping the fruit. On the other hand, Haley, the kindergarten teacher from Las Vegas, looked like they'd asked her to step into a vat of spiders. Kristina, the Criminal Justice professor from Seattle appeared to be stomping out crime, one grape at a time.

Then there was Suzanne. With every step she took, the blonde nurse from Wisconsin grew even paler than was natural for her Scandinavian heritage.

"Get Ian over there," Lexie called out to Emma. "Let's get some footage before she pukes."

Ian obliged, but before he could step into the pool, the poor girl bent at the waist, heaved, and emptied the contents of her stomach into the pool full of grapes.

"Cut!" Lexie yelled as she waved people over to deal with the mess.

Emma assisted, leading the sick contestant over to a chair in the shade. Lexie approached, but kept her distance. Just in case. She couldn't afford to be sick if what the woman had was catching. "Are you okay?"

"No. I woke up with an upset stomach. I hoped it would settle, but it hasn't. Obviously." She wrapped her arms around her middle. "I'm sorry."

"Not your fault. Unless you're pregnant. Are you?" Her expression told Lexie all she needed to know. "Don't answer that." She waved another assistant over. "Take her to the food services tent. See if they've got some ginger ale or something. Stay with her until she feels better."

"Thank you," Suzanne said with an apologetic look. She followed the assistant like a lost puppy.

"Is she okay?"

Lexie switched her attention to Ian, who'd joined them in the shade. "She will be. In about nine months." Ian raised an eyebrow. "She may not have known it when she signed the contract. It took weeks for Angellica to figure it out, and she's having triplets."

"Just so we're on the same page here," Ian glared at her. "I'm not giving her a charm."

"Wouldn't expect you to." She grabbed his arm and dragged him out onto the lawn. "Go stomp some grapes and let me take care of the personnel problems."

"I'm going. I'm going."

And I'm going insane. It was the only explanation for the way her body reacted every time Ian came near her.

***

"I'm going to have to call the set builders to see if they

have some spackle."

"Why? What in the world would you need spackle for?"

"Hon, if you'd open your eyes, you wouldn't have to ask."

Lexie refused to open her eyes. The lights rimming the makeup mirror made her already tired eyes water. Besides, she'd already seen the dark circles under her eyes. No need to see them again. "You're a miracle worker, Rafe. Make the fatigue go away."

"Did you sleep at all last night?" He dabbed at the sagging skin under her left eye.

"Maybe." When she drifted off as the sun was rising, she'd dreamed of Ian. Flashes of those dreams remained when she dragged herself out of bed a few hours later. In some he had horns like the devil while chasing her down in his patrol car. In others, she was naked, bent over the trunk of his cruiser, her hands cuffed behind her while fully clothed Ian searched her. Thoroughly. Her own whimpers had woken her. The coldest shower she could stand hadn't done a thing to alleviate the lingering ache between her legs.

"It was a yes or no question, Lexie. Either you slept, or you didn't. From the looks of the bags under your eyes, you didn't. What's going on? Trouble with the contestants?"

"No. Well, nothing more than usual." Rafe had been head of their makeup department from the beginning. "Every season has its challenges."

"The bachelor?"

"He's…difficult. But nothing I can't handle."

"Hmm. Do I need to talk to the handsome Deputy Nightingale?"

Lexie chuckled. "No. I think he's made up his mind already, and that doesn't bode well for the next couple of weeks."

"Wow." He brushed something over her lips. "That was fast. Is he for real, or has he settled on one early because he thinks it's what's expected of him?"

"Because the name of the show is *Love at First Sight*?"

"Yeah."

"One thing I know about Ian is that he doesn't do anything because he thinks it's expected of him. If he did, he'd be working with his family's business. No. He genuinely thinks he's found *the one*." She just wished he'd chosen someone he could have, but imagining him doing the things he'd done to her with someone else made her heart feel like a stone inside her chest. Ian wasn't hers, and he never would be. That was the cold, hard truth she'd better learn to live with.

"That's good for the show, then. Right? We've never had anyone actually fall in love at first sight. Which one is she? Did I do her makeup, or was it Alice?"

"Nice try, but I'm not going to tell you. You're a terrible gossip, and you'd tell her or worse, tell all the others they aren't the one." Lexie sighed. "I've got enough problems with this production as it is."

Rafe dropped his brush on the table below the mirror. "All done, doll."

Whipping off the cape Rafe had used to protect her dress; Lexie studied herself in the mirror. "You're a miracle worker, Rafe."

"I had a lot to work with, boss. You have the most expressive eyes I've ever seen, and your skin is flawless. If it weren't for the lights on the set, you wouldn't need any makeup at all."

"I'm calling BS on that." Though his comments put a smile on her face. "You don't have to kiss up to me, Rafe." She'd never fire him. He was the best makeup artist in the industry, and he'd had several offers to abandon ship and had chosen to stay with her. You couldn't buy loyalty like that in Hollywood.

Rafe made a show of zipping his lips and then air-kissed her cheek. "You know all your secrets are safe with me, girlfriend."

"I know my secrets are safe. It's everyone else's that I'm worried about." With a smirk, she brushed past her favorite makeup artist, making a beeline for the exit. His mocking laughter followed her all the way to the door of the event center where the evening's cocktail party shoot would take place.

***

"What's the matter now?" Lexie breezed past Emma, who'd clearly been lying in wait for her. They needed to get as much footage as possible before Ian had to leave for his shift with the sheriff's office.

"I've convinced the preggers one to stay on until tomorrow night's charm ceremony. She's clear that Ian won't give her a charm, for obvious reasons."

Lexie came to an abrupt stop and turned to face her assistant. "That's not why you were waiting for me. Spill it, Emma.

I can take it."

Emma scrunched up her face like she'd bitten into a lemon. "Well…uh…someone leaked some raw footage. It's a short clip, but it's gone viral. Over a hundred thousand views so far, and almost that many shares."

It wasn't the first time unedited footage had been leaked. She preferred to let the marketing geniuses handle the show's publicity, but fans of the show loved it when they got a sneak peek at a season. "Please tell me it wasn't that woman puking into the grapes."

"It wasn't the woman puking into the grapes."

"The catfight at the pool?"

Emma took a step back as she delivered the bombshell. "No, but you're getting closer."

Understanding dawned. Head spinning, Lexie bent at the waist, one hand braced against her thigh, the other found purchase against a wall. Someone had leaked the footage of her diving into the pool. Bare, marked ass, clearly visible. "Have the network execs seen it?"

"Um… they want to talk to you ASAP. I told them we're on a tight schedule and have to get the cocktail party footage before our bachelor goes to his day job. Well, his night job, in this case."

Emma was rambling, but Lexie had caught the important part. The execs would never interrupt a production to talk unless they were delivering bad news. Time was money, and money was the only language they spoke. *My career is over. Done. Caput.* She'd be lucky if they let her stay on to finish the season. Heck, she'd be lucky if they didn't pull the plug on the entire show. And it was all Ian's fault.

If he hadn't insisted the production be moved to New Jersey.

If he hadn't suggested the traffic stop activity.

If he hadn't marked her.

None of this would have ever happened.

If I hadn't let him mark me.

If I'd used my safeword.

If I'd stepped out of his grasp.

This is what happens when you let others take control.

Yeah. It's all my fault.

"Lexie?"

"Huh?"

"What do you want me to do?"

Lexie forced herself upright. After two deep, calming breaths, she shook her arms to release the tension. "Get everyone on the set. If anyone asks, tell them I'll be there in a few minutes. I'll sneak on set and do my usual hide-in-plain-sight routine." Emma looked at her like she'd lost her mind, and maybe she had. She was certainly teetering on the edge of sanity as she tried to think of ways to salvage the show and her career. "I'm fine, Em. I just need a few minutes to process; then I'll be there. Get the cameras rolling, okay? We don't want Ian to be late for his shift."

It took two laps around the building before Lexie stopped shaking. Two more before she admitted to herself that she'd enjoyed everything Ian had done to her during the fake traffic stop. And two more before she vowed never to let a man have that kind of control over her ever again.

She'd hoped to sneak into the ongoing taping, but the second she eased into the most out-of-the-way spot on the set, Ian's gaze found her, taking in every inch of her before settling on her face. His brow knit with concern—a sure sign she'd done a terrible job of masking her feelings. The moment he extricated himself from the three women huddled around him, Lexie shook her head, silently pleading with him to stay where he was. She wasn't in any mood to deal with Ian Nightingale or pretend to be flattered by his attention.

Crap. Every step he took in her direction chipped away at the fragile walls she'd hastily built to protect herself. The fake smile he'd had for the other women had fallen away, replaced by an expression that warned her not to put up a fight. He was going to have his way, and God help her, she was going to let him. Her career was over, so what was the point of arguing now?

"What's wrong?"

"Nothing."

"Don't lie to me, Alexa. Something's happened. What is it?"

"I can't talk about it here. Go back over there and schmooze with the ladies. We'll talk later."

His gaze bored into hers until she blinked and looked away. "Nope. Not getting away with it, Lex." He captured her hand in his and tugged. "Come with me."

129

CHAPTER TWENTY-FIVE

Something was wrong. Really wrong. Ian didn't know what it was, but he was going to get to the bottom of it. He'd read so many things in the depths of Lexie's gaze—anger, disappointment, lust, and resignation—that he didn't know where to start with her. The lust he understood. He'd been in a state of perpetual need since the day she'd set foot on Nightingale land. The ill-advised interlude out at the clearing where he planned to build a home for himself had only made his life more miserable. Lexie was his, and, like it or not, he was hers. Convincing her was the part he got hung up on.

But that could wait. She'd been fine when he'd seen her at the grape stomping that morning, so whatever had put her in this mood had happened since then.

"Ian. Stop!"

She'd said stop, not red. He halted in his tracks, but kept her hand in his. "We can't have this discussion here."

"We don't have anything to talk about."

"Yes, we do." He crowded into her personal space. Close enough to smell her lavender-scented shampoo mixed with the essence of her. It was an intoxicating mix that fired his libido. "We have a lot to talk about." With his free hand, he stroked the slope of her jaw. "You're going to tell me what has you grinding your teeth."

"I'm not grinding my teeth."

He dragged his thumb over her tight lips. "No lies, Alexa."

"Or what?"

It was his turn to clench his jaw. He wanted nothing more than to see her expression when he answered her question, but they needed to be someplace private, not this fishbowl full of hidden cameras and microphones. "Not here."

"Here is fine, Ian."

"No. It's not."

"I'm not going anywhere with you."

Ian hid the smile threatening to split across his face. Her hand was still in his, but the desolate expression had left her face, replaced by one he could work with. Defiance. Leaning down, he brushed his lips over the shell of her ear. A shiver racked her entire body, bringing that smile to his lips after all. "You're coming with me, Alexa. Then you're going to come *for* me. As many times as it takes to get you to tell me what's going on in that pretty head of yours."

Straightening to his full height, he cradled her jaw in his free hand and tilted her chin until her gaze met his. Her pupils were dark pools of desire, confirming what he'd always believed. Alexa Hanson was sexually submissive. "Trust me."

It wasn't a question. Her cheeks flushed, and she shuttered her eyes, giving him what he'd demanded. Her trust.

His car was at Wade and Serenity's house, but his dad's old pickup truck, which he refused to get rid of, was parked next to the tasting room, where it served as a photo backdrop most of the time and backup transportation when needed. Lexie kept pace with him across the parking lot. He hoisted her into the passenger seat and then buckled her in before rounding the hood and climbing behind the wheel. The keys were in the ignition, a testament to his dad's faith in people's good nature.

The AM radio, tuned to a local talk show, coupled with the wind whipping through the open windows of the cab, alleviated the need for conversation. Besides, the things they needed to say to each other required their total focus.

When they pulled into his designated parking space in front of his condo, he killed the engine and pocketed the keys.

Lexie reached for the latch on her seatbelt. "Not yet." He captured her hand before she could release the latch. "Do you have your phone?"

"Yes." She fished it out of the tiny evening bag that matched her gown.

"Call your assistant. Tell her you're at my house and that you won't be back until tomorrow morning."

He expected the flash of angry disbelief, but the gentle nod of acceptance took him by surprise. "I'll just text her."

"No. Call. She needs to hear your voice. If you text her, she might think it's me, not you. Put it on speaker."

Another nod. She pressed a few buttons on the phone. It rang a couple of times then Emma's voice, laced with concern, filled the cab. "Lexie! Oh, my God! Are you okay? Where are you?"

"I'm fine, Em. I'm with Ian, at his place. I needed to get away for a while, and he was nice enough to get me out of there." She hurried on, not allowing her assistant to respond. "Go ahead and wrap things up for tonight. Send everyone home for now, but tell them to be ready to tape the cocktail party and the charm ceremony tomorrow afternoon."

"Lex? Are you sure you're okay?"

Lexie glanced at him. "I'm fine. Just need a little space tonight."

"Okay, but don't do anything stupid. All this will blow over."

"Gotta go, Em. I'll see you tomorrow." She abruptly ended the call, but he'd heard enough to know he'd been right. There was something wrong, and his girl was going to lay it at his feet so he could deal with it.

"Good girl." He took her phone and powered it off before slipping it into the inside pocket of his jacket. "Don't move. I need to call the station and let them know I won't be in tonight."

Lexie looked straight ahead as he made his lame excuses to his boss. They could do without him for one night, but Lexie needed him, and he wouldn't let her down. Before powering off his own phone, he sent a text to Wade, letting him know not to meet him for breakfast in the morning. "When we get inside, I'll show you where my bedroom is. I want you to go inside and take that dress off. If you have anything underneath it, you can leave that on. Once you've done that, I want you to wait for me on your knees, legs spread, eyes cast down. You can sit back on your heels, but I want your hands on your thighs, palms up.”

"Ian. No.”

“This is non-negotiable, Alexa.”

“Take me home then.”

“No.”

“This is kidnapping.”

“Not the first time I've been accused of kidnapping you.”

“I'm not going to play your little sex games.”

“I don't play games, Alexa. Everything I do is done with intent.”

“Yeah, and what do you intend to do with me?”

“Everything.”

CHAPTER TWENTY-SIX

Lexie stared out the windshield, her gaze unfocused. Her life was in the crapper, the production was out of control, and her job was on the line. All because she'd let this man do things to her no other had dared. Confidence fit him like a bespoke suit. But confidence wasn't something you put on when you wanted to. It was something a person earned by successfully navigating through the valleys of life and coming out on top of the mountains. Her life had been one endless trudge through the deepest valley, or so it seemed, and until Ian came along and threw her off track, she'd thought the mountaintop was in sight. Despite the bright sunlight outside the truck cab, her view was obscured by the darkest of clouds.

Silence stretched between them as she contemplated his words. The promise of multiple orgasms had convinced her to leave with him, but now, his demands were both intriguing and frightening. Part of her wanted to do exactly what he wanted, but another part feared losing control. Wringing her hands in her lap, she cast her gaze to the dashboard. "I don't know what *everything* is."

"I'll explain, but let's have this conversation inside where it's cool. I promise I won't do anything to you that you don't want, and I'd never harm you."

"You hit me, Ian."

"I spanked you, and I bit your ass. Yes, those hurt, but caused no permanent harm."

"Semantics."

"Truth, Alexa. You could have used your safeword or moved out of my grasp, but you didn't." He tugged at his tie and popped the top button on his shirt. "Please, can we go inside? You can keep your dress on until you're ready to take it off."

"What makes you think I'll want to take it off?"

"You will. We're going to talk about our needs and my expectations, and when we're done, you're going to do exactly as I say."

"Your confidence is annoying." When had she become such a liar? His confidence was a pheromone she couldn't resist. Which was why she hesitated to go inside with him—afraid once they were alone behind closed doors, she'd do anything he asked. Or demanded. And that scared her down to the marrow of her bones.

"I know what I'm doing, Alexa." He released his seatbelt and popped his door open. "Come inside. We'll have something cold to drink and talk."

Orders issued, Ian stalked toward the front door of his condo without looking back to see if she was going to follow. Lexie watched through the windshield as he unlocked the door and disappeared inside, leaving the door ajar, making it clear the decision was hers to make. The old truck didn't have air conditioning but with the windows down, the ride over hadn't been too bad, but sitting still, even with the windows open, was akin to baking in an oven. The beautiful gown she'd chosen for the cocktail party seemed to get tighter with every breath she took, and if she sweated in it anymore, it might never come off of her. She'd love nothing more than to take it off so she could breathe again, but could she do it for Ian? She closed her eyes and imagined herself in the position he'd described. It had sounded absurd and demeaning at first, but seeing the image in her mind's eye, it felt anything but. Her heart pounded with anticipation, and her lady parts throbbed with arousal at the idea of Ian's gaze lingering on her body while she waited for his next command. She couldn't help but recall the feel of his hands on her, between her legs, holding her steady while he marked her. She'd never let anyone have that kind of control over her before. But Ian was right. A simple word from her would have made him stop. If she knew anything about the man, it was that he meant what he said. He would have released her if she'd said the word.

Opening her eyes, she saw the door to his condo remained open. A metaphor not lost on her. Walking through the portal would change her life.

The decision is mine.

If she stayed out there long enough, Ian would eventually return and drive her back to the set. Or… Lexie clutched her evening bag to her stomach. The old door squeaked on its hinges as she pushed it open and dropped her feet to the hot asphalt.

It took a moment for her eyes to adjust from the blinding sunshine outside to the soft indoor lighting. Once acclimated, she eased inside, closing the door behind her. Her shoes tapped lightly against the tiled entryway, but her footsteps weren't anywhere near as loud as the beating of her heart as she made her way deeper into Ian's home. Her first glimpse of the main living space surprised her. She'd expected bachelor chic—lots of black leather, chrome, and glass. Instead, Ian's home décor was ultramodern and sleek, with white walls, floors, and furnishings. Strategic lighting trained on colorful paintings softened the starkness of the space, as did the brightly colored throw pillows, blankets, and rugs scattered about. Giant windows that looked out onto a small but well-landscaped yard flanked a traditional wood-burning fireplace on both sides. A large island sectioned the small but well-appointed kitchen off from the rest of the room.

The condo might be cookie-cutter on the outside, but this one had undergone extensive renovations. Nothing here was builder-grade. It made the little house she rented back home in the San Fernando Valley look like a shack.

"Welcome to chez Nightingale."

Lexie jumped at the deep, disembodied voice and spun around. Ian had ditched the suit for a Nightingale Vineyard T-shirt and jeans that looked to be as old as the pickup that had gotten them there. As he approached, she noticed his bare feet.

"I hope you don't mind. That suit was killing me." He moved behind the island, opened what looked like a cabinet, reached inside, and brought out two cold bottles of water. "You must be dying in that dress." He set a water bottle on the corner of the island and then gave it a shove toward her. "I laid one of my shirts out for you." He pointed in the direction he'd come from. "My bedroom is that way. Go change, then come back, and we'll talk."

She couldn't resist the lure of cold water or the chance to get out of the confining dress. Grabbing the bottle off the island, she walked down the hallway he'd indicated until she found an open door. Peeking inside, she saw a crisp white button-down shirt laid out on the corner of a king-sized bed. Ian's bed. Like the other part of the house she'd seen, the room was stark white with splashes of color in the paintings on the walls and on the pile of throw pillows on the neatly made bed. Glancing around, not a thing seemed out of place. It was hard to imagine anyone lived there, but as she closed the door behind her, she noticed a row of small picture frames on the dresser. She twisted the cap off the water bottle and took a giant swig before venturing closer. The photos were casual ones, probably taken with someone's phone and printed off. They were all of Ian and his family members over a period of years. Lexie was drawn to a recent one that included his brothers, his parents, and Wade's fiancée, Serenity Granger. Wade wore a white suit and the biggest smile she'd ever seen on a person. A mirror ball hung above their heads, which explained the colored lights dotting the photograph. *Must have been a party.* She carefully placed the memento back where she'd found it. An only child, she had a few photos of herself and her parents before her mother disappeared, but they all looked staged compared to the easy smiles and comradery Ian's family exhibited. Truthfully, she could barely remember her mother. She'd been eight when her mother disappeared on her way to pick Lexie up from school. A year went by without a word or a clue as to what had happened to her. Then she and her dad moved to Temecula to be closer to her paternal grandparents. That's where she'd met Angellica. They'd been best friends ever since.

Knock. Knock. "You okay in there?"

Lexie startled. "I'm fine." She hastily slid the back zipper down on her dress, letting the heavy beaded silk fall to her feet. One step, and she was free. A second step and Ian's shirt was in her hands. "Give me a second." She silently cursed the buttons for being on the wrong side of the placket, making it difficult to work them through the holes. Finally getting enough buttons done up to be decent, she rolled the cuffs back until she could see her hands, then reached for the doorknob.

"Sorry." Ian cocked an eyebrow and then gave her the once over. "I was looking at one of the pictures on your dresser. I think it was taken at a party?"

He nodded. "The night Wade proposed to Serenity. We had a lot to celebrate."

"Well, it's a great photo of all of you."

Ian's gaze shifted to the framed photos on his dresser, then to the floor where her discarded dress still rested. "Come on. I fixed us a snack." At the mention of food, Lexie's stomach growled loud enough to be heard in the next county. "When was the last time you ate?"

"I had breakfast." Her stomach let out another snarl as she followed Ian back to the kitchen where he lifted her onto the island like she weighed nothing.

Placing both his hands on the stone countertop on either side of her hips, he boxed her in. "Let me guess, you had coffee and two bites of a muffin from food services before someone needed you?"

He wasn't far from the truth. She'd had half a cup of coffee and had intended to eat the bagel she'd picked up in the food services tent, but there'd been a problem with the permits for the fireworks display she wanted for the final charm ceremony. No permit meant no fireworks which meant a huge budget savings. "Close enough."

"What about lunch?"

"What's that?"

His gaze turned to stone. "That's not funny, Alexa."

No, it wasn't, but she was out of her element here and had fallen back on lame humor to help even the odds. "I'm sorry. I know I should eat better, but my job is demanding."

"You don't know what demanding is, sweetheart, but you're about to find out."

He opened a drawer beside her right leg and drew out a length of chrome-plated chain. The sound of it hitting the quartz countertop sent a chill down her spine. He opened another drawer. Two leather handcuffs joined the chains. "What are you going to do with those?"

CHAPTER TWENTY-SEVEN

"I'm going to restrain you. Then I'm going to feed you, Alexa."

"I…I can feed myself."

"All evidence to the contrary." He held her prisoner with his eyes while he traced the lines of her face with his index finger. "Let me take care of you, sweetheart. I promise I won't do anything you don't want me to." He brushed his thumb over her lower lip. "You'll be able to release yourself any time you want, and your safe word is still red. Use it, and I'll stop whatever I'm doing."

Lexie searched his face for any hint of deceit and found none, but she still wasn't sure if she wanted to play this game with him…whatever the game was. "I don't know…"

"Your assistant knows where you are and who you're with. I won't harm you, Alexa. I'm a meticulous man. I take care of what's mine."

"I'm not yours."

"But you want to be."

Stunned by his arrogant and all-too-correct statement, Lexie didn't object when he placed a fur-lined cuff around her left wrist and attached a length of chain to it with a simple snap hook a child could open. Her heart pounded as he fastened the remaining cuff around her other wrist. "Ian?"

"Yes, sweetheart?"

"I…"

With the cuff secure, he took both her wrists and held them lightly in his hands. His gaze met hers, and she couldn't look away. "Breathe, Alexa. It's a simple restraint. One you can get out of at any time without my help."

Her breath hitched as she tried to fill her lungs.

"Like this, sweetheart. In through the nose. Out through the mouth." He demonstrated the technique and when she tried it, he performed it along with her. When they'd repeated it three times, he smiled and squeezed her hands. "Good girl. Perfect. Keep breathing. Just like that." His gaze remained on her face as he slowly maneuvered her hands behind her back and secured the chain between her cuffed wrists. Letting go, her hands fell to the countertop beside her hips. It wasn't as uncomfortable as the steel cuffs he'd put on her during the bogus traffic stop, but she still felt vulnerable. "Bring your hands together and release the clasp."

It was ridiculously easy. She brought her hands to her lap and fingered the links of the chain.

"Now you do it. Hands behind your back, Alexa, and fasten the clasp."

She jerked her gaze to his. "What?"

"Fasten the restraints, Alexa. Show me you want this. That you trust me."

Did she trust him? Did she want whatever this was?

"If you want me to stop, use your safeword, or release the cuffs. Either one will signal an end to our scene."

"Scene?"

"It's a term you should be familiar with. In this scene, you trust me to feed you and take care of you." He stroked the line of her jaw with his index finger. "Let me take care of you."

Maybe it was the way he asked instead of ordering, or maybe her empty stomach overruled her good sense, but holding his gaze with hers, she slowly put her hands behind her back and fastened the clasp. Dropping her hands to the countertop, she pulled the chain tight and was instantly hit with a tsunami of emotions. Fighting for breath, she dropped her chin to her chest and tried to focus on getting air into her lungs. Ian clasped her shoulders and then drew his hands down her arms to her shackled wrists. "Breathe, Alexa. You're in charge, sweetheart. Nothing happens that you don't want. Remember?"

She nodded as she blew a breath out through her lips.

"Thank you for trusting me." His fingers, featherlight on her cheek, sent tendrils of heat straight to her core. "Submission looks good on you. Your cheeks are flushed, and your skin is hot." With one finger beneath her chin, he tilted her face up so their gazes met once again. "I want to see all of you." His other hand went to the front placket of her shirt. "May I?"

Lexie's heart shifted into overdrive. It was one thing to consent to the restraint, but to let him undress her? She had nothing on beneath the shirt other than a lace thong that did nothing to cover her.

Ian fingered the top button and then let his hand slide away to brush lightly over her left breast. "Maybe later?" He stepped away, coming back in an instant with a charcuterie board that had been sitting on the counter next to the refrigerator. "I promised to feed you, and that's what I'm going to do."

Gently spreading her legs, he stepped into the V he'd created and held a grape to her lips. "Open up, Alexa."

Every morsel she took from his fingers earned her praise from his lips. "So good, sweetheart."

"Good girl."

"You're doing great, Alexa."

As her stomach filled, she almost forgot about the cuffs and relaxed into the scene, though she still wasn't sure what that meant. Before her mouth went dry, he presented a water bottle with a straw and coaxed her to drink. Then he fed her more until she pressed her lips together, refusing another bite. He set the almost empty board aside and then came back to stand between her thighs. "Are you ready to tell me what had you so upset earlier?"

The nightmare her life had become came flooding back into her consciousness, and she shook her head. "No."

"Then let me take your mind off of it for a little while longer." Both hands went to the top button of her shirt. He paused a moment, silently giving her time to protest. When she remained silent, he popped the first one free, then the next. And the next. When the last one gave way, he dropped his hands to her knees. She was still covered, the shirt only slightly gaping open. "I want to see you. Touch you."

Not a question, but still asking her permission. Lexie bit her lower lip and nodded.

"Say it, Alexa. Tell me what you want me to do."

The change in his voice, the command, sent her heart racing again. She could tell him no. Use her safeword. She fingered the chain restraining her hands. A flick of her thumb would release the clasp. He'd given her control over the scene. *It's my choice. I can end it here. Or I can let him make this horrible day into something else.* Something she had wanted since the moment she'd seen him standing off-set in Malibu with a box of strawberries in his hands. Hands that were presently resting on her knees. Not moving. Not taking more than what was offered. Awaiting her permission to move.

Her life had gone completely off the rails in the last few hours, so what would be the harm in taking something for herself? Mustering all the bravado she could, she met his gaze with hers. "I want you to see and touch me. Everywhere."

Ian cocked an eyebrow. "Everywhere?"

"Yes, please."

CHAPTER TWENTY-EIGHT

Ian had, out of necessity, learned to be patient. But waiting for Lexie to decide if he could continue was slowly killing him. He was sexually dominant, but knowing that didn't give him permission to take what wasn't freely offered. Especially from a woman who didn't know what ceding control to a man like him could mean for her. He'd seen it many times. Strong, independent women wanted to control every situation, but once they finally let someone else have the reins, so to speak, they were able to experience pleasure on a whole new level. And there was nothing Ian loved more than earning a woman's trust and then giving them what they never knew they needed in return.

"I want you to see and touch me. Everywhere."

Hardly believing his ears, Ian cocked an eyebrow. "Everywhere?"

"Yes, please."

He wasn't one to argue when a woman asked for what she wanted, but in this case, he took an extra heartbeat to study her expression. Her pupils were blown with arousal. Her cheeks and chest were a becoming shade of pink that made him want to see everything she was offering. He felt he should remind her, just in case. "You can change your mind at any time."

"I won't. Touch me, Ian. Make me forget this shitty day."

He slid his hands up her thighs, letting his arms act like a snowplow, parting her shirt, exposing her creamy flesh one inch at a time. When he reached the juncture of her thighs, instead of delving beneath her panties like he desperately wanted to, he slid his hands around to her hips then up, along her ribcage until her breasts came into view. His fingers itched to touch, but as brave as she'd been to tell him what she wanted, he sensed she needed time to acclimate. Time to forget about the cuffs on her wrists and just feel. He could give her that.

With movements so slow his arms ached, he carefully skirted her breasts, his hands slipping beneath the fabric covering her shoulders. He brushed his thumbs over her collarbone, then softly swept the shirt off her shoulders, pushing it down her arms until it joined the leather cuffs imprisoning her wrists.

Leaning back, he looked his fill. He'd seen plenty of women, but none wore their submission the way she did. Posed like this, immobilized by his cuffs, his shirt. His body wedged between her thighs. "You're breathtaking, Alexa. If I were an artist, I'd paint you just like this."

"Tell me what you see."

God, would she ever stop surprising him? He searched his normally intelligent brain for the words to describe her. "Wanton beauty. Arousal in your eyes. Nipples begging for attention. A damp spot on the scrap of lace between your legs. Leather and chains at your wrists are evidence of your trust. Your submission." He lifted his gaze to hers. "You're the most beautiful woman I've ever seen, Alexa. I need to touch you. To taste you."

Her chest and face flushed a darker shade of pink. "Please, Sir."

Sir.

Holy shit. Ian bit the inside of his cheek to keep from howling. To keep from taking her right then and there like the caveman inside him demanded. He'd brought her here for her own good, not to satisfy his growing hunger for her. Of all the things he'd expected to hear her say, that one syllable wasn't among them—yet it was something he hadn't dared hope for. He hadn't earned the honorific. Didn't deserve it. Yet.

Despite the honorific echoing in his brain, she was far from his. She'd told him nothing about the things weighing her down, and wouldn't until he'd proven he was a man of his word. He'd promised to make her come as many times as it took to get her to talk to him—to confide in him.

Cradling her face in his palms, he brushed his lips over hers until her lips parted in invitation. Only then did he back away, keeping her face in a gentle grasp. "Keep your eyes open and on me, Alexa. I'm going to eat you for lunch, and I want you present for every lick, every bite, every suckle. I want you to know it's me and no one else making you come."

With her bottom lip clamped beneath her teeth, Lexie nodded her acceptance of his terms. Ian held back the groan desperately trying to work its way out. "That's my girl." Using his thumb, he freed her kiss-swollen lip. "My beautiful, sexy girl." She was all that and more, but she'd never believe him if he told her now. Forcing his gaze from her kissable lips, he cataloged the slope of her shoulders and the swell of her gorgeous breasts. Testing their weight with both hands, he bent and swiped his tongue over one nipple, then the other, until both stood at attention. Squeezing one, he took the other into his mouth and sucked the bud to the roof of his mouth. Lexie cried out and squirmed beneath him, her chest rising and falling with her rapid breathing. He switched sides, repeating the not-so-gentle handling. She deserved tender worship, and she'd get it, just not today. Today, she needed him to take her mind off her troubles. She needed to *feel*, not think.

Satisfied he'd gotten her attention, he thumbed the elastic band of her thong and jerked it down over her hips. Lifting her legs, he slid the scrap of cloth down to her ankles. He positioned her heels on the edge of the counter, then pressed down on her knees, spreading her open. The womanly scent he recalled from the day he'd spanked her wafted over him, and he knew he was lost. Only one thing would stop him from tasting her now. Glancing up, his gaze met hers. Her pupils were blown, her cheeks red, and her lips parted. "I'm going to eat the fuck out of you right now, Alexa." Her groan was a bolt of lightning to his dick, but this wasn't about him. It was about her. Pressing her knee down with one hand, he fondled her folds with the other, spreading her juices around and teasing at her entrance until her eyes closed and her head dropped back between her shoulders. Ian plunged two fingers into her wet heat. The sudden invasion brought her head up and her eyes locked with his again. Then he bent and put his mouth on her.

"Ian!" Her hips rose to meet his tongue. Holding her down with one hand pressed against her stomach, he ate his fill. Lexie was wild beneath him, taking what she wanted while he gave her what she needed. His fingers sought and found the magic spot that made her thighs tense and her breath hitch. He could do this all day, but he'd promised her orgasms, and he was a man of his word. Thrusting a third finger inside her, he stretched her opening, then curled his fingers upward, tapping against her G-spot. Her legs trembled as her body reached for the crest. Ian flicked his tongue over her clit, then sucked the swollen nub between his lips. He grazed his teeth over her clit at the same time he put pressure on her G-spot with all three fingers. Lexie flew apart. If his neighbors were home, they'd probably be calling the cops; she screamed so loud. Through it all, Ian kept his mouth on her and his fingers inside her tight sheath. When her body went lax, he rose, and cradling her nape with one hand, he brought their lips together, letting her taste herself. Her channel continued to intermittently squeeze his fingers as he wrung every ounce of pleasure out of her.

Finally, he withdrew his fingers and cupped her swollen pussy in the palm of his hand while he placed soft kisses on her lips, down the slope of her jaw, then to the sensitive spot behind her ear. He nibbled at the lobe until a shiver racked her body, and she tried to clamp his hand between her thighs. With one last tug on her ear, he whispered, "Time to talk, Alexa."

CHAPTER TWENTY-NINE

Talk? He wanted to talk? His hand rested between her legs like he owned her, and after the orgasm he'd orchestrated, maybe he did. She'd never experienced anything like what he'd done to her. Tugging on the fur-lined cuffs at her wrists sent a thrill straight to her core, her hips involuntarily thrusting up to meet his hand.

"I've got you, sweetheart." God, the man had the sexiest bedroom voice. Deep and soft, it was both arousing and soothing at the same time. "Tell me what had you all in a huff earlier, and I'll give you another orgasm." To emphasize the point, he cupped her pussy with a firm hand.

Lexie groaned and ground against his palm, seeking more of what she was afraid only he could give her.

"Tell me, sweetheart." His fingers delved between her folds, teasing. "Let me help you."

"Please." She bit her bottom lip, her focus entirely on what he was doing to her oh-so-sensitive flesh. Begging wasn't her style, but these were extraordinary circumstances. The rules didn't apply.

"Not until you tell me what had you so upset." He fingered her opening. Rimming, but not delving inside where she needed him. "No more orgasms until you tell me what happened today."

Her gaze shot up to his. "You're blackmailing me? With orgasms?" She struggled to get free, but when he captured her breast with his mouth and sucked the nipple against the roof of his mouth, her core clenched with need. Crying out, she arched her back, inviting him to do more. He switched breasts, sucking hard on her nipple while simultaneously plunging two fingers inside her channel. Lexie bucked against his hand, but as soon as she did, he withdrew to cup her pussy in that possessive way he had. He released her nipple with an audible pop. Raw need coursed through her arteries like molten lava. Her breasts tingled, and her pussy wept for more. For completion. He didn't have to say anything. His actions made his intent clear.

"Okay. Give me a second, and I'll tell you."

"That's a good girl." He massaged the aching flesh between her legs. "Give me what I want, and I'll let you have what you need."

His gentle caress was both a promise and a distraction—one she could get used to. She'd heard of edging before and thought this might fall into that category. Lexie took a calming breath, then forced her brain to recall the events of that morning.

"I'm probably going to lose my job."

His hand stilled but remained possessively over her tender parts. "What? Why?"

"Someone leaked footage of me diving into the pool yesterday. The clip has gone viral. People all over the world are laughing about the bite mark on my ass."

"They can't know it's you."

"No, but the network execs know me." Ian's hold tightened, and his eyes blazed. "Relax. They haven't seen my ass, but they know me, and they have the footage from the entire fiasco. It didn't take a rocket scientist to figure out who the ass belonged to."

His hold eased, and the massage resumed. "Is that all?"

"No. The entire production is out of control. We're over budget and strapped for time. As much as I want you to make good on your promise," she cast her gaze to where his hand rested between her legs, "I need to get back. We've got to tape the charm ceremony tonight."

Without warning, Ian plunged two fingers deep inside her, then bent, closing his mouth over hers, swallowing her gasp. His tongue mimicked the motion of his fingers, tapping at the roof of her mouth as he tapped at her G-spot. Flames licked at her body. Having been to the edge and denied, she was desperate for release. She fought the restraints, her fingers itching to guide his hands, to do whatever she could to reach the promised pinnacle. In that moment, nothing mattered except the tight coil in her belly and her need for release.

Suddenly, Ian broke the kiss, leaving her gasping for air. No sooner than she'd filled her lungs, he bent to her chest, took a nipple between his teeth, and tugged. Pain shot straight to her pussy like a lightning bolt, triggering an orgasm that rode the edge between pain and pleasure. Her lungs seized, and her head spun as her vaginal walls convulsed around Ian's intruding fingers. Unable to lie down, she bowed over Ian's head. He still had her nipple in his mouth, but he switched to gently sucking the tortured nub and laving it with his tongue.

Struggling to breathe, Lexie whispered his name.

Ian released her breast, but his fingers remained inside her, stroking now, in and out, slowly milking the last vestiges of pleasure from her walls. With his free hand, he reached behind her and flicked the clasp open, freeing her hands. Cradling the back of her head in his palm, he eased her back onto the cold quartz countertop. "Easy, Alexa. Relax. Breathe. Let me take care of you."

Continuing to lazily massage her inner walls, his free hand caressed her breasts, massaging and teasing at the same time. Boneless, she lay there, letting him touch her as her body slowly recovered from the most intense orgasm she'd ever experienced. When, at last, he withdrew his fingers and cupped her possessively, she closed her eyes and succumbed to the emotions she'd tamped down. Tears flooded her eyes, streaming down across her temples. Sobs racked her body.

Ian gently urged her up to a sitting position and brought his shirt up over her shoulders to cover her. Her ankles were still trapped by her thong, but he made quick work of those to free her legs. Whatever muscle mass she'd had before had turned to jelly in Ian's hands, so when he picked her up, cradling her against his chest, she didn't even try to fight him. When he lowered them to the well-loved sofa she'd seen earlier, she curled into his lap and let him hold her.

"Shh. It's going to be okay, Alexa. Everything is going to

be okay." His deep voice soothed, but it couldn't take away the pain of failure, and his strong arms couldn't repair the damage she'd done to her career.

She didn't know how long they sat there, but when she'd cried all the tears she had in her dark shadows had stolen the color from the room. Pushing against Ian's muscled chest, she tried to sit up, but arms like steel bands held her tight.

"Stay a minute longer, sweetheart."

"I need to go. *We* need to go. We've got to tape the charm ceremony."

"We'll go, but first, tell me what I can do to fix this. It's my fault you're in trouble with the network."

Lexie wiped at her eyes, surprised to find fresh tears pooling along her lower lids. She'd had plenty of time to think about the reason she was in her present predicament and came to one conclusion. "It's not your fault, and there's nothing you can do. Except not give me a charm. I need to get back behind the cameras, Ian."

"Let me at least talk to your supervisor. I'll take the blame for everything."

She shook her head. "No. I made my bed. I'll lie in it. There's got to be a way to salvage the show." Placing her fingers on his cheek, she positioned his face so his gaze met hers. "Don't give me a charm tonight, Ian."

"If I don't, will you agree to see me off-set?"

"You know I can't do that. What we did today…it was wonderful…perfect. And I needed it, but it can't happen again. I'm not the woman for you, Ian. I have a life, and hopefully a career, in California. I've worked too hard to give it up. And you have your career. Serenity told me you plan to run for sheriff in the next election. I can't take that away from you, and I know you don't want to take my career away from me."

CHAPTER THIRTY

Ian hated that Lexie was right. He had a well-planned career path that included running for sheriff. If he moved to California, he'd have to start over, and as she'd said, he'd worked too hard to get where he was. Quitting wasn't an option. For either of them. And as much as he loved her, yes, loved her, he couldn't ask her to give up her career either.

Knowing he had no choice but to let Lexie go felt like a mortal wound, but he wouldn't succumb without a fight. He had a contract to fulfill, and he'd use it to his advantage. "I'm going to give you a charm, Lexie." She opened her mouth to protest, but he gently pressed her lips closed. "I promised to play the part with honesty, and I will, but to do that, you have to be one of the finalists. Please don't ask me to lie to two women. Lying to one will be bad enough."

"I'm just a placeholder, and everyone knows that. Everyone but you. You talk about being honest, but you haven't given any of the women a chance. They deserve better than that."

"You're wrong, Alexa. I've given them plenty of chances and there isn't a single one of them that holds a candle to you." Trying to keep his composure, he inhaled deeply and then let the breath out slowly. "I agreed to do the show for two reasons.

Serenity said the publicity would be good for wine sales. The other reason was more selfish. I wanted to spend time with you. That was my only goal, Alexa. But as time went on, I realized my reasons went deeper. I love you. I'm *in* love with you. Looking back, I think I fell for you the day we met. So, maybe the other women never had a chance, but I can't help the way I feel."

Lexie pushed out of his lap, and he let her go. Despite the thundercloud hovering above her as she paced his living room, he couldn't help but think how much he liked having her in his space, wearing nothing but one of his shirts. "You're delusional. You know that, right?" He'd only done up a couple of buttons, and he hadn't done a good job of it. Every time she turned a certain way, the ill-fastened placket gaped open, revealing some of her more interesting body parts. When she turned the other way, the hem riding high on that side provided a glimpse of the curve of her ass where it met her thigh. He vividly recalled spanking her and then putting his mark on her. Attempting to relieve the pressure on his throbbing cock, Ian shifted in his seat. He hadn't been with a woman since he met Alexa. He'd had plenty of opportunities, but found reasons to decline every time.

"Call it what you will, but I know what I know, Alexa." Rising, Ian moved into her path. She attempted to go around him, but he easily blocked her. "Stop pacing. You're wearing a rut in the hardwood." He reached for the lowest button on her shirt, and she swatted his hand away.

"What are you doing?"

"Fixing the buttons. You can't leave here in the dress you came in, and you can't wear my shirt out with it gaping open, either." He reached again, and she let him work the button free this time. "No one sees what's mine, Alexa. Not unless I give them permission."

"What?" She slapped his hand away again and began doing the buttons up herself. "First, I'm not yours, and second, if I were, it would be up to me who I showed myself to. You'd have no say in it."

Ian swallowed the growl rising up his throat. He had no intention of letting anyone else see or touch her ever again. He'd only said that to make a point. Apparently, she hadn't gotten the message yet. "You. Are. Mine. Don't even think of letting another man see what's mine."

"Maybe you should have thought of that before you bit my ass. Your possessive streak may have cost me my job. Hell, my career. If I get fired for this, I'll never get another job in television, and it will be your fault."

Pointing out that she could have said no, and that it wasn't his idea for her to wear a swimsuit that didn't cover her butt, or to dive into a pool with cameras rolling, would serve no purpose. Those had been her decisions, but he was a grown-ass man. His shoulders were wide enough to carry her burdens. "Maybe." He shrugged. "There's no point in debating the issue, but if you think I have regrets or that I'm going to apologize for putting that mark on you, you're sadly mistaken." He closed the little distance between them, his hands automatically landing on the outside of her thighs. Slowly, he rucked the tail of her shirt up until he was touching bare skin. He slid his palms around to caress her butt cheeks, all the while watching her emotions play across her face. Anger morphed into disbelief, which shifted to acceptance. Then, the one he'd been waiting for—desire. Her pupils dilated, and her lips parted. Her skin heated, and a becoming flush crept from her chest, visible where she'd left the top two buttons undone, up the slope of her neck and across her face.

Ian squeezed her ass cheeks. "In fact, I'm going to do it again. Turn around, Alexa, and put your hands on the bar stool."

It took a moment for her to digest his words, but like the good girl she was, she followed his instructions. Ian felt the loss of her flesh beneath his palms when she turned around, but the sight of her slightly bent over, the tails of his shirt hitting just below the curve of her ass, made up for it. The need to mark her, to claim her in every way possible, roared through him like a runaway freight train. He palmed his cock, pressing as hard as he could against it in an effort to assuage his need. Lexie needed him to assert his dominion, not use her for his own gratification, and he wouldn't let her down. "I'm going to put my mark on you, Alexa, then I'm going to make you come on my fingers. Say yes if you agree to let me do these things, or walk away now. The choice is yours."

Her knuckles were white where she gripped the edges of the bar stool. Ian held his breath, waiting for her to decide. If she walked away, his chances of possessing her in the future would walk with her. But if she said yes… His dick jerked just thinking about making good on his promise.

Ian thought he might pass out from lack of oxygen before she made up her mind. Then, the faintest whisper met his ears. Unwilling to accept anything except a firm yes, he demanded she repeat herself.

"Yes. For God's sake, Ian, get on with it."

Smiling to himself, he moved in behind her. Bracketing her hips with his hands, he pressed his groin against her cloth-covered ass, letting her feel his erection. "This is what you do to me, Alexa. Only you make my dick this hard." Gathering the fabric with his fingers, he slowly exposed her ass. Torturing himself, he nudged his groin against her perfect globes, cursing the layers of cloth still between them. "One day, Alexa, you'll give yourself to me. One day, you'll say you're mine."

Pulling away, he went to his knees. The mark he'd left the other day was still there, but faded. Even knowing the trouble his actions had caused Lexie, he wasn't sorry he'd marked her. If he had his way, she'd bear his mark somewhere on her body every day for the rest of her life. An image of her wearing his collar popped into his brain. His cock throbbed at the visual. He allowed a feral growl past his lips, then he put his mouth on her and clamped his teeth down on her unmarked buttock. Lexie cried out but didn't try to get away from him. He tasted the salt on her skin and groaned as her unique fragrance wafted up to his nostrils. He filled his lungs with her drugging scent and mentally told his dick to stand down. Ignoring his own need, He held the shirt at the small of her back with one hand then probed between her legs with the fingers of his free hand. He spread her juices through her folds and up to her clit. He flicked the tiny nub with his thumb; the move earning him a curse he took as encouragement. Continuing to play with her clit, he gave her ass one last, hard suck, then popped his mouth free. The angry red spot would turn into an unmistakable dark bruise soon. He flattened his tongue over the spot, soothing it with several licks. Hand still between her legs, he stood and bent over her, bracing himself with his free hand next to hers on the bar stool. He growled into her ear. "No one sees my mark but you and me. When I ask to see it, you'll show it to me. No matter where we are or what we're doing. Understand?"

She nodded, but remained silent. Ian pinched her clit. "Say it, Alexa."

"I'll show you the mark anytime you ask."

"Anywhere I ask."

"Anywhere you ask."

God, she was perfect! He hadn't gotten everything he wanted, but he'd achieved more than he'd hoped for. He had another week to convince her to stay, to give them a chance. Sliding the hand at the small of her back around to her front, he spread his fingers over her stomach, his pinky finger close, but not touching her clit. Bent over the stool and wearing nothing but his shirt, her chin dropped to her chest, and her legs spread in submission; she was the most beautiful woman he'd ever seen. His gaze dropped to the bruise already forming on her ass, and he damn near came in his pants. Closing his eyes, he inhaled her scent deep into his body and held it there until his lungs burned. Exhaling, he praised through gritted teeth, "Good girl," then plunged two fingers into her so hard she rocked up on tiptoes. Her whimpers as he fingered her hard would play on an endless loop and fuel his solo orgasms for the foreseeable future. She rode his hand, her hips bucking as she sought her pleasure. Ian inserted a third finger, stretching her opening wide enough to take his cock. Lexie's initial cry quickly morphed into a moan as she adjusted to the intrusion. Then she ground down on his hand, impaling herself on his digits. Ian froze, three fingers buried to the last knuckle inside her.

"Please."

"Please, what, Alexa?"

"Make me come." She tried to move her hips, but with one hand on her lower belly and the other buried deep inside her, he had her right where he wanted her.

"I'm a man of my word, Alexa." He inched the hand on her belly lower, shifting it so his middle finger hovered above her clit. "I said I'd make you come on my fingers, and I will. But know this, too—you're mine. Your orgasms are mine. You won't touch yourself without my permission. If you're horny, you tell me, and I'll decide if you've earned an orgasm or not." He tapped her clit once. "Do you understand?"

He thought she was going to come apart when he tapped her clit, but she somehow kept it together with only a whimper and a strangled cry of frustration. "Say you understand, Alexa, and I'll let you come."

CHAPTER THIRTY-ONE

Lexie had never wanted to come so bad in her life. She was a hot mess. Hot being the operative word. She was burning up from the inside out. Nothing was off limits if it meant he'd let her come. Eyes squeezed shut, her concentration laser-focused on Ian's fingers and the need clawing at her, she forced the words past her lips. "I understand."

Ian crooned into her ear, "Good girl." Then he delivered, as promised. He fingered her clit with one hand while the other rocked her so hard her feet left the floor with each upward thrust. There was no time to think, to analyze her decisions, to worry about anything beyond the massive orgasm coiling tight in her belly. Her skin tingled, and her thigh muscles stiffened. She hovered on the precipice. "That's it, sweetheart." She felt more than heard his voice as it rumbled in his chest pressed against her back. "Come for me."

At his command, every muscle in her body tensed. Then, with one last tap to her clit, Lexie's world exploded like a supernova, scattering bits and pieces of her to the universe. She cried out as pain and pleasure warred, pleasure winning out as she slowly reassembled into a new version of herself.

"There you are." Lexie opened her eyes to find herself

cradled in Ian's lap on the sofa. "I was beginning to think you were going to sleep the rest of the day away."

"What?" She tried to sit up, but his arms were like steel bands, one around her shoulders, the other across her waist. "What? How?" She feebly pointed across the room. The last thing she remembered was holding onto the barstool while Ian did obscene things to her body.

"Don't tell me you can't remember your orgasm." He lifted his hand from her waist and wiggled his fingers in front of her face. "The way you squeezed me, I'm lucky to still have functioning digits."

"Oh, God!" Lexie closed her eyes and buried her face against his shoulder. Seeing his fingers made her aware of the ache between her legs. Instinctively, she closed her thighs and then instantly regretted doing so. She wouldn't be forgetting what he'd done to her anytime soon. Or ever. "I…we…"

"What, Alexa.?"

"We shouldn't have done that. This is so wrong." She tried to scoot off his lap, and this time, he let her, even steadying her with his hands on her hips when she lost her balance. "I can't be having sex with you."

"You didn't have sex with me. I gave you a couple of orgasms. *We*," he wiggled a finger between the two of them, "didn't have sex. Trust me, I'd know if we had." His gaze dipped to the obvious bulge below his belt. "After tonight's charm ceremony? I've got a week to decide which of the two remaining women I want to propose to, right? I can invite either or both of them to spend a night with me. Right?"

The thought of Ian doing the things he'd done to her with one of the other women on the show made her heart stutter and drop to her toes. She swallowed back the sick feeling in her throat and shook off the unwarranted jealousy. Who he slept with shouldn't make any difference to her, but that sinking feeling in the pit of her stomach told her otherwise. She paced away from him, hoping the distance would help clear the last of the post-orgasmic cobwebs out of her mind. "My career is on the edge of the crapper. What we did," she waved vaguely in the direction of the kitchen island, "can't happen again. I'm a professional, and I have to act like one. Rule #1 on any set is don't sleep with the talent!"

"Again, we didn't have sex. You had an orgasm. All I did

was facilitate it."

Three. Three of the best orgasms of her life. But that wasn't the point. "Ugh! You're impossible, Ian Nightingale. We've got to get back to the set. Time is money, Ian, and the budget can't handle any more delays."

Ian stood and stretched his arms above his head. "Okay. I'll take you back."

"We need to put our clothes back on."

"I'm fine the way I am."

"No, you're not. If we arrive in different clothes than we left in, speculation will run wild, and any chance I have of salvaging the production and my career will take a dive right into the aforementioned crapper."

Ian placed his hands on his hips and studied her expression. She did her best to appear a serious professional while wearing nothing but a man's rumpled dress shirt. Ian, still in jeans and a ragged T-shirt, was sexy as hell. If she put him on camera dressed like that, his hair in disarray like someone had been running their fingers through it, the ratings would skyrocket. Women would drool all over their television sets.

"Fine. We'll wear what we left in, but I hate wearing suits. After the Charm Ceremony, I'll provide my own wardrobe."

Lexie shrugged. She didn't have it in her to argue with him anymore. The style change might be just what she needed to save the production from the proverbial trash can. "No. Wear what you've got on. Let the last two women make a decision whether to accept the charm based on the real you."

"No one knows the real me more than you, Alexa. No one." He jammed his hands into the front pocket of his jeans. "Go on. Put your dress back on. I'll wait here."

"I need my panties."

He drew his left hand out of his pocket. A familiar scrap of fabric dangled from his index finger. "You mean these?" He shook his head. "Nope. They're mine now."

Lexie watched helplessly as he stuffed them back in his pocket. "I must have been out of my mind when I asked you to audition for the show."

"You knew we were meant to be, same as me." Ian dropped back onto the sofa and rested his bare feet on the coffee table. "I'll play the pretend game with you in public, but not when we're alone. When it's just you and me, we'll be ourselves. No fake smiles. No pretense." He spread his arms wide. "What you see is what you get."

Lexie nodded, agreeing to his terms. It wasn't like she'd be spending much time alone with him. Unless he insisted on giving her a charm. Even then, the execs might pull the plug on the show before she actually had to spend a night with him. Or fire her and reshoot the charm ceremony so he could pick someone to replace her. "Okay." She nodded again. "Since we're alone, I'm going to be honest with you, Ian. The first time I saw you, lurking just off-set at the Malibu shoot, I imagined being with you. I pushed you to interview—"

Ian waggled his index finger. "Tsk, tsk. You blackmailed me, Alexa."

Gritting her teeth, Lexie amended her statement. "I blackmailed you into interviewing, then I *pushed* the execs to make a deal with you to be on the show."

"And, why did you do that?"

"Will you shut up and let me have my say?" He made a show of zipping his lips, but his smile remained. He loved pushing her buttons and God help her, she reacted every time. Huffing out a breath, she took a moment to remember what she'd been saying. "I did it because I wanted to get to know you better. Your brother, Sean, thinks you're a hero. The way you stepped up for him when he was frantic to find Angellica was impressive." She wiped her clammy palms on the tails of the borrowed shirt. "I didn't expect…this. I'm not a submissive person, Ian."

He dipped his chin and observed her through his lashes. "Oh, really?"

"Despite what happened here today and during the traffic stop shoot, I'm not…the person you clearly need." There. She'd said it. The words tasted like lies, but she refused to dwell on that. Whatever this insane attraction to him was, there was no future for them, and the sooner they both recognized it, the better.

"Are you through?"

In more ways than one. Lexie nodded, but kept her thoughts to herself.

"First, I'm no one's hero." She opened her mouth to argue the point, but he held up his hand, stop sign fashion, and she swallowed her retort. "I stepped up for Sean because he's family.

He'd do the same for me. Second, I'm the only person who gets to decide what I need." He stood, closing the distance between them. When his toes met hers, he continued. "Third, you think submissive is the same as weak. Weakness doesn't appeal to me. Strength does, and you're the strongest person I know. You *are* submissive—in the only place I want you to be—the bedroom. It takes strength to relinquish control to another when you're at your most vulnerable. You submitted to me during the traffic stop and again today, and I proved to you that a little pain can be cathartic, as can intense pleasure. Whatever you need, Alexa, I'll give it to you. I *need* to give it to you."

CHAPTER THIRTY-TWO

Lexie swallowed hard. Ian wasn't wrong. But he wasn't right, either. The trouble was, she was having a hard time deciding which of his statements were right and which ones were wrong. The whole domination/submission thing had her so confused. Want and need were things she understood, but they, too, had become jumbled in her mind.

I want Ian, but I don't need him. Any man would do. Wouldn't they? Fearing she wouldn't like the answer to the question, she refused to dwell on it.

I don't need him to give me orgasms. Again, there were other men out there, and she'd never shied away from pleasuring herself when the need arose. But nothing felt as good as Ian's tongue against her clit.

I don't need him to spank me. But the sting of his hand on her ass—the feel of his strong thighs beneath her and his hard shaft gouging into her hip weren't unpleasant memories.

I don't want him to mark me. She shifted her feet; the motion bringing the latest mark he'd put on her into sharp focus. For as long as she lived, she'd never forget the way his mouth and hands had felt on her—the thrill of having him claim her in such a primal way. He wasn't a knight in shining armor, but his possession made her feel safe. Protected. Safe enough to give over full control of her body in return for mind-altering pleasure.

But none of that made any difference. Lust was something you could get over, and get over it, she would. Once there was a continent between her and Ian, forgetting about him would be a simple matter. Out of sight. Out of mind. He'd find someone else to possess, and she'd have her freedom and, hopefully, her job.

"What you *need*, Ian Nightingale, is to get back to the set so we can get this production back on schedule." He opened his mouth, no doubt to argue with her again, but she shut him down with a hand held out like a stop sign. "No. We're through with this discussion. I'm not the woman you need, Ian. I can't do whatever this is in the long term. Yeah, it's been fun, and I've enjoyed being the recipient of your undivided attention…"

"Don't forget the orgasms."

Lexie glared at him. "And the orgasms, but the life you're talking about is a fantasy. It's not real, and it's not sustainable. *The show* is reality, and we've got to get back to it."

"You've got it all wrong, Alexa. What happened here today is reality. The show is fake. Contrived relationships for entertainment purposes. What I want, what I need with you, is real. Pretending it isn't won't make it go away."

"You know what's going away, Ian? Me." She looked around for the small handbag that was more for looks on the set but contained her phone because she was never without her connection to the real world, aka her job. Spying it on the island, she brushed past Ian. "I'll call a car to pick me up." She opened her purse, only then realizing she no longer had her phone. She turned a furious glare on the man responsible for all her troubles. "Give it back."

"I'll give it back once you're in the truck with me. You aren't riding in a stranger's car wearing nothing but my shirt. I'll take you back. Give me a minute." He wasn't asking, and since he had a point about her attire, she waited while he dug a plastic grocery bag out of a drawer in the kitchen and then disappeared in the direction of his bedroom. He came back a minute later, handing her the bag. "Your dress and shoes."

Lexie took the bag.

Ian picked up a set of car keys from the table next to the front door. "Let's go. The sooner we get this over with, the better."

He didn't say a word to her on the way back to the winery, and she was too worried about losing her job to engage him in an unwanted conversation. They'd both said their peace and hadn't agreed on anything, so what more was there to say? Other than give me back my panties, but his word on that had sounded final, and if she was being truthful with herself, imagining her panties wrapped around his shaft while he jacked off was hotter than Hades.

They pulled up right in front of the Wardrobe tent, and Lexie jumped out. Before closing the door on the truck, she leaned in. "Fifteen minutes, Ian. Don't take a minute more." She slammed the door and turned to go inside the tent.

"Got it," he called out through the open window. He put the old truck in gear and left her standing there wearing a shirt she had no intention of giving back and holding a plastic bag containing her clothes.

"Girl! What happened to you?" Rafe ran to meet her as she entered the tent. "People are talking." He waggled his eyebrows as he drew out the last word. His gaze swept over her attire, appraising and drawing conclusions that were probably more or less correct. "Let me guess. He ripped the dress off of you?"

Holding the bag containing the dress and shoes out for him to take, Lexie shook her head. She hoped the dress could be salvaged, but the way her luck was running, it was destined for the trash bin. Adding the replacement cost to her already strapped budget would be the last straw. "Just too sweaty to put back on, and probably wrinkled beyond repair."

"Sweaty." The makeup artist practically purred the word. "Do tell."

"There's nothing to tell. We went for a drive in a truck with no air conditioning. I was sweating like the proverbial stuck pig in that thing, so I took it off. We're shooting the charm ceremony in fifteen minutes. I need a new dress." She glanced around at the deserted tent. "Where's everybody at?"

"It's late, hon. All the wardrobe staff left for the day. They said something about union rules and no overtime."

"Great. My day just keeps getting better and better."

Rafe gave Lexie another appraising look. "I don't know, Lex. The boyfriend shirt is a good look on you. Maybe you should just wear that with a pair of heels. Maybe add a belt, Christy

Brinkley in *National Lampoon's Vacation* style."

"I thought you liked your job."

"Oh, I do, hon. Especially on days like today. Wait right here." He sashayed off, presumably to find her another dress.

One thing at a time, she reminded herself. *Get through this shoot and worry about the final week's events tomorrow.* If there was a tomorrow for her. Avoiding calls from the network execs invited more trouble, but if she could right the ship before it sank completely, she'd have an argument for them to let her complete the project.

Lexie rejected two dress options without trying them on. The third option had a halter-style bodice and shimmering pleated skirt that moved with the slightest breeze. The voluminous skirt hid her curves, which explained why none of the other women had chosen it. It screamed, *don't look at me,* which was the opposite of what the women wanted. Even if they didn't receive a charm tonight, a seductive dress would guarantee them more screen time, possible job offers, and post-production talk show interviews. Several former contestants had gone on to lucrative careers in television. But that wasn't her goal. She already had a job in television and wanted to keep it. After a quick stop in the Makeup where Rafe did his magic, she joined the other contestants inside the event center, where they were to await the call to the set.

The atmosphere on the cocktail party set was different than previous gatherings of all the contestants. Instead of clustering together in small groups to chat and cheer each other on, the women were scattered across the fake room like one of them had the plague—only no one knew who the infected one was. So they all just kept their distance while secretly sizing up the competition with sly glances. Lexie had seen it before, but it felt different being one of the contestants and even worse when all eyes charted her entrance. "Ladies," she said, offering them a tight smile as she made her way to her usual hiding place. She received a few murmurs that might have been *hello* in return, but could have been something less welcoming. This was it. They were all hoping to be one of the two who would receive a charm tonight. All except her. Even though she'd begged Ian to choose someone else, he hadn't been swayed. She was going to receive a charm tonight, whether she wanted one or not.

I don't want one.

It was a lie she'd been telling herself ever since she'd

stepped into the contestant role. One she'd told Ian multiple times, but there, in her corner, she secretly admitted that she wanted a charm. Not just a charm…

I want him.

Even if the things he wanted, no, *needed*, from her were impossible, she still harbored feelings for him she couldn't shake. From the moment she'd noticed him at the shoot in Malibu, she'd known there was something between them. The show producers called it love at first sight, but it had been more than that. Her skin had tingled with awareness, and her insides had gone on high alert. She'd heard one contestant during a previous taping say it felt like her ovaries had exploded. That pretty much summed it up for Lexie. Even though she'd been annoyed at his tactics, she'd yearned to be close to him. It made no sense then, and even less sense now that she knew what he expected from her, but still, she couldn't shake her excitement. Fingering the bracelet bearing the charm he'd given her a week ago, she wished with all her heart that she could accept one from him tonight.

Lexie's assistant arrived, clipboard in hand, and began ushering them out to the gazebo in the order they had discussed earlier. Lexie would be last and take the corner spot in the back row where all anyone would see of her was her head. Not even that if she could manage to duck behind the contestant in front of her. Once she rejected the offered charm, she'd slink off the set and get busy planning the activities for the last week of taping. She'd survive. Ian would be furious, but he'd survive, too. And, the plot twist would be great for the show's ratings. No one had ever refused to accept a charm before. It was a brilliant idea, if she did say so herself.

CHAPTER THIRTY-THREE

"Riley, will you accept this charm?"

Ian, wearing a suit that appeared to have been custom-made for him and most certainly hadn't come from Wardrobe, looked and sounded sincere. Like he genuinely cared for the former beauty queen from Frognot, Texas. *He's a better actor than he thinks he is.*

And I'm a horrible actor. Knowing she'd be next to answer that very same question, Lexie squirmed like ants were crawling over her entire body. Good actors put aside their feelings in order to be convincing in a role polar opposite of who they were. Gentle people played murderers. Arachnophobes played spider researchers, and so on. All Lexie had to do was play the cold-hearted bitch for the three seconds it would take to break Ian's heart. And hers.

I can do this. She licked her lips and clenched her hands into fists.

The beauty queen squealed and jumped Ian, wrapping her arms around his neck, squishing her ample tits against his chest. Being a gentleman, he had no choice but to hug her back. "Yes. Yes. Yes. I'll accept your charm."

Ugh! So dramatic. So fake.

She's fake. Not Ian. Never Ian.

Come on. Wrap this up. Move on! I want to get this over with.

Lexie glanced off-set at her assistant, mentally willing her to move things along. The sooner they finished taping this segment, the better. It was still early on the west coast. She'd have time to send a clip to the network exes and explain how the plot twist would work out. They'd tease the audience for weeks ahead of airing this episode. Then they'd hit them with the best plot twist ever. It would be ratings gold! She'd salvage the entire season and her job at the same time. She'd probably get a raise. Or a promotion. Or fired. It could go either way.

With his hands on the beauty queen's waist, Ian pried her off him, setting her on her feet. Her excitement was palpable as Ian held her wrist in the palm of one hand while he tried to attach the charm to her bracelet.

Hold still. Let him fasten the charm on.

I'm dying here.

That was no lie. With every second that passed, the crack in her resolve grew bigger until she doubted her ability to say the one word she needed to say. "No." she tested it on her lips. Not even a whisper, but still loud enough to get an elbow to the ribs from the woman next to her. Lexie steeled herself. Any second now, Ian would call her name. She envisioned herself gracefully making an opening between the women in front of her, stepping past them, Ian's loving gaze following her every step as she approached him. Imagining the look on his face made her gut churn. Up until now, they'd both been honest with each other, even if their individual wants and needs made it impossible for them to be together. The lie she was prepared to utter would seal their fate.

It's the only way.

Only, it wasn't. After kissing Ian on the cheek, Ms. Beauty Queen returned to her place in the lineup. Lexie wanted to wipe the smug look off the woman's face, but throttled back her dislike. After Lexie turned down Ian, he would choose another woman. A runner-up, per se. He had to. That's the way the game was played. Once again, she tested the single syllable on her lips and found it even harder to utter. If she couldn't do it across the room from Ian, could she do it to his face?

The show's host cleared his throat. Lexie's gaze shot up as

the man waited for the women fawning over the beauty queen's newly acquired charm to quiet. Once he had everyone's attention, he stated the obvious. "Ladies, there's only one charm left." He nodded to Ian. "Choose wisely."

Ian shot his cuffs then his gaze swept the assembled contestants, coming to a stop on the woman next to Lexie before sweeping back the other way. Was he trying to be discreet? Or was snubbing her some sort of message? Lexie's gut churned as Ian picked up the last charm from the tray beside him.

This is it. Showtime. She gripped her skirt with both hands, preparing to lift it free of her feet the moment he called her name. Face-planting on her way to reject him wouldn't do. She had to appear dignified. Confident. Or he'd never let her go. Blood roared past her ears, and with her gaze fixed on the shoulders of the women one step down and in front of her, she almost toppled forward when she heard Ian's voice.

"Harper."

An audible gasp rose from the other contestants and the production crew off set. Lexie jerked her gaze to Ian. He wasn't looking at her. He was looking at the woman *next* to her.

Harper. The actress from some place in Virginia no one had ever heard of. Statuesque, with a mane of strawberry blonde hair, she was the quietest one of the bunch. If they gave a Miss Congeniality award, she'd win it, hands down. Everybody loved her. She didn't rock the boat. Didn't call attention to herself intentionally. She didn't need to. She was lovely in the vintage Hollywood style that drew eyes her way without her doing a thing to encourage the attention.

Time moved in slow motion as the proverbial seas parted, allowing Harper to step down. It took a lifetime for the woman to cross the gazebo. All the while, Ian's gaze never left her. Once she stood before him, he stretched his palm out, revealing the charm. The studio lighting flashed off the polished silver as the overhead camera zoomed in on the tiny piece of jewelry.

Lexie shook her head as her worst nightmare unfolded in front of her. He'd chosen someone else. Just as she'd asked him to.

Damn him!

Damn him all to hell!

Tears streamed down her cheeks. The word, no, rattled through her brain, but her vocal cords and numb lips refused to cooperate. Her knees threatened to give out on her as she watched the train wreck happening before her.

"Harper, will you accept this charm?"

"Yes! Of course, I will."

Of course, I will. Lexie's brain mocked the woman's words. It was petty jealousy, but up until Ian called the other woman's name, Lexie hadn't known how deep her feelings for Ian went. Now she knew, and her heart lay shattered at her feet. He'd made his intentions plain. He wanted her. He loved her, but she'd pushed him away. Told him what she wanted, *needed*, him to do, and he'd done it. He'd chosen someone else. He'd let her go.

He'd been adamant that he wouldn't do it, so she'd devised a plan to reject him and force him to choose another. And then he went and did something like this.

Why? Had everything Ian said to her been a lie?

Chaos reigned for a few minutes as the latest charm recipient returned to her place. Lexie clenched her trembling hands together in front of her and played the part of the crushed contestant for the cameras. She forced a smile to her face and muttered her congratulations.

Her assistant called for order, and the shoot resumed. The host returned with instructions for the rejects to say their goodbyes, and ignoring all the other women, Lexie was the first to approach Ian. She thought she saw a flash of regret in his eyes before he reached out and took her hands in his.

"It's been a pleasure getting to know you, Alexa. I hope you find what you're looking for." He squeezed her fingers gently, then bent so his cheek rested against hers. He whispered in her ear. "I'll always love you, Alexa. Always." The kiss he placed on her cheek weakened her knees. The words spoken only for her had the ring of finality to them. She wanted more than anything to say them back to him, but when he pulled away, his eyes were cold, and his jaw set. He'd made up his mind to let her go, and there'd be no changing it.

CHAPTER THIRTY-FOUR

"Have another drink." Wade waved the bottle of fifty-year-old whiskey in front of Ian's face.

Ian shook his head and instantly wished he hadn't. He was scheduled to work the day shift tomorrow, and he'd already had more to drink than was prudent. "Nah. I'm good."

"Maybe you should take tomorrow off." Wade set the half-empty bottle on the coffee table then joined Ian on the sofa. "You're going to hate yourself in the morning."

He already hated himself, but not for the reasons his brother thought. "If I don't have anything to do, I'll just sit around and second-guess my decision. Work will keep my mind off my stupidity."

Serenity breezed into the living room carrying a giant bowl of popcorn and a handful of napkins. "Don't beat yourself up over it, Ian. You did what she asked you to do." She picked up the liquor bottle and returned it to the bar cart in the corner of the room. After placing the popcorn bowl beside Ian's feet on the coffee table, Serenity curled up on the old love seat that had been in the Granger house as long as he could remember. She leaned over, took a giant fistful of popcorn then sat back. "One of these days, she'll be sorry she chose her job over you."

Leave it to Serenity to boil a complicated mess down to one sentence. Ian drained the last of the whiskey in his glass then helped himself to a fistful of popcorn. Anything to keep his mouth occupied so he wouldn't spill his guts to his brother and future sister-in-law. He'd already said enough to have them feeling sorry for him. He didn't need them to bash Lexie on top of everything else. He'd done what he'd done because she'd asked him to, and because it was the right thing to do. Her job meant a lot to her, and she'd been right about neither of them wanting to uproot themselves. No matter how perfect Lexie was for him, he wasn't going to leave Riverside or the sheriff's department. Not when the current sheriff planned to retire next year. Ian had put in the years and had the experience to take on the office. The informal poll he'd commissioned showed he'd win if the election were held this year. He had a good shot at winning next year, especially if Sheriff Ritter endorsed him. Which the man had already agreed to do. So, yeah. Ian wasn't going anywhere.

Hopefully, not giving Lexie a charm would go a long way to salvaging her job. He hadn't heard from her since she'd said goodbye to him for the cameras. He'd hoped she'd be the last to approach him so they could linger after the taping and talk, but she'd thwarted that plan by being the first of the rejected women to leave the set. She'd given him no time to explain why he'd changed his mind, and the hurt he'd seen in her eyes gutted him. But there was no going back now. He tossed a kernel of popcorn in the air, catching it in his mouth. Apparently, he wasn't near drunk enough if he could do that. "All I want is for her to be happy." Another kernel. Another catch.

Serenity turned the television on with the remote and began flipping through the channels. Wade held out his hand. "Here. Give me that. We aren't watching a sappy rom-com tonight."

Sen handed over the device then sat back, arms crossed. "Rom-coms are funny and uplifting. Exactly what Ian needs tonight."

"Oh, no." Ian stood. "All Ian needs is a good night's sleep." He stepped over Wade's outstretched legs. "You two lovebirds can fight over the remote. I'm going to bed."

Wade muted the television. "You know she's staying in my house. You could go talk to her."

Ian paused at the bottom of the staircase. God, it hurt knowing she was a short golf cart ride away. *Thanks for the reminder, bro.* He picked up the suit coat he'd hung on the newel post when he'd come in from the taping. "She doesn't want to talk to me." Without a backward glance, he trudged up the stairs to the guest room where he'd been staying during the taping.

From the upstairs room, he had a view of the pool all the way across his family's vineyard to the mountain ridge far in the distance. In between, dots of light marked various homes and buildings on the Nightingale property, including the house Wade had built for himself almost a decade ago. It had sat empty since he'd moved into Serenity's aging home until the production company rented it out for Lexie. Having her so close to the action was good for business, but not so good for Ian. He crammed the last of the popcorn kernels into his mouth and chewed; his gaze focused on the pinpoint of light he knew represented Wade's house.

Was Lexie still awake? Thinking about him? Or had she put him out of her mind? Was she sleeping like a baby? Her worries solved now that he'd essentially booted her off the island? *I hope so.* If anything good was to come from the acid eating his insides, he hoped Lexie had found peace in her world. He'd never been in love before, and recognizing the self-sacrificing emotion, he hated it. He doubted he'd ever get over Lexie, but he would move on. Eventually. Love again? No. Never. But he'd play. It had been a while since he'd gone to either of the two clubs he belonged to in the city. In the past, he'd always found someone there willing to go to their knees for him. *Too willing,* he thought, recalling why he'd stop going. None of the subs there had presented a challenge. All he had to do was point at the floor, and they'd obey. After meeting Alexa Hanson, easy hadn't been enough. Turns out, he liked a challenge.

Lexie challenged him at every turn, and he'd taken the bait—hook, line, and sinker—never thinking she was a catch-and-release type of person.

He'd learned a lot about himself in the last few weeks. Dominant tendencies came naturally to him, and he'd never had reason to question his need to be in charge of his partner's pleasure. His ability to read people was partly what made him a good cop, and it served him well as a Dom, too. It was all in the body language. And it was Lexie's body language, not her words, that changed his mind about giving her a charm.

She'd been afraid of what he made her feel. He'd seen it in her eyes and in the way she held herself apart from him. How she'd used her job as a shield between them so she wouldn't have to face the truth about herself. She was sexually submissive. Down to the marrow of her bones. And that scared the living daylights out of her. After he'd put some distance between them, he'd realized he had to let her go. Maybe she'd come to terms with her submissive side in the future. Or maybe she wouldn't. For her own good, he hoped she did. He hated to think of her going the rest of her life without experiencing the kind of pleasure he knew she was capable of, but on the other hand, the idea of her kneeling for someone else brought him to his knees.

Ian dropped to the floor and sat with his back to the wall beneath the window. Legs bent, he rested his elbows on his knees and dropped his head into his upturned palms. *Christ.* How the hell was he going to complete this charade with the two women he'd given charms to, with Alexa imprinted on his very being? *Impossible.* Especially with Lexie standing behind the cameras.

He couldn't do it, but he had to. He'd signed a contract. Hell, his family's business had signed contracts. *I should have taken a leave of absence and gone to California to do the show.* That would have kept his family out of his mess but wouldn't have changed anything between him and Lexie. As long as she denied her submissive side, there couldn't be anything between them.

Ian kicked his legs out in front of him and dropped his head back against the windowsill hard enough to shake him out of his maudlin thoughts. Tomorrow, he'd move back to his own place across town. Being this close to Lexie and not being with her was torture. How he was going to get through the next week with her calling the shots, he had no idea.

CHAPTER THIRTY-FIVE

"Hey," Lexie shoved her suitcase through the door with her foot. She let her carry-on slide down her arm to the tiled entryway floor, then shouldered the door shut behind her. "I made it," she said into the phone wedged against her shoulder.

Her best friend, Angellica Capello, now Nightingale, squealed so loud Lexie feared for her eardrum. "I'm on my way. Don't move!"

Lexie opened her mouth to tell Jelly not to bother coming, but her protests were met with silence. She'd already ended the call. She thought about calling her back but was too tired to argue with her. Besides, it had been too long since she'd seen her best friend, and tired as Lexie was, she needed someone to talk to. Her life had gone from almost perfect to a shitshow in a matter of days. She'd hoped Ian not giving her a charm would appease the network execs, but that hadn't been the case. When her phone rang at 3:00 a.m., midnight California time, she'd known before she even took the call that her career was over. And she'd been right.

She'd spent the remainder of the night packing and, thanks to Uber, made the first flight out of Newark to Los Angeles that morning.

Since Angellica and her new hubby, Sean Nightingale,

Ian's other brother, lived in Temecula and Lexie's house was in the San Fernando Valley, several hours drive on a good day, Lexie headed straight for her bedroom. She'd tried to sleep on the plane, but every mistake she'd made since she met Ian played on a loop through her brain, ensuring she couldn't sleep a wink. Then there'd been the toddler in the seat behind her who apparently had yet to discover words and screeched the entire five-hour flight. Lexie might have had some sympathy if they'd been happy screeches, but they weren't. They sounded exactly like Lexie felt, and she'd wished she could get away with venting her misery in the same way. Alas, that would have gotten her kicked off the plane and probably on a no-fly list somewhere, too. Suffice it to say, she didn't think there was anything in the world that would keep her awake now. Kicking off her shoes, she belly-flopped onto the bed and went lights out as soon as she closed her eyes.

The ringing of her phone, accompanied by someone pounding on her front door, woke Lexie. The light streaming through the gap in her curtains told her she hadn't slept long. Her aching head and stiff body told her she hadn't slept long enough. A quick glance at her home screen confirmed that Jelly was responsible for the door pounding as well as the phone call.

"Alright, already!" Lexie sat on the edge of the bed and rubbed the sleep from her eyes. "I'm coming!" Both offending sounds ceased. Lexie dodged the suitcases she'd left in the tiny entryway and yanked the door open. Bright California sunlight seared her retinas. She brought a hand up to shield her eyes. The first thing she made out was a wine bottle waving six inches from her nose. Then Jelly's face came into focus.

"Surprise! We brought wine!"

We? That's when she noticed Jelly's husband, Sean Nightingale, standing on the porch, his arms wrapped possessively around Jelly's growing belly. She should have known he wouldn't let his wife, pregnant with triplets, drive all that way by herself. If he was anything like Ian, he probably didn't let Jelly out of his sight. It was understandable and sweet in a caveman sort of way, but the last thing she needed right then was a reminder of the man who had rejected her.

Jelly thrust the bottle into Lexie's hands then spun and placed a decidedly not PG kiss on Sean's lips. When they parted, she patted him on the chest. "I'm good. Thanks for driving."

Sean swept a lock of stray hair out of Jelly's eyes. "No problem. I'll be at the hotel. Call me when you're ready to leave, and I'll come get you."

"It might be late."

"Anytime, Jelly Bean. I'll be up."

I didn't even want to know if that was code for something sexual, but suspect by the grin on his face that it was. And, Jelly Bean? What the hell?

Sean glanced over her friend's shoulder. "Lexie." His gaze and the dip of his chin conveyed a lot. He was trusting Lexie with the most precious things in his life, and he'd kill her if anything happened to them.

Lexie gave him a slight nod in return.

After placing his hand on Jelly's stomach one more time, he returned to the Land Rover waiting at the curb.

Lexie smirked. "Okay, *Jelly Bean*, get in here so Papa Bear can leave." With a final wave goodbye, Angellica followed Lexie inside. "Is he always that protective?"

"Pretty much." Her friend made herself at home on the sofa. "It can be annoying at times, but then I think how much worse it would be if he didn't care at all, and I realize how fortunate I am. He's a good man."

Lexie had met all three Nightingale brothers and could say the same for Wade and Ian. She suspected they took after their father, but had yet to meet the man. "I'm happy for you, Jelly." She held up the bottle of wine. "No label?"

"We're still trying to decide on a design so we can bottle the rest of it."

"Are you going to tell me what's in it?"

"Nope. I want you to try it first and tell me what you think."

"You've tasted it?"

"The doctor said I could have the occasional sip, which Sean took to mean one sip a week. I've already had my quota for the week, so that's all yours."

"Thanks. I'll be right back." Lexie took the bottle to the kitchen. After opening it, she poured herself a glass and then grabbed a water bottle for Jelly from the refrigerator. "Am I going to love or hate this?" Lexie asked as she handed over the water bottle, then settled on the sofa, wine glass in hand.

"Love it."

"Okay. Here goes." Having a best friend whose family had been in the wine business for generations, Lexie was well-versed in the correct way to sample a new wine. As she lifted the glass to her nose to take a whiff, she tried not to think of the "dates" she'd planned for Ian and the two women he'd chosen as finalists for his affections. He'd be taking them each to the Nightingale Winery Tasting Room for a private tasting he would conduct before introducing them to his family. Even though Ian wasn't active in the family business, it was important to him that his partner in life have some knowledge of the wine industry. A discerning palate wasn't a necessity, but it would go a long way to making her fit in with his relatives.

Lexie took a delicate sniff. "Uhm," she hummed. "There's a lot going on there, but cherries and oak stand out." Lifting the glass, she swirled the liquid around in the bowl, watching how it clung to the sides before forming rivulets, or legs, as they were known in the wine world. "Great legs. I bet it goes down smooth." The last stage was actually tasting the wine. Lexie took a moderate swig, let it rest on her tongue for a heartbeat before swallowing. Her eyes widened. She licked her lips, savoring every drop. "Damn, Jelly Bean! This might be the best thing I've ever tasted." Her friend preened while Lexie took another healthy sip. "How did you come up with this?"

"It's all Sean's doing. I'm good with blending wines, but he's a genius. It's a blend of a Nightingale Merlot and a Capello Cabernet Savignon."

"This is why he bought Capello Vineyards." She'd thought it odd when Sean purchased the century-old vineyard so far away from his family's wine empire in New Jersey. "He already knew how well the two would blend."

Jelly nodded. "Pretty much. He'd blended some already bottled vintages and risked everything he had on his experiment."

"You're going to be rich. People will pay out the wazoo for this."

"That's what we're hoping. I'll let Sean know it has your seal of approval." Jelly shifted on the sofa so she was fully facing Lexie. "Enough about the wine. Tell me why you're back early."

CHAPTER THIRTY-SIX

Lexie drained the last bit of liquid gold from her glass then retrieved the bottle from the kitchen and refilled her glass. She was right, the blend went down smooth. Unlike the telling of her story. That was a bitter pill to swallow.

"I messed up, Jell." Angellica didn't respond, which meant she was reserving judgment until she'd heard the entire story. Lexie took a tiny sip from her glass and then spilled the entire story in all its ugly glory. "I still have a job, just not on the show. I'll probably be mopping floors or reading scripts from the slush pile, but I'll have a paycheck."

"Maybe this is a good time for you to explore other options, Lex. *Love at First Sight* wasn't your dream job. For as long as I've known you, you've wanted to do something else, something with more grit. Maybe you should try following your dream for a change."

Jelly wasn't wrong. Creating artificial love matches had never been her end game, but it had paid the bills. "I wouldn't know where to start."

"You've always wanted to delve into cold case files, one in particular. You could start with that one. Work on it in your spare time and see what you can find. Television is your first love, but podcasts are big these days. The equipment is affordable, and you could work from home—again, in your spare time. When the podcast takes off, and you get enough sponsors, you could quit your day job and research full-time."

"I don't know if I'm ready to dig into my mother's file yet."

"Then don't. Find another case to explore." Jelly tossed her now empty water bottle on the coffee table. "Enough about work. I'm sure you'll figure something out. Let's talk about Ian."

Lexie shook her head. "Let's not and say we did."

"Nope. I let you distract me with work talk, but that's over. It's time to talk about the man you're in love with and avoiding."

"I'm not avoiding him. I was removed from my job and recalled to California."

"Hmm. Telling that you didn't say you weren't in love with him."

Lexie curled her feet underneath her and sipped her wine. It was useless to deny her feelings for Ian, but those same feelings were the reason she hadn't told him she was leaving. She didn't trust herself around him.

"You could have stayed long enough to tell him you were leaving, but you didn't. That's avoidance."

"Looks who's talking. You hid out in my house to avoid talking to Sean."

"That was different."

"I don't see how."

"I wasn't in love with him."

"Liar."

Jelly shrugged. "Okay. I was in love with Sean, but I didn't think he was in love with me. Ian, on the other hand, told you he was in love with you, and you pushed him away. For what?"

"My job." The excuse sounded pathetic, even to her own ears.

"How did that work out for you?"

"It didn't, Jelly. Is that what you want to hear? I lost my job, but it was all Ian's fault."

"How do you figure that?"

"He refused to play by the rules. He didn't even pretend to like any of the cast. He spent all his time trying to lure me away from the cameras so he could…do things to me."

"Tell me about that traffic stop again."

"Why?"

"Because I want to count how many times you told him no during that encounter."

Lexie felt her face flame. "Okay, so I didn't explicitly tell him no, but he knew I didn't want to do all those things."

"Yet, you were given the chance to walk away, and you didn't take it. Want to tell me why?"

Lexie got up to pace the small living room. Ian's bite mark from the traffic stop shoot had faded away, but the more recent one remained. She felt it every time she sat down and every time her ass jiggled when she walked. It was one of the reasons the cross-country flight had been so miserable. Its presence made her think of Ian and the way he touched her. The way he looked at her. The way he *saw* her. No one else had ever looked beneath her skin the way he did. "He scares me."

"What?" Jelly struggled to her feet. "Did he hurt you? Are you okay? I'll kill him with my bare hands."

"No. No, Jell." Lexie shook her head. "Ian would never harm me. He's a hero. A real-life hero. He's got a savior complex a mile wide."

"And that scares you?"

"Yeah." She took Jelly's hand and led them both back to the sofa. "No one has ever seen me the way he does." Lexie reached for her wine glass and took a fortifying sip. "You can't tell anyone what I'm about to say. Especially Sean."

"If his brother hurt you, then I won't make that promise, Lex."

"As I said, Ian would never hurt me. His savior complex is…complicated."

"I swear to God, woman, if you don't tell me what you're talking about right this minute, I'm going to call Sean and tell him to murder his brother."

Lexie placed a staying hand on her friend's arm. "Ian is dominant."

Jelly's brows met in the center of her forehead. "Ooookaaaay."

"He's a Dom. You know, like Christian in that book."

Understanding dawned, and Jelly's gaze bored into Lexie.

"Christian Gray hit what's her name."

"He might have been a sadist, too, but Ian's not like *that*. He's observant. He saw that I was upset, and he wanted to take my mind off my troubles."

"So he *hit* you?" It was difficult to determine which emotion was stronger beneath Jelly's words, anger or disbelief.

"No. He gave me three orgasms and bit me on the ass again. I told him not to give me a charm. He refused to cooperate, then he took me back to work where he did exactly what I asked him to."

"He gave you three orgasms? In one day?"

"In about an hour. Give or take. But you're missing the point, Jell."

"Forgive me. I'm having a hard time wrapping my head around this. You walked away from a man who gave you three orgasms in the span of an hour—and marked your ass like a caveman. Are you insane?"

"I don't know why I thought you'd understand. Maybe I am insane." She drained her glass and promptly refilled it.

"Oh, I understand. I think." Jelly placed her hand on Lexie's forearm. "You aren't afraid of Ian. You're afraid of the things he makes you feel. You know as well as I do that there are all kinds of television jobs in New York, so making this about your work is just a convenient excuse. A shield you put up so you don't have to admit the truth."

Lexie scoffed. "And what truth would that be?"

"That Ian saw through the walls you put up. He saw behind the mask you put on for work. He saw the real you. And the real you liked everything he did to you." Jelly pushed off the sofa. "Wait right here. I've got to pee."

As soon as she heard Jelly returning, she called out. "You're wrong."

"No, I'm not." Jelly eased back onto the sofa. "Ian's the first man you've been with that you couldn't control."

Lexie shook her head. "Not true."

"Name one man you've dated who wasn't under your thumb the entire time you were together."

"There was…Geoff."

"He wouldn't tie his shoelaces unless you told him to."

"Tim."

"You mean, Timid Tim? The guy who insisted all the lights were off before he'd get naked? That doesn't count. He was just putting off the inevitable."

Lexie shrugged. "I don't know why he thought that would work. All I had to do was touch him to figure out I'd need a spotlight to find his dick. A bedside lamp wouldn't have made any difference."

"Anyone else?"

"No." Lexie picked at a pulled thread on her leggings. "You might have a point."

"I know I do. So, are you ready to admit you like the good-looking, heroic, bossy, dominant type?"

CHAPTER THIRTY-SEVEN

"Are you ready?"

The sooner the farce was over, the better. He'd hoped to have a minute with Sean before taping this segment of the show, but Sean arrived with just enough time for the makeup people to wipe the shine off his face. His brother owed him, and Ian had every intention of collecting on the debt. Ian gave the faintest nod to the production assistant, then made his way to the front door. His family, minus his new sister-in-law, who was too pregnant to make the trip, sat at a table in the tasting room, ready to meet the two women who wanted to become the newest Mrs. Nightingale. He'd told them ahead of time that neither of the women they were to meet today would ever become his wife, and they'd agreed to play along. They all had something to lose if Ian came off looking like an ass on national television. The adage that all publicity was good publicity wasn't necessarily true these days. A negative social media post could wreck their reputation and tank sales faster than a bachelorette party could suck down a case of wine.

The final two contestants waited outside, arm in arm, looking like the best of friends. Ian knew otherwise. This show of solidarity was just that, a show. They were pissed, and he couldn't blame them. He'd met with them individually to tell them where they stood, and then he'd approached the production assistant and told her there was no need for his family to suffer through two fake interviews. The faster they all got this playacting over with, the better.

Pasting a smile on his face, Ian approached the ladies, giving them each a friendly peck on the cheek. "It's so good to see you," he crooned. "Thank you both for coming." For the benefit of the show, he recited the scripted words. "As you know, I'm not personally involved in the family business, but it's important that my wife understands my connection to the wine industry. Nightingale wine flows through my veins and always will. Our family is very close, and I could never bring anyone into the family that they didn't approve of." He paused for dramatic effect. "That being said, they respect my decisions and always have. That's why I'm certain they're going to love both of you." Ian stepped between them, offering each an arm. "Come on. Let me introduce you to the Nightingales."

Everyone stood as they approached. Introductions were made, and pleasantries exchanged. The scripted conversation went as well as could be expected, given the circumstances. They all knew it was a sham, but smiles remained in place, and they all played their parts. As previously planned, his mom and dad left with one of the women to do a private interview at one of the picnic tables outside while Wade and Serenity held a wine tasting at the bar for the other woman. The women would switch places after a few minutes, and the same script would repeat itself. That left Ian alone with Sean.

It only took them a few minutes to tape their scripted conversation, and as soon as it was over, Ian waved Sean into the storage room and closed the door behind him. "Have you seen her?" he asked his brother.

"I assume you mean Lexie."

"Who the hell else would I be asking about? She's your wife's best friend. They're thick as thieves."

"You're right about that, and though I sympathize with your situation, I'm glad Lexie's back home. Angellica needs her right now."

God, he felt like an asshole for not asking about Sean's wife first. "How's she doing? And the babies?"

"They're all fine, thanks for asking, but Angellica needs a

woman to talk to, you know? I'm sympathetic and all, but there's no way I can truly understand what she's going through. It helps to have Lexie there to talk to."

"I'm glad she's there, then."

Sean slapped him on the shoulder. "No need to lie to me. Mom and Dad filled me in. Do both those women know you aren't going to propose to them?"

Ian rubbed the back of his neck. "Yeah. You know me. I couldn't let them think any of this was real. They hate me, but they're going along with it, anyway. I think they both expect to get more acting deals once the season airs."

Sean nodded. "I hope they do. They deserve something for seeing this through. But that's not why we're standing in the storeroom, is it?"

"No. I want to know about Lexie. Is she okay? Did she really get fired because of me?"

"They demoted her. She's a script consultant now? I think that's what Angellica said. She sits off-set with the script in hand and prompts the actors when they forget their lines. She's working on a soap opera or a daytime drama?" He waved a hand dismissively. "Something like that."

"This is all my fault."

"I'm not going to argue with you, Ian, but from what little I've been told, Lexie played a part in her own downfall. And before you get all bent out of shape, Angellica didn't tell me anything. Everything I know comes from Lexie herself. She didn't want me to be mad at you."

The door swung open, and Emma stuck her head inside. "There you are. Come on, it's time for the big goodbye scene with the contestants. Their families are coming in later tonight. We'll tape the meet her parents segments tomorrow."

"Be right there." Once she'd gone, Ian faced his brother. "I don't want to get you into trouble with Angellica, but can you keep an eye on Lexie? Let me know if she needs anything?"

Sean gazed at him with a critical eye. "You're serious about her."

"No shit, Sherlock. I'm in love with her. She's the one."

"You sound like you're certain about that."

"I am. I'll do anything for her, including let her go if that's what she really wants, but I'm hoping some distance will help her see what we have together."

"What, exactly, do you have together?"

"An endless love."

The door squeaked on its hinges, and Emma poked her head inside again. Neither man moved, their gazes locked.

Emma's voice boomed through the cavernous room. "Get out here. Both of you. Now!"

Sean nodded. "Okay, baby brother. I'll spy for you, but you better not mess this up. Angellica will kill me if she finds out I helped you hurt her best friend."

"I can't make that promise, but I'd rather cut my dick off than hurt Alexa."

His brother cringed. "Yikes. I hope it doesn't come to that."

"It won't. And, thanks. I appreciate your help." Ian grabbed his older brother in a fierce hug. "You always were my favorite brother."

With a final back slap, Sean pushed away from his baby brother and headed toward the door. "Fuck you, man. Overkill on the bullshit. You worshipped Wade when you were a kid, and don't pretend otherwise."

Ian kept pace with him. "I was too busy trying to keep you and Serenity alive back then to worship Wade. The two of you owe me your lives, and you know it."

Sean paused before opening the door. "You were a little tattle-tale shit. You spoiled all our fun."

Ian laughed. "And you can thank me by keeping an eye on my woman."

Sean rolled his eyes and then pushed the door open. "Showtime, asshole."

CHAPTER THIRTY-EIGHT

Lexie eyed Sean as she filled an insulted tumbler from the chilled water dispenser in the refrigerator door. This was the first time she'd been alone with him since he'd returned from taping the last segments of the reality show two weeks ago. With Jelly on bed rest for the final few weeks of her pregnancy, Lexie had taken all her accumulated vacation days to help her friend out. So far, all she'd done was keep Jelly fed and hydrated while they binge-watched old TV shows together. She was dying to question Sean about the show she'd once been in charge of and to ask about Ian. Sean had been home for two weeks, and it crossed her mind that he was avoiding her, though she doubted that was the case. He wouldn't neglect his pregnant wife to avoid talking to her best friend, and since she and Jelly had been inseparable the last few days...

"Is there anything I can do for you while I'm here?" Lexie checked the water level in the tumbler, pulled it out from under the dispenser, and screwed the lid on. "Jelly takes a lot of naps. I feel like a bum just sitting around waiting for her to wake up."

"I appreciate you keeping Angellica company. There's a lot going on right now with introducing the new wines. Losing those few days last week put me behind. I'd like to catch up so I can take more time off when the babies come. Knowing you're with her gives me the peace of mind to work."

"The wine you guys brought over the night I got home was superior. Jelly said it's one of the new ones?"

"Yeah. It's the reason I bought this vineyard from her father. I took some bottles back to New Jersey with me so the family could taste-test them, too."

Lexie immediately thought of Ian. He wasn't directly involved in the family business, but he knew wine. It was in the Nightingale's blood, she supposed. "How did it go over?"

Sean's smile lit the room. "I think I finally won them over to my way of thinking. They, and everyone else, thought I was nuts to blend wines from two different parts of the country."

"Ian didn't think you were nuts."

Sean cocked his head to one side. "Ian talked about me?"

"He was explaining to me why he never wanted to work in the family business. He said Wade was a genius when it came to the wine business and that you're a genius at blending wines. He didn't think there was anything left for him to do."

"Did he tell you he's a sommelier? Passed the certification before he graduated college."

Lexie let that bit of news sink in. "No. He didn't mention that."

"Don't be offended. He doesn't tell anybody. I'm not sure our parents know, but for what it's worth, there will always be room for him at Nightingale's, and he knows it. I think he feels guilty for wanting something for himself that isn't wine-related, so he makes up excuses for doing what he was meant to do. None of us are pushing him away from the family business. On the contrary, we're proud of him for following his heart."

"Why do you think he agreed to do the reality show? It doesn't sound like something he'd do."

Sean leaned his hips against the counter and crossed his arms over his chest. He focused his gaze on Lexie. "Two reasons. It would be good for Nightingales. He was right. It's going to be excellent publicity for us. And yes, I think it's his way of contributing to the business. Might even ease his guilt a little bit. I hope so, anyway."

"And the second reason?" she prompted.

"You."

Lexie's heart lodged in her throat. "Me?" she croaked out.

Sean shrugged. "My baby brother is stupid in love with you, Lexie. He feels horrible about you losing your job. Thinks it was all his fault."

"He thinks that because I told him it was his fault." Lexie sagged against the island. "I was so mad at myself for being impulsive that I took my anger out on him."

"Do you still blame Ian?"

"No. I mean, if he hadn't…done the things he did…none of the other stuff would have happened. But I could have said no." Heat crept up her face. Thinking about all the things she'd done with Ian brought back feelings she'd tried to run away from. But putting a continent between them hadn't been enough to keep the feelings at bay. "I'm sorry. I shouldn't be talking about this with you." Embarrassment added flames to her already red cheeks.

"Maybe you should talk to Angellica."

Lexie nodded as she walked toward the back staircase. "Thank you. I might do that." Out of breath when she reached the second-floor landing, Lexie grabbed the banister, sank down to the top step, and flopped onto her back to stare at the ceiling. Her stomach was in knots, and she could hardly breathe for all the thoughts swirling in her brain. She'd been doing so well up until she'd met Ian Nightingale. She had a career she didn't love but was good at. She had her little house in the valley and a small, well, tiny, nest egg. Then *he* had walked into her life, and like any rooster in the henhouse, created havoc. Her life hadn't been the same since. But could she place all the blame on Ian?

No. I pursued him. Blackmailed him into auditioning for the show, then pushed his audition through. If I'd let things be, he might not have been chosen for this season's show.

Lexie's stomach tumbled.

And then I wouldn't know the thrill of his touch. Or the peace of submitting to him.

She bolted upright so fast her head spun. Bracing her forehead against the newel post, she faced the reality of her situation. *I'm in love with him.* She thumped her head against the polished wood in rhythm with her thoughts. *Hopeless. Hopeless. Hopeless.*

"Lexie?"

Crap! Wrapped up in her own misery, she'd forgotten all

about Jelly. "Coming!" She darted into her best friend's bedroom. An apology for taking so long died on her lips when she saw the pain etched on Jelly's face. "Oh, no! What's wrong?"

Jelly struggled to sit up. "Babies." Lexie set the water bottle on the nightstand and then slipped her arm around her friend, helping her into a sitting position.

"What about the babies?"

"Are coming." She panted the words out.

"Now? They aren't due for two more weeks!"

"Tell them that!" Jelly grabbed her abdomen and screamed through the pain.

"Okay. Okay. We have a plan for this." She fished her phone out of her pocket and dialed Sean's number. He answered on the second ring.

"Lexie?"

"Sean. It's time. The babies are coming!"

There was a moment of dead air, then Sean calmly spoke. "I'm on my way. Stay with her. I'll bring the car around." The line went dead.

Lexie returned her attention to Jelly. "Sean's on the way. Let's get you ready to go."

CHAPTER THIRTY-NINE

The next few hours were chaotic, with a mad dash to the hospital followed by phone calls and worry that drained Lexie's strength and consumed her thoughts. Through it all, Sean remained calm. A rock that infuriated her even as she leaned on him for her own emotional support. Childbirth wasn't child's play. It was serious shit. Multiply that by three, and the odds of something going wrong rose exponentially.

On one of his rare excursions outside the birthing room, Lexie asked him how he could remain so calm when his wife was in labor with triplets. "Everything is going to be okay. I saw it, remember?" He was referring to a vision he'd had before Jelly had become pregnant. In his vision, the two of them had been in the kitchen with one baby in a bouncy seat on the island and three little boys running rampant around them. "I hate that Angellica has to go through so much pain, but she's strong. She'll get through this. I know it."

Lexie wanted to scream at him. Tell him his vision was for years in the future, not the here and now. But on one of the few occasions she'd ventured in to see Jelly, his calm demeanor appeared to be exactly what her high-strung friend needed. So, Lexie kept her mouth shut and tried to have the same faith in

Sean's vision that he had. She was pacing the waiting room when a flurry of activity had her looking up from the dull green tile floor.

The Nightingales stormed down the hall, Ian leading the way.

The moment he saw her, he stopped dead in his tracks. The river of relatives continued to flow around him and into the waiting area. Serenity was the first to reach her. "Lexie! How is she? Any word yet?"

Deb Nightingale, the matriarch of the clan wrapped Lexie in a tight hug. "Thanks so much for the call. What's happening? Am I a grandma yet?"

Wade and his dad halted next to Ian, their gazes sharp as they waited for Lexie to speak.

"Sean came out about half an hour ago and said everything was looking good. The babies' heartbeats are strong, and Angellica is, in his words, a goddess." Recalling the look on his face when he said it brought a smile to her face. "Sean is so freakin' calm it annoys the hell out of me, but he's exactly what Jelly needs right now."

"That's my boy," Paul Nightingale chimed in. "A chip off the old block."

Deb gave him a look. "You were anything but calm," she recalled. "When I was in labor with Wade, you were so nervous the doctor asked me if I wanted him to escort you to the waiting room for the duration."

"Did not!" Paul scoffed.

"Did so!" Deb sidled up to her husband and wrapped an arm around his slim waist. "By the time Ian came along, you'd learned to bring a couple of bottles of wine along to settle your nerves."

Everyone laughed. Ian held up a tote bag with the Nightingale logo on it. Six corked bottles peeked out of the top of the bag. "I thought these were for Angellica," he said, handing the bag off to his father.

"Nope. These are for me. Play your cards right, and I might share."

Wade eyed his family. "Did anyone bring glasses?"

Lexie pointed to a water cooler in the corner. Beside it was a stack of plastic cups. "Will those do?"

Paul produced a corkscrew from his pocket. "Yep. Son,"

he nodded to Wade, who took the hint. Serenity followed her fiancé, leaving Ian standing next to Lexie while Deb looked over the wine selection.

"Alexa."

God, how she'd missed hearing him say her name in that deep, sexy way he had that made her knees go weak. "Ian. How did you get here so quickly?" She couldn't exactly avoid talking to him, but if she kept their conversations on neutral ground, she might survive the next few days.

"Wade had the jet on standby. We were practically in the air before you got off the phone with Mom."

It was easy to forget how wealthy the Nightingales were until they did something like this. That they'd all hopped on the plane to support Angellica and Sean spoke to how close they were. "I didn't expect the whole family to come. Not on such short notice."

Ian smirked. "Mom has been planning this trip since Sean called to tell her she was going to be a grandmother. She'd have our heads if we didn't come along."

"I like your mom. She's got her priorities straight."

"I'm glad you like her. She likes you, too."

His soft-spoken words felt like a spear to her heart. She'd lost more than a chance to be with Ian. She'd lost her chance to be part of his family. Being an only child, Jelly was the closest thing to a sister she had. It was hard not to be a little jealous of her best friend, who was now a part of this big, loving family. Lexie's emotions swelled, clogging her throat. Before she could respond to Ian's declaration, Wade approached and handed them both plastic cups filled with wine.

"Come on." He waved them over to where the rest of the family stood around a magazine-covered coffee table. "Dad wants to make a toast."

"Isn't that a bit premature?" Ian asked. "The babies aren't here yet."

The elder Nightingale spoke up. "I want to toast to all my boys and the lovely ladies they had the good sense to fall in love with." He raised his cup high. His gaze swept the small gathering before stopping on Lexie. "May they all be as blessed as Deb and I have been."

Lexie squirmed under his piercing gaze. Was he trying to

tell her something?

Everyone exclaimed, "Cheers!" at once.

Lexie took a tiny sip from her cup, her gaze shifting automatically to Ian standing beside her. Her heart kicked against her ribs, and her body quickened just like it had the first time she laid eyes on him. She'd been naïve then, not understanding the kind of man he was or what he would ask of her. Now that she knew, she couldn't stop thinking about what it would feel like to give him what he wanted. What he said she wanted.

Perhaps sensing her gaze on him, Ian glanced her way. His eyes blazed with a fire she knew all too well. "Can we have a word? In private?"

A quick glance assured her the rest of the family were trying to guess what Sean and Jelly would name their brood. Lexie nodded toward the hallway. Ian followed her to another alcove near the elevator where they wouldn't be overheard.

CHAPTER FORTY

Ian reached for her free hand. At his touch, electricity tingled along her skin. His gaze met hers and held. "I've missed you."

There was no sense in lying. He'd always had an uncanny ability to read her expressions. "I've missed you, too.

"I'm sorry you lost your job. It was all my fault. I should have kept my hands and my mouth to myself."

"No." She shook her head. "You were right. I could have said no to you, but I didn't. I didn't want to." It was time to tell him the truth. She took a deep breath and then let it out. "I was scared to admit you were right. About everything. My job was nothing more than a paycheck, but I let it consume me. It was sucking the joy out of my life. You saw the toll it was taking on me and offered me a way to release the stress." She swallowed, forcing down the fear of admitting the whole truth. It was now or never. "No one has ever seen me the way you do. It scared me, Ian. The way you touched me, the things you made me see about myself, the things you made me want—it was all new and scary."

"I shouldn't have pushed you—"

"No. You were right, Ian. About all of it. My job. My need to submit. I'm still scared. I know I need to follow my heart. I need to take my career in a new direction, and I need…I need you."

Ian let her hand drop, but only so he could take the flimsy plastic cup from her hand. After placing both their cups down on a nearby bench, he took both her hands in his. His gaze met and held hers. "Nothing has changed for me, Alexa. I'm still the same man I was before. I want you, but more than that, I need you on your knees for me."

"I know, and I won't lie to you. I'm afraid of what that means for me, but I can't stop thinking about you. About the things you said and did. About the way it made me feel. I want to feel that way again, and I can't imagine trusting anyone but you to make that happen."

"Then let's get out of here."

Regret overwhelmed her. "We can't." She glanced down the hallway toward the waiting room. "We can't leave until the babies are here, and we know everyone is okay."

"One of the things I love about you is your loyalty and compassion for your friends." He squeezed her hands. "We'll stay, but I'm taking you out of here as soon as possible."

Hurried footsteps and hushed voices drew their attention. Wade and Serenity headed their way. "There you are!" Wade sounded like he'd just located bigfoot.

Serenity tugged on Lexie's sleeve. "Come on! The babies are here! Sean said Angellica is asking for you."

That's all Lexie needed to hear. She bolted along the hallway, eager to make sure her best friend was okay and to see the babies for herself. A bevy of footsteps rushing behind her spurred her on.

"Through there." Deb Nightingale pointed toward the birthing rooms. Lexie had been there several times already and knew the way. She stopped to give Deb a hug and offer her congratulations before hurrying to see the new family.

Lexie lightly rapped on the door before pushing it open and peeking her head in. Controlled chaos was the only way to describe what was going on. No one seemed to notice her, so she stood rooted to the spot, taking it all in. The room was filled with nurses, and maybe a couple of doctors doing God knows what. Her heart tripped over itself as the reality of the situation sank in. Angellica had just given birth to three baby boys! Love for the babies she'd yet to see or hold filled her heart. Feeling like an intruder, she was about to leave when she heard Angellica's voice. "Where's Lexie? I thought you said she was outside."

Relieved to know she was truly wanted amid all the chaos, she waved her arm in the air like a schoolgirl and called out, "I'm here!" Heads came up, and then bodies moved, providing her a line-of-sight to the woman of the hour. Angellica looked like the angel her name implied. Tired and perhaps more rumpled than her usual put-together self, she radiated love and feminine accomplishment. A tiny, wrapped bundle lay against her chest, a head of dark hair barely visible. A tidal wave of emotion swept over her. Not jealousy. But longing. She'd never thought about having children, but seeing the emotions play across her friend's face brought the emptiness of her life home to her like nothing else ever had. Sweeping her emotions aside, Lexie stumbled forward on numb feet. "Oh. My. God. You did it, Jelly!"

"I did. I mean, *we* did." Lexie followed her gaze. Sean stood next to the bed holding two identical bundles to the one Jelly cradled in her arms.

Lexie didn't know where to look first. When Jelly adjusted her bundle, Lexie leaned in closer. "He's beautiful, Jelly! Are they identical?"

"Down to their cute little toes," Sean answered. He shifted, allowing Lexie to see for herself. "Want to hold one?"

"May I?"

In answer, Sean dipped a shoulder, allowing her to lift one of the precious charges from his arm. Tears blurred her vision as she gazed at the perfect little human in her arms. "I've never seen anything more beautiful. But how are you going to tell them apart?"

Angellica chuckled. "For now, they each have a toenail painted a different color. Until we get to know them a little better, that will have to do."

"Have you decided on names yet?" They'd been pouring over lists of possible names for months, and the last she'd heard, hadn't settled on anything.

Jelly gazed at the baby in her arms. "Now that I can see their little faces, I think I know, but we need to discuss it. Until we decide, they're A, B, and C. That's C you're holding. I think." She glanced at her husband.

Sean nodded. "Yeah, Angellica has A. I've got B, and

you're holding C. As for the names, I think we know, but we don't want to say anything until we're sure."

"I get it. You want to get it right the first time."

"Absolutely," Sean agreed.

Lexie wanted nothing more than to stay and ask all the questions running through her brain, but there were others outside who were waiting to get their hands on the babies. And Ian was waiting for her, too. She gently placed her precious bundle back in his daddy's arms. "I'm so proud of you." She pressed her cheek next to Jelly's. "There's a waiting room full of people who are dying to see you, so I'm going to get out of your way. If you need anything at all, call me."

"Sean said you called my dad?"

"I did. He's up in Napa visiting friends. He'll be here tonight."

"Thank you."

"It was nothing, Jelly."

"It was a lot, and we owe you," Sean said. "Send my parents in next?"

"Will do. Again, my congratulations, Mom and Dad!" She'd never forget the look on her friends' faces when their new sobriquets registered. She left the room with a giant smile on her face and more love and longing in her heart than she'd thought possible.

Ian took one look at her and rushed to her side. "Is everything alright?"

Lexie wiped tears from her cheek. "Everything is perfect. Sean asked to see your parents."

"Mom. Dad? It's your turn." They didn't need to be told twice. Lexie grabbed a tissue from a box on an end table as she tried to get her emotions under control. "Hey, you two." Ian caught his brother's attention. "I'm going to take Alexa home. She's been here for hours and needs to rest. Call me if Sean needs anything?"

"We can stay," Lexie argued. "You haven't seen the babies yet."

"I'll come back later." He took her by the elbow and escorted her toward the door. "The babies have dozens of people here to take care of them. My priority is taking care of you."

Lexie's skin tingled at his touch and a warmth settled in

her belly at his words. For once, she didn't want to argue with him. In the hallway, Ian slid his hand down to hers. He wove their fingers together in a grip that felt intimate, yet possessive. As they waited for the elevator car, Lexie closed her eyes.

Ian took advantage of having the elevator to themselves. Keeping her hand in his grip, he tugged her in front of him and banded his free arm around her waist. Bending over her, he nipped at the side of her neck. "Thank you," he said, "for trusting me."

Lexie pulled back so she could see his expression. "With what?"

"Your stress. You don't think I missed the way the tension left your body back there, do you? Every muscle in your body was tight, but the minute I took your hand, you released the stress." He gently brushed a lock of hair over her shoulder. "When was the last time you ate?"

Lexie had whiplash from the abrupt change of subject. "I don't know. What time is it now?"

"If you can't remember, then it's been too long." Cradling the back of her head in his free hand, he tilted her head, exposing more of her neck to his feasting lips. Lexie melted against him, her body admitting all the things she'd been afraid to say before. "I'm going to feed you, Alexa. Then you're going to have a hot bath and a nap."

"But…"

He flashed her a devastatingly tender smile. His tongue tickled the shell of her ear. "Don't argue with me, Alexa. You'll need all your strength for what I'm going to do to you."

His tone, part promise, part warning, sent a shiver of desire along her spine. Her nipples tingled and tightened. Her core melted. A whimper passed her lips.

Ding! Ian released the grip he had on her head but retained possession of her hand as the elevator doors swished open on the ground floor.

CHAPTER FORTY-ONE

A black limo waited in the drop-off zone outside the front entrance. The driver saw Ian coming and opened the rear door for them. Lexie climbed in first. After giving the driver instructions to drop them at the hotel and then return to pick up the rest of the family, Ian joined her in the backseat. The passenger compartment was luxurious and quiet, and the car's suspension was heavenly. Snuggled in the shelter of Ian's arm, Lexie nodded off to sleep.

A feast awaited them in Ian's suite. "Change of plans. I'll feed you while you take a bath." Too tired to argue, she allowed Ian to lead her past the meal set out on a table near the balcony door, through the bedroom, and into the largest bathroom Lexie had ever seen. He sat her down on the closed toilet seat while he turned taps to adjust the water temperature in an ornate claw-foot tub. A heavenly scent filled the room—compliments of the generous helping of bubble bath he poured into the running water. While the tub filled, Ian stripped her of her clothes, setting her body on fire with every touch, every kiss to her exposed skin. By the time he lifted her and gently eased her into the fragrant water, all she could think about was being with him. But he had other plans.

It wasn't in her nature to let others make decisions for her, but Ian's tender care, his gentle insistence that she relax and let him take care of her, convinced her to let him have his way. Lounging like a queen, she accepted morsels of food from his fingertips and sips of wine from the finest crystal until she couldn't take another bite. Satisfied he'd sated her hunger, she relaxed in the water and let him wash her. When his fingers probed between her legs, she spread herself wide and let him sate another hunger.

Limp as a rag doll, Ian carried her to bed and tucked her in. With a chaste kiss on her forehead, he turned out the light and left the room.

Lexie woke to find Ian watching her from an armchair in the corner of the bedroom. He wore jeans, a crisp white button-up with the sleeves rolled to expose his wrists. His feet were bare.

"Hi." Realizing she was naked, Lexie clutched the covers to her chest as she propped up against the headboard. Ian's gaze felt like the sun and had her warming from the inside out. Heat suffused her face. "I must look a fright," she said as she brushed her hair away from her face, "but thanks for…everything." The food, the bath, the nap…the orgasm. God, could her face get any redder? "I needed…that." He'd taken care of all her needs, and it had felt surprisingly good to let him.

"Yes, you did, and you're welcome." Ian didn't move an inch. There was something about the self-control that rolled off him in waves and his steady gaze and deep, rich voice that sent tingles of awareness skittering across her skin. "Do you remember what I told you in the hospital elevator?"

She'd never forget. "Yes. You said I'd need all my strength for what you were going to do to me."

He nodded. "Very good, Alexa. Tell me, do you feel rested? Are you hungry? Do you have any urgent needs?"

Lord, did she have needs, but she didn't think those were the kind he was referring to. "Uhm. I need to go to the bathroom."

"Then do so. Take your time, but leave the door open. When you're done, come back and stand where I can see you." When she hesitated, he prodded, "There's no need to be modest around me. I've seen you naked. In fact, when we're alone, you'll wear as little or as much as I want you to. Your body belongs to me, and inside our private quarters, I'll dictate what you do with it. Is that clear?"

Numb, Lexie nodded.

"Go on, Alexa. Do what you need to do. I've waited long enough."

There was no way to access the en-suite without giving him a view of her ass. Seeing as he'd had his mouth there more than once, being shy about him watching her walk to the bathroom didn't make any sense. But this was different. This was her following his instructions, submitting, in the most basic way, to his control. *Go pee. Come back. Show yourself to me.* A few weeks ago, she would have told him to go to hell, but that was before she'd had a taste of what it meant to be a submissive. Scratch that. To be Ian's submissive.

Lexie didn't dare look at him as she pushed the covers off and climbed out of bed. The walk to the en-suite felt like a mile and once inside, knowing he was out there, listening, made her bladder seize up. Her brain and her body were at war with one another, and there was nothing she could do about it. Giving up control of her body was so much harder than she'd ever imagined, and lord, she'd imagined plenty. Tears formed, and her body trembled. *I can't do this.*

"Look at me, Alexa."

She didn't realize she'd closed her eyes until Ian's commanding voice startled her. Remembering her vulnerable position, she snapped her knees together and fisted her hands in her lap. Only then did she look at the man standing in front of her.

"I thought you would appreciate the privacy, but I was wrong." He stretched his hands out in front of him. "Give me your hands."

Lexie clenched her jaw and reluctantly placed her hands in his.

"Open your legs."

It took everything she had to obey. When she'd exposed herself to him, he praised, "Good girl. Now, keep your eyes on mine, and let it go."

She shook her head. *I can't. Good lord, I can't.*

"You can do it, Alexa. This is nothing compared to the intimacies I have planned for you." He squeezed her fingers. "Do this for me so we can move on."

He was so calm and cool while she was breathing like she'd run a marathon, uphill all the way. She didn't know how long she sat there, staring into his eyes, but eventually, her bladder released a hot stream of liquid into the bowl. The relief overshadowed the embarrassment of peeing in front of Ian.

"That's my girl." She expected him to let go of her hands, but he gently guided them up and behind her head. "Keep your hands here. Don't move."

Lexie watched as he unrolled a length of toilet paper. Her entire body trembled as he wadded it up, then reached between her legs to dry her. "I'll always take care of you, Alexa, no matter what your needs are." He dropped the paper in the bowl and reached around her to flush the toilet. Cool air caressed her tender tissues. "Stay there."

Ian wet a washcloth in the sink then returned to wash between her legs. Words of praise tumbled from his lips. "Good girl."

"So beautiful."

"Obedience like this deserves a reward."

He did a thorough job of cleaning her as well as arousing her. By the time he tossed the soiled cloth in the hamper, she shook with need, and hot juices dripped from her vagina.

"Keep your hands behind your head," he instructed as he helped her to her feet and out into the bedroom. A firm hand on her shoulder urged her to her knees. "Sit back on your heels and spread your thighs."

Lexie fought an internal battle with herself, but it was Ian's praise, "I can smell your arousal from here, beautiful girl. Open for me," that had her complying with his commands.

"Perfect." Her eyes tracked him as he crouched to examine her breasts and then between her legs. "Put your hands behind your back, Alexa."

Her arms shook as she followed his instructions. Ian got to his feet and circled around behind her. She shivered as he traced the line of her spine with a fingertip. "Gorgeous." Hands massaged her arms from shoulder to wrist. "Remember the first time I cuffed you?" His fingers encircled her wrists. "You fought with yourself that day, just like you are now. The most primal part of you wants to give in to your desires, but society has taught you that the only way to be a successful woman in today's world is to hang onto control with both hands and to never let go."

Metal rattled behind her. Fear spiked her heart rate. "Relax, Alexa." He took her hands in his. "Breathe through the fear." The cuffs clinked shut. Ian clasped her hands in his again. "Good girl." Then he tugged her hands apart, and they went! Still holding her hands, he pressed his front to her back and brought their clasped hands around so she could see two sets, one on each wrist. "Hands on your thighs, sweetheart."

Heart jackhammering her ribs, she let her hands drop to the top of her thighs. The cold metal felt like ice against her heated skin.

Still behind her, Ian praised, "Such a good girl. Now, open your mouth for me."

She'd no sooner opened her mouth than Ian stuffed a red ball between her lips. He pulled the strap tight around her head, securing the gag in place. Lexie closed her eyes and fought the panic sweeping through her.

Ian crouched in front of her. A fingertip traced her upper lip. "God, you're beautiful like this." Lexie popped her eyes open. A whimper died against the gag. "Shh, baby. Breathe with me, through your nose." He inhaled, his gaze, locked on hers, encouraged her to mimic his breathing pattern until they were breathing in sync. "That's it, Alexa. You're doing great. So beautiful. So perfect."

CHAPTER FORTY-TWO

Ian withdrew a red rubber ball from his pocket and placed it in her right hand. "If you need me to stop, let go of the ball. I'll stop whatever we're doing, and we'll discuss. If we can't resolve the issue, the session will be over. Nod once if you understand."

Lexie tightened her hold on the ball. Ian stroked the inside of her arm until her grip eased. "Good girl." His gaze met hers again. "Nod once if you understand and wish to continue."

She dipped her chin once.

"That's my beautiful girl." He got to his feet and extended a hand to help her up. Lexie allowed him to help her to the king-sized bed, where he placed her in the middle and raised her arms above her head. The mattress dipped as he leaned over her and secured the cuffs to something, the bedframe, maybe, beneath the tufted headboard.

Hands on either side of her head, his gaze met hers. "You're doing good, sweetheart. Remember to breathe. Relax and forget about everything but your own pleasure. Can you do that for me?"

Lexie nodded, though she wasn't at all sure she could do what he asked.

"Remember to drop the ball if you need or want me to

stop." He kissed her forehead. "Just to make sure you understand how this works when I say go, I want you to count to ten, then let go of the ball. Okay?"

Lexie nodded again.

"On my word," he repeated before disappearing from her line of sight. "Go!"

One.

Augh! Ian shouldered her thighs wide. Then his mouth was on her, his tongue swiping her from back to front. Lexie closed her eyes, squeezed both her hands into fists, and spread her legs as wide as they would go. Ian licked her again, this time, spearing his tongue into her opening while he fingered her clit. She forgot all about counting as he drove her insane with his lips, teeth, and tongue.

Lexie writhed, her hips working against his face, seeking that last bit of friction to push her over the edge. But every time she got close, Ian backed off just enough. He kept her on edge until her voice was hoarse from screaming against the gag, and tears streamed down her temples onto the mattress. Desperate for relief, she remembered the ball and, one-by-one, peeled her fingers away until it rolled off her palm.

Ian was above her in an instant, his knees wedged between her legs, preventing her from gaining her own pleasure. Lexie silently cursed him with one part of her brain while another part begged him to finish what he'd started.

"Look at me, Alexa." It was his dominant voice, the one that commanded her to listen. Lexie opened her tear-filled eyes. "Nod once for yes. Shake your head for no. Do you understand?"

Lexie nodded.

"Are you all right?"

Lexie shook her head.

"Did you lose count?"

A nod.

"I thought so. We'll talk about disobeying me later, but for now, I need to know why you stopped me." His gaze locked with hers and she got the impression he could see right through to her soul. His next question confirmed it. "Do you need to come?"

Another nod. Sobs racked her body. Snot clogged her airways. Instantly, Ian reached behind her head and released the clasp on the gag, allowing her to take in a full breath. He grabbed a fistful of tissues from a box on the nightstand, wiped her eyes, and helped her blow her nose.

"Yes or no answers," he commanded. Lexie nodded her agreement.

"Did I hurt you?"

"No."

"If I promise to let you come, do you want to continue?"

"Yes."

"What a good girl. I'm going to leave the gag out, but I'm going to blindfold you instead. Are you okay with that?" Ian waited while she let the idea settle. His expression gave no indication of what answer he wanted to hear. "It's up to you, Alexa."

"Yes."

"Good girl." He bounded off the bed. "Give me a sec." In no time, he was back, a dark silk tie dangling from his fist. Lexie swallowed hard as he secured it over her eyes.

She imagined a blindfold wouldn't be that different from just closing her eyes, but she soon realized it felt very different. The silk of his tie blocked all light, and he'd tied it tight enough she couldn't open her eyes at all.

"This is a form of sensory deprivation," he instructed. "Without your sight, you'll depend more on your other senses to determine what's going on around you."

The mattress dipped to one side. The fabric of Ian's jeans scraped over her right leg. She imagined him standing next to the bed, watching her. "Keep your legs spread. You're not to come until I tell you to. Do you understand?"

"Yes." She nodded because she wasn't sure she'd actually said the word out loud.

"I'll be right back. Don't move, Alexa."

Lexie lay perfectly still, listening as his footsteps retreated. To the bathroom, she surmised, though she didn't hear a door shut. After several minutes of silence, she began to doubt herself. What if he left and didn't come back? Would the maid eventually find her? She frantically rubbed her face against her shoulder, hoping to dislodge the blindfold, but it wouldn't budge. Tugging on the handcuffs confirmed they were secured to something immobile. In a panic, she thrashed around as much as the restraints allowed her. As soon as her thighs came together, her heightened state of arousal came back with a vengeance. She clamped her legs tight and tried to turn herself over so she could get herself off against the mattress. It took several tries, but she eventually managed it. Crawling up onto her elbows, she was able to angle her hips so she could grind her clit against the bed.

The first drag of sensitive skin against expensive bed linen drew a sigh of relief from her lips. She did it again and again until she teetered on the edge of pleasure. She'd get herself off, and then she'd figure out how to get out of the cuffs.

So close.

So, so close.

Something whistling through the air was the only warning she got before pain exploded across her ass. Lexie froze; a cry of frustration, fear, and anger spewed from her lips. Realization dawned. She hadn't bothered to remove the blindfold, but now she pried it up and off with her thumbs. She jerked her head around to face Ian. Anger and disbelief made it easy to find her voice. "You hit me? Really?"

"I punished you. With my belt because it was either that or my hand, and you didn't deserve my hand."

"I didn't deserve to be spanked with your belt, either." She tugged on the cuffs. "Let me go."

The mattress dipped. Strong hands bracketed her hips. Then Ian tossed her onto her back as easily as she'd toss a pillow. She'd expected his anger, but his expression gave nothing away. Was he mad? Amused? Fed up with her? Lying there, fully exposed and at his mercy while he still wore the clothes, minus the belt he'd had on when he'd arrived at the hospital, made her feel vulnerable and inexplicably aroused.

He braced himself over her, his gaze demanding her attention. "I said I'd be right back. What did I tell you before I left?"

It was hard to think when all she wanted was for him to touch her. To make her come.

"Alexa? What did I tell you?"

"Uhm…not to move?"

His smile felt like the sun breaking through the clouds. Warmth spread over her entire body. "Very good." He stroked a thumb over her bottom lip, and her mind went blank. "So, why did you move?"

"Because…I was…you left me horny! I needed to come so

bad!" She sounded like a petulant child, but she'd never been so horny in her life. She fought back tears. Why wouldn't he just let her come?

"I promised to take care of you, Alexa. Did you think I would leave you here to suffer?"

She shook her head, and the tears she'd fought so hard filled her eyes. "No." Her bottom lip trembled. "But it hurts. It hurts so much."

"The belt?"

"No. Needing to come."

"Ahh. I see." He placed a hand on her stomach. "Open for me, Alexa."

She spread her legs, and he slipped his hand down to cup her aching flesh. Lexie groaned and flexed her hips in a wanton attempt to find the release she craved. Ian jerked his hand away, leaving her desperate for his touch. Again.

"Your orgasms are mine, Alexa. I decide when and how you experience them." He dragged a finger from her chin, down the slope of her neck, then along her sternum to her navel, then stopping at the cleft between her legs. Gooseflesh broke out over her entire body. "I promise when I let you come, all the waiting, all the wanting, all the hurting will be worth it." His finger dipped between her swollen folds. "Do you trust me to keep my promise?"

One finger. One single digit. That's all it took to make her forget why she'd been mad at him. "Yes." He rubbed her clit in a circular motion—just the way she liked it.

Lexie groaned and worked her hips, once again so close to the promised orgasm she saw stars beneath her tightly closed eyelids. *Don't stop. Don't stop. Don't stop.* Lexie's entire body stiffened, her back arched, preparing for flight.

CHAPTER FORTY-THREE

Suddenly, instead of flying, Lexie crashed into an abyss of frustration. Sobs racked her body. Her pussy throbbed with unfulfilled need. "So beautiful." Ian's voice, his stupid praise, grated on her last nerve. In a desperate attempt to ease the ache, Lexie clamped her legs tight, but Ian's hands were there, urging her thighs to part. "Shh, sweetheart. I promised to let you come, and I will."

Then his hand was there, cupping her swollen flesh in a gentle but firm hold. He fingered her folds, seeking her opening. Lexie flexed her hips, begging for more. More of his touch. More of his promises.

"That's it, sweetheart. Take what you want." She flexed again, and Ian thrust a finger into her. Lexie cried out, her body moving of its own volition.

"More. Please, Ian. I need…"

He gave her what she needed, stretching her, filling her with three fingers before she could finish her thought. Then he was on the bed, stretched out beside her, his hand working between her legs. "Close your legs around me, sweetheart. Ride my hand. Ride it hard."

Lexie clamped her legs together, trapping Ian's hand

exactly where she wanted it. Nothing existed in her world, no worries over the state of her career, no worries over her best friend or her new babies. Nothing existed but the white-hot need twisting her insides into a tight coil and the man telling her bliss was hers for the taking. As much as she wanted it, the promised orgasm seemed to always be just out of her reach. Tears streaming down her temples, she pleaded. "Ian. I…I…can't…"

He moved so quickly that she wasn't sure what was happening until she felt the flat of his tongue lap against her clit. She screamed and bucked her hips, but with his fingers still deep inside her and his other hand on her stomach, pressing her into the mattress, she had nowhere to go. He pumped his fingers into her once, twice. Then his mouth was on her, his tongue lashing at her clit. The second he sucked the tiny nub into his mouth, every muscle in her body seized. Another draw of his lips sent a bolt of electricity through her system. Frayed nerve endings triggered muscle spasms that radiated from her core to the tips of her fingers and toes. She heard herself scream as she spun through space into an unknown universe where pleasure and pain were one and the same.

The last thing she heard before she passed out was Ian's voice. "Good girl."

Lexie woke not knowing what day it was or even caring. *Extraordinary sex will do that to you.* It was a theory, given that she only had one data point to base it on. Testing her musculature, she found herself sore in unexpected places. Who knew sex could be a full-body experience? Smiling, she stretched, only then realizing she was still naked, but her hands were free, and she was alone in the decadent bedding. Rising to one elbow, she squinted into the darkness, not really surprised to find Ian watching her from a plush armchair in the corner. He wore the same clothes he'd had on when he arrived at the hospital earlier…that day? "What time is it?" She asked.

"You slept a few hours."

Lexie let his non-answer sink in. "And you sat there the whole time and watched me sleep?"

He shrugged. "You were pretty out of it. I wanted to make sure you were all right." He motioned to the nightstand. "There's water and a couple of chocolates from the minibar for you."

"Thank you." He'd added ice to a wine glass and filled it with water. She took a few sips, then replaced it on the bedside table. The chocolates looked fabulous, but she wasn't sure her stomach was up to it. "I think I'll pass on the chocolates." She leveraged herself to a sitting position while holding the covers like a shield. Why, she didn't know. He'd seen every inch of her and touched her in places few had ever been allowed.

"Don't hide from me, Alexa." His voice took on that bossy quality that made her lady parts tingle. She let the covers drop. "Good girl." Her traitorous nipples stood at attention. Lexie swung her feet to the floor, but before she could stand, Ian was there, an arm around her waist, helping her to her feet. His touch was electric but comforting in a way she didn't want to think about. Her bladder was screaming at her, but recalling the last time she'd tried to relieve herself, she balked at his help.

"I can do this on my own."

"Let me help you to the bathroom, then I'll leave you alone. I promise."

Her legs *were* shaky. The last thing she needed was to fall and bash her head on something. This wasn't her. She didn't get weak-kneed after sex, and she never passed out after an orgasm. But there was no getting around it. He'd screwed her six ways to Sunday—with just his fingers and his mouth! And she needed his freakin' help to get to the bathroom. Lord, help her if he actually fucked her. She probably wouldn't walk for a week. With a reluctant nod, she gave in. "Okay. But you aren't going in with me."

"Got it. But give me a shout if you want to take a shower or a bath. I'm not sure you're up to either one on your own yet."

Her brain instantly flashed back to the way he'd tended to her in the bath earlier. He'd reduced her to a quivering mess—again, with just his fingers—then tucked her into bed to sleep it off. "Maybe in a bit?" A shower sounded fantastic, but there was no way she was letting him give her one. She wasn't going anywhere near those lethal hands of his anytime soon.

"Fine. I'll order some food. Oh, and there's a comb in my kit." He pointed to the leather bag on a table underneath the marble countertop.

"Thanks." Bracing herself against the vanity, she waited until Ian shut the door before daring to look in the mirror. She'd feared the worst and wasn't disappointed. Her hair resembled a bird's nest, and her bloodshot eyes would frighten a demon. Sighing, she took care of her most urgent needs, then, after washing her hands and face, she dug around in his kit until she found the comb he'd said was there. A brush would have been better, but beggars couldn't be choosers.

Beggars.

I begged him to make me come.

Memories flooded back in, making her acutely aware of every inch of skin he'd touched and every sore muscle in her body. She rummaged through his kit again, found a bottle of over-the-counter pain relievers, and popped two in her mouth, washing them down with water from the tap. *Crap!* Even her jaw hurt from the gag he'd used.

Lexie clamped the fingers of her right hand around her left wrist. The cuffs hadn't been tight, but it didn't take much imagination to recall the weight of cold steel against her skin and the way his restraints had made her feel. *Not frightened.* Ian wouldn't hurt her. Not in a million years.

Helpless.

Nervous.

Aroused.

Yeah, those fit.

That last orgasm took her places she'd never been before, so much so she blanked out afterward.

That's what you get for burning the candle at both ends. You can't stay awake after a not-self-inflicted orgasm.

Fatigue. That's all it was. It had nothing to do with his magic hands or his magic mouth. It had everything to do with her lack of a sex life and the stress she'd been under lately. The handcuffs, the blindfold, the gag. None of them had been necessary. She could have gotten off a lot faster if she'd had any say in the matter. But she hadn't had any say and that last orgasm had been off the charts.

Lexie studied her reflection in the mirror. Other than a faint pink stripe across her butt where he'd spanked her with his belt, she didn't look any different than when she'd entered Ian's hotel room.

But she felt different. Shouldn't she look different, too?

"You okay in there?" Ian's voice sent a shiver down her

spine and called attention to the residual ache between her thighs. She placed both hands on her stomach.

"I'll be out in a minute." Watching in the mirror, she shifted her right hand lower, angling it so her middle finger parted her folds. Her heart raced, and her skin felt like it was on fire as she gently explored her tender flesh. Her fingers felt nothing like Ian's. Hers were too slim, too soft, yet she didn't want to stop touching herself. Because beneath the tenderness was an ache deep inside her that Ian had yet to assuage.

Using her free hand to brace against the countertop, Lexie spread her legs and hunched her shoulders and back, allowing her hand to go lower, her fingers to delve deeper. Imagining her inadequate fingers were Ian's cock, she closed her eyes and plunged three fingers into her heated depth. She pressed her lips into a tight line to stifle the moans and whimpers working their way up her throat. Then, the heel of her hand accidentally brushed against her clit. A gasp burst from her lips before she could stop it.

The door swung open, letting in a gust of cool air and an irate Ian Nightingale. Lexie froze as his assessing gaze swept from her reddening face to her reflection in the mirror that hid nothing from him. She made to move, but he held up a hand. "Don't."

A tear spilled over and slid down her cheek. Embarrassment at being caught warred with frustration at being interrupted. She needed to come. Again. Which made no sense at all, given the two orgasms she'd had in the last few hours.

What was happening to her? She didn't do things like this. Ian Nightingale had her twisted in knots. Had her wanting things she didn't understand. Had her wanting him. Every inch of him.

"Is that what you need?" He nodded to her reflection. "A meaningless orgasm?"

She shook her head. "No."

"Yes."

"I don't know." Tears ran unchecked down her cheeks. Her knees quivered, but she didn't dare move her hand from between her legs to help support her. She was wrong to touch herself this way, but something, her pride, her stubbornness, wouldn't let her ask for what she wanted.

"You aren't being honest with me or with yourself, Alexa." His gaze was as heated as his words. "You know what you need. All you have to do is say you belong to me, and I'll take care of your every need. I knew you were mine from the moment I saw you, and you knew it, too. The only difference between you and me is I accepted it from the beginning, and you've fought it until it brought you to this." He motioned at the spot where her hand was clenched between her thighs. "I love you, Alexa. I thought you were ready to admit that you love me, too, but I was wrong. If you were, you wouldn't be alone in a hotel bathroom trying to find the missing part of yourself when it's right outside the door.

"Go ahead. Chase an empty orgasm. It won't fill the empty spaces inside you."

Hand on the doorknob, he began to close it behind his retreating back then stopped and looked over his shoulder. "There's no one else for me, Alexa. Only you. I have endless patience. I'll be waiting when you come to your senses."

The door closed quietly behind him. Lexie's knees gave out, and she collapsed to the cold floor in a blubbering heap.

CHAPTER FORTY-FOUR

"Three infants are a lot of freakin' work." Lexie fell onto the sofa face down. One leg and one arm dangled off the edge.

"Thank goodness for private nurses," Jelly said from where she was sprawled on the opposite sofa. "With the one we hired yesterday, I think we have it under control now."

The babies had been in the hospital for a week before the pediatrician was satisfied the Nightingale household was ready to take them home. The babies were fine. It was the parents who weren't prepared. From the unfinished nursery to the yet-to-be-hired staff, nothing had been in place when they brought the infants home. Jelly's in-laws, Paul and Deb, had helped all they could, and Jelly's dad did what he did best—he threw money at the problem. Nursery furniture was purchased and delivered along with a mountain of diapers and other accessories. Ian, Wade, and Serenity stayed long enough to hold their nephews and congratulate the new parents before flying back to New Jersey and their jobs. That left Sean, Jelly, and Lexie to care for the precious bundles until the hired nursing staff arrived to take charge.

"I think this is the first time I've been horizontal since you brought the little terrors home."

"Speaking of horizontal," Jelly pushed to a sitting position.

"When are you going to tell me what happened with Ian?"

Lexie buried her face in the plush cushion to stifle a groan. When the need to breathe overpowered her reluctance to talk, she sat up, mirroring her best friend's position. "Nothing happened."

"You are the worst liar in the entire world, Alexa Roberta Hanson."

Lexie caught the throw pillow, tossed her way, and sent it back to the other side of the coffee table. "I never should have told you my middle name," she groused as she picked at the fringe on another throw pillow. That secret had come out when she was ten, and Angellica had never forgotten it.

"I'm glad you did, and little Alexander Robert will be thankful one day, as well."

"I can't believe you named your second-born after me."

"Third-born, remember? We had to honor the grandfathers first. Sean Paul and Tomas Capello Nightingale."

Lexie sighed. "You're going to have your hands full, Jelly."

Her friend flashed a tired but proud smile. "I know, but they're so darned cute, Lex. They look so much like Sean it's crazy. Those Nightingale genes are something, I'm telling you." She ducked her head and eyed Lexie through her lashes. "Which brings me back to my original question. It's going to be weeks before I experience the wonders of my Nightingale man. Let me live vicariously through you, so spill the wine, girlfriend. I want to hear all about it. Sean said you left the hospital with his little brother, and no one saw either of you for nearly twenty-four hours." She tucked her feet beneath her on the couch. "Talk, and don't leave anything out."

"I don't know where to start."

"At the beginning. How did he convince you to leave the hospital with him? I thought you didn't want to see him again."

"I don't know, Jelly. I thought I didn't want to see him again, but when he walked into the waiting room, I knew he wasn't there for me, but…then he noticed what no one else had. He saw how tired I was and he went into protective mode." She shrugged. "I was exhausted from worrying, and I hadn't eaten in I don't know how long, and I was a little jealous of you and your new family. So, yeah, I was feeling sorry for myself, and Ian's offer to take care of me sounded pretty good at the time."

"At the time," Jelly prompted when Lexie paused to get

her thoughts together. "But not now?"

"It's a long story, Jell, and you should be napping."

Angellica shook her head. "Nope. The nurses are watching over the brood, and I've been waiting weeks to hear what happened. If you don't tell me, I'm going to call Ian and ask him. That's how desperate I am for adult conversation."

"Okay, but you can't breathe a word of this to Sean."

"Cross my heart." Jelly drew an invisible X across her chest with one finger.

Lexie held her friend's attention for nearly an hour as she recalled the time she'd spent with Ian. "When I finally pried myself off the bathroom floor, he was gone. He'd folded my clothes and left them on the end of the bed next to a room service tray."

Jelly's eyebrows rose nearly to her hairline. "He made sure you were fed before he left?"

Lexie nodded. "Yep. When I went down to the concierge to ask him to call me a cab, he said there was a limo waiting for me, and sure enough, there was. I took the limo back here, and the next morning, another one was outside to take me back to the hospital where I'd left my car."

"Wow. Lexie…"

"I know. You don't have to say it. I'm an idiot. What kind of woman doesn't want a man to take care of her like that? But…" she shook her head. "It's what he wants in return that has me twisted up in knots."

"He wants your submission."

Lexie made a humming sound and flopped onto her back to stare at the ceiling.

"Was it so bad? Being cuffed and blindfolded?"

Lexie cut her gaze to her friend. "Yes. And no."

"Explain."

"I don't think I can. I don't understand it myself."

"Did he hurt you?"

"Only in the best possible way. It was a lot to process, Jell. I don't think I was ready for all of it at once, but when it was over, and I was in the bathroom…I needed…"

"What?"

"More." Her core clenched at the stark truth she'd avoided. "I needed him. Inside me. We'd done so much, but never that, and I didn't have the guts to tell him."

"You've never had any trouble telling your lovers what you want before. Why was it different with Ian?"

"I've thought about that, and you're right. I've always known what I wanted and didn't have a problem asking for it or *telling* them what I wanted. But with Ian...I'm not in charge."

"We're back to that?" Jelly took a long draw from her ever-present water bottle. "Why do I get the feeling that you're leaving something out?"

Lexie scrunched her face up. "Because I am?"

Jelly's steady stare made Lexie squirm. "I knew there was more to the story. Go on. Spill it."

"He said he loved me. And he thought I was ready to admit that I loved him."

Angellica straightened her spine. "Do you love him?"

Lexie nodded. "Yeah. I do. But..."

"The submission." Jelly waved off the statement like it was a pesky fly. "You admitted the orgasms were over the top, Alexa. Correct me if I'm wrong, but he's only asking for your submission in the bedroom. Not out in the real world, right?"

"Yeah."

"So, what is your problem? Get down on your knees and give that man what he wants."

"But..."

"No buts. Forget about your job here. You can find another one. New York is only an hour away from Riverside. Did you even think about that? Go tell him you love him, then move your ass to New Jersey, and don't look back."

"Who's moving to New Jersey?"

Sean's deep voice, so much like his brother's, made her heart leap into her throat. He joined his wife on the sofa, wrapping a possessive arm around her shoulders. They shared a kiss that had Lexie easing off the sofa to give them some privacy.

"Where do you think you're going?" Jelly asked.

"Uhm. To my room? You two look like you could use some alone time."

Jelly pointed to the spot Lexie had previously occupied. "Sit. Tell her to sit, Sean."

"Better do as she says," Sean advised, "or I'll never hear the end of it." He dodged the elbow to the ribs from his wife, smiling as she smacked him on the leg instead.

Lexie sat and dragged the fringe-edged throw pillow back into her lap. "I don't want to be in the way."

"You're never in the way," Sean assured. "Our house is your house. You're family, Lex."

"Not yet, she's not, but if I have anything to say about it, she will be soon."

Sean raised an eyebrow at his wife's statement. "Oh? Did I miss something?"

"Please, don't," Lexie pleaded.

"Shush, woman. You've been my sister from another mister since we met in third grade, and now you've got the power to make that a legal reality, and I'm not going to sit back and let you blow it."

"Legal reality?" Sean's brow furrowed. "Are we adopting Lexie?"

"No. She's going to marry Ian."

"What? Did Ian propose?"

Lexie sighed. "No. He proposed something, but it wasn't marriage." She stood. "This conversation is over. If you need help with the babies, I'll be in my room."

"Packing," Jelly yelled at her retreating back. "I'm going to call Wade and see if you can use the company jet."

"I'll call him," Sean said. "She's really going to marry Ian? He didn't knock her up, did he?"

"Yes, she's going to marry Ian, and no…"

Their voices faded out as she climbed the stairs, but the idea Jelly had put in her head lingered as she lay on her bed staring at the ceiling. There were jobs to be had in New York City. Scads of television networks and movie and theater production companies had offices and studios there. She didn't like the idea of living so far away from her best friend, but the Nightingales had a plane, and Jelly was a Nightingale now. It sometimes took hours for Lexie to drive the short distance between her house in the valley to Jelly's house in Temecula. The plane ride, minus the hassles of flying commercial, didn't sound all that bad in comparison. And it wasn't like they spent every weekend together now, anyway. Over the last few years, they'd been lucky to get together in person on the odd holiday.

As soon as she closed her eyes, Sean's last question popped into her brain and refused to go away. No, she wasn't pregnant, but the idea wasn't near as frightening as she thought it would be. Ian would be a great father. That endless patience he spoke of would serve him well in that capacity, as would his white knight syndrome. Any child would be lucky to have him as their protector. And any woman would be lucky to nurture his child.

Lexie absently rubbed her belly, imagining Ian's child growing there. She'd never thought about having children. Her career had consumed her life for so long that there hadn't been room for daydreams of love, marriage, and motherhood. And there'd never been anybody she could see herself wanting kids with.

Does Ian want kids?

They hadn't talked about anything beyond what he expected of her. Suddenly, she had to know. Sitting up against the headboard, Lexie found Ian's number in her contact list, and before she could talk herself out of it, she pushed the call button.

CHAPTER FORTY-FIVE

Ian's phone beeped with an incoming call. Already on the phone with Sean, he held the device from his ear to check the caller ID. A smile lifted his lips and his heart. "Hey, I've got another call. Can I get back to you?"

"Sure, but don't mess this up, or Angellica will kill both of us."

"I'll do my best," he promised before ending that call and accepting the incoming one. "Alexa. To what do I owe the pleasure?"

"Do you want kids?"

The question rocked him back on his heels. She couldn't be pregnant. Not with his kid, anyway. The idea of her carrying some other dude's baby made his blood run cold. "Why are you asking?"

"Because I think I do, and if you don't, that's maybe a deal breaker."

"So, this is a hypothetical question?"

"What other kind would it be? Though it might not be if you'd done what I wanted and fucked me. You Nightingale's are potent. Just ask Jelly."

Ian breathed a sigh of relief even as a white-hot lust had

his dick straining against his uniform pants. It was common knowledge that Sean had gotten Jelly pregnant the first time they'd been together. Despite Jelly being on birth control and Sean wearing a condom, they were now the parents to identical triplets. So, her observation wasn't unfounded. "Point taken." He paused to collect his thoughts before continuing. "To answer your question, sweetheart, I'd like nothing more than to conceive a child with you. In fact, I wouldn't mind having an entire baseball team with you."

Silence met his declaration. "Alexa? Are you there?"

"I'm here." It was barely a whisper. Then, "I've got to go."

"Alexa?"

"Alexa?"

Ian stared at the home screen on his phone. It was just like Alexa to call him out of the blue with a question that set his body on fire then hang up on him. And he still had half a shift to get through before he could go home and take care of his raging hard on.

He was in no condition to talk to either of his brothers, but he'd promised to get back to Sean about the company plane situation. A text would have to do.

Tell Wade to send the plane to Temecula. It can sit there until Alexa decides to use it.

Do not pressure her to use it.

His brother sent him a thumbs-up emoji, and that was that. If Sean couldn't convince Wade to free up the plane for…well…for however long it took for Alexa to get her shit together, Ian would appeal to his oldest brother in person. Wade had a soft spot for Ian. Always had. Maybe it was because there was enough of an age difference that Ian had never been direct competition for Wade—on any front—or maybe it was that Ian had never expressed an interest in the family business. Whatever it was, Ian had taken advantage of it for years. Wade would deny it, but Ian was his favorite. That thought brought a smile to Ian's lips and provided enough distraction for him to focus on his job again. A report of a traffic accident on the main road out of town forced all thoughts of his personal life to the back of his mind for the remainder of his shift.

"Care to explain why Sean called me to request I send our plane to California to pick up Alexa?"

Shit. Ian shrugged as he exchanged a twenty-dollar bill for a brown paper bag that smelled like heaven. He should have taken his chances with the contents of his refrigerator instead of stopping in at Dott's Diner for takeout. He knew he'd have to face Wade at some point but had hoped to put off the big brother inquisition for a few days. At least until he'd made sense of Alexa's phone call. But he should have known Sean's request would generate questions, and Wade kept close tabs on Ian's schedule—so he'd know when he needed to worry about his baby brother and when he didn't— he claimed. The truth was, he was a nosy SOB, and he liked to meddle in other people's business. "No. I don't believe I do." He pushed his way past his brother and out onto the sidewalk. As expected, Wade fell into step beside him.

"I thought you two were through."

"I don't know where you got your information from, but it's wrong."

"She left. You're still here. She didn't come back with you when we went out to see the babies. What else was I supposed to think?"

Ian stopped in his tracks. He checked to make sure there weren't any more nosy people around then set his brother straight. "You're not supposed to think anything. Alexa is as much a Nightingale as Angellica or Serenity. She just doesn't know it yet." He thought about the call from her earlier. "She's coming around. She's asking the right questions."

"Why didn't *you* ask me for the plane?"

"It was Sean's idea, and I was busy." He pointed at the badge pinned to his shirt like Wade didn't know Ian had a job. "I figured it didn't matter who made the request. She's one of us."

Wade held both hands up in surrender. "Okay. I get it." He dropped his hands, and a smile broke across his face. "Is she pregnant?"

Ian glared at him. "No. Is Serenity?" he jabbed back.

His brother's smile grew impossibly bigger. "As a matter of fact…but I'm not supposed to say anything."

"Holy shit!" Ian wrapped his brother in a bear hug. "Congratulations, man!"

"Shh!" Wade pushed out of Ian's embrace. "Sen says it's too early to say anything, but I've been busting at the seams to tell everyone."

Genuinely happy for Wade and Sen, Ian filed the news

away in his vault. "No one's going to hear it from me, but you'd better not say anything about my situation to anyone either. I mean it, Wade. Alexa is mine, and she knows it. Sean and Angellica are already pushing her to come back here—that's where Sean got the idea about the plane—and I don't need anyone else pressuring her into a decision she's not ready to make. She'll make up her own mind in her own time."

"My lips are sealed."

"Wait. Do you need the plane? Are you guys doing the Vegas thing, too?" As soon as Sean found out Angellica was pregnant with his triplets, he'd whisked her off to Las Vegas and married her.

"Are you kidding? You think Serenity would go for a quickie wedding in Vegas? She's planning an extravaganza at the winery in a few weeks."

"Isn't that sort of short notice?"

"Not for Sen. She's been planning this ever since I put a ring on her finger. All she has to do is give all the vendors the date, and voila, instant wedding. Which brings me to something else I've been meaning to ask you. Will you be my best man? I'd do co-best men, but Sean isn't going to leave his family behind to come, and they can't travel yet."

"Seriously?"

"I expect to be your best man soon, but yeah. Will you do it?"

"I'd be honored, and likewise. You and Sean, once I convince Alexa that she can't live without me."

Wade stuck out his hand, and they shook on it. "It's a deal then. Invitations are being printed now, so be on the lookout for yours."

They parted ways, each with a smile on their face. Ian nuked his burger when he got home then popped open a beer and sat at the island to eat. Memories of the day he'd brought Lexie to his condo flooded in. She'd been worn thin, and in desperate need of a break from everything weighing her down. Images of her wearing nothing but his shirt, restrained and open to him on that very island, made his mouth water for her. Out of necessity, he'd pushed thoughts of a pregnant Alexa from his mind, but now he gave them free rein. She'd be radiant. A goddess he'd lust for every hour of every day. She'd get so tired of having his dick inside her that she'd probably want to cut it off just to be rid of him, but that would be hard to do with her hands shackled and secured above her head. He'd spend hours inside her. Not moving. Just possessing her. Loving her.

She'd be a great mom. He'd seen the way she mothered all the contestants on the show while they tested her patience at every turn, and he couldn't forget how protective she was of her best friend. She'd fight dragons for the ones she loved. He smiled at the image forming in his head. *Alexa Nightingale—Dragon Slayer.* It had a nice ring to it.

It would take someone with Alexa's organizational skills to make sure the passel of kids he imagined them having made it to all their practices, lessons, and play dates. And she'd do it all while holding down a full-time job. Not that she'd need to work. He had more money than they could ever spend, but Alexa needed an outlet for her creative energy, and he'd never deny her anything she needed.

There was only one problem with the utopian vision in his head. He had to get Alexa onboard with it.

CHAPTER FORTY-SIX

She shouldn't have called him. Hearing his voice reminded her of all the things she was missing out on by being a continent away from him. His answer to her question put images in her mind she couldn't shake. Every time she closed her eyes, she saw adorable babies secure in Ian's arms. Safe. Loved. Adored. He'd be a fierce protector, but she only had to look at his relationship with his brothers to see how easily he loved. He'd do anything for Wade and Sean, and they'd do anything for him. A prime example was the private jet parked at the local airport—waiting for her to step aboard. Wade had sent it at Sean's request, but both brothers had done it for Ian.

"How long are you going to sit here denying that you're hopelessly in love with my brother-in-law?" Angellica folded a tiny onesie and placed it on top of the giant stack of matching baby clothes.

Lexie picked another gauze blanket out of the laundry basket and folded it before adding it to the mountain of blankets she'd already folded. Three times the babies meant nine times the laundry. Or so it seemed. "If I left, who would help you fold all these clothes?" As dodges went, it was lame as it got, but she was running out of reasons she shouldn't get on that jet.

"I've got plenty of help around here, and you know it, so don't use the babies as an excuse." Jelly started a new stack of folded onesies, then turned her full attention on Lexie. "We love having you here, and you know you're always welcome. In fact, I expect you to visit often, but I refuse to be the reason you don't chase your dreams."

"What dreams would those be?"

"A home. A family. Love. As long as I've known you, you've wanted those things, so don't tell me you don't want them now. And if you tell me you don't want them with Ian, then I'll know you're lying. I saw the way you looked at him the night he came to your house pretending to be a floral deliveryman to see if I was hiding out with you. You were a goner then. I'm pretty sure that's the reason you let him in to see me in the first place. I know it's the reason you blackmailed him into auditioning for the show."

Angellica knew her too well. She couldn't argue with a thing she'd said. "There's more to it than what I want, Jelly. It's what Ian wants that's holding me back."

With pursed her lips, Jelly tapped her index finger on her chin while she studied the ceiling. "Hmm. He wants to take care of you. He gives you multiple, mind-blowing—your words, not mine—orgasms. He's richer than Midas and knows his way around a wine cellar. Oh, and he owns handcuffs." She dropped her gaze to Lexie. "If you don't want him, I'll take him."

"Only one Nightingale per person. Those are the rules."

"I love you like a sister, Lexie, but I have to say, you're overthinking this. You overthink everything, which is exactly why Ian and his handcuffs are what you need. Think about it, Lex. Have you ever had mind-blowing sex with anyone else?" She held her hand up like a stop sign. "Don't bother to answer that, because the answer is no. And the reason the answer is no is because you were always in control of the situation. You were so busy thinking about what you wanted the guy to do next that you didn't get lost in your own feelings. Then Ian came along and refused to let you call the shots. And guess what? You had mind-blowing sex, that's what." She softened her tone. "I know that scared the bejeesus out of you, but I don't know anyone who would walk away from that. But you. Maybe."

"But…"

"No buts, Alexa Roberta Hanson. I'm telling you right

now to get on that plane and go tell Ian that you love him. The two of you can work this out, but not when you're three thousand miles apart and not talking to each other."

There were a million rebuttals on Lexie's tongue, but rather than continue arguing with her best friend, she held them in. None of them were good anyway. Jelly was correct on all counts. The only reason she was still in California was cowardice.

Jelly and Sean had everything under control. They didn't need her.

Her job was shit, and it never had been what she wanted to do. She could look for another job in New York or start that podcast Jelly kept telling her to try.

Submitting to Ian wasn't the only thing she was afraid of. She was afraid of change.

But everything is changing whether I want it to or not. I'm changing. And I'm not at all sure I want to.

But there was no stopping change. Or her runaway thoughts.

"You really think we can work this out?"

"I hope so, but there's one thing I know for sure. If you don't try, you'll regret it for the rest of your life."

"That's a bit dramatic, don't you think?"

Jelly stacked the last little folded onesie then leaned forward, bracing her forearms on her thighs. "You know you're a part of my family, which means you'll be invited to all our holiday events, and the boys' birthday parties, and all that stuff. Forever. Right?"

"Right."

"Ian is going to be invited, too. So, how are you going to feel when he shows up with his girlfriend or his wife? He loves you, but he's a man, Lexie. If you don't work this out with him, he'll eventually move on, and so will you, I suspect. He'll find someone who won't be you, but they'll be close enough to hold his interest. You'll find some weak substitute who'll handcuff you when you tell them to, but won't know what to do with you unless you walk them through it. And then it won't be the same. Because they won't be Ian."

Jelly's words painted a tableau Lexie didn't want to see, but nevertheless rang true. "Okay. Okay. I get it."

"Good." Jelly sounded way too satisfied with herself for

Lexie's taste. "So, what are going to do about it?"

Exasperated with herself and her best friend's meddling, Lexie stood to pace the room. Questions swirled in her head like a hurricane, scattering her thoughts so fast she couldn't grasp a single one long enough to examine it with any depth. One hand on her hip, the other pressed to her forehead, her feet worried a path into the throw rug. "He's asking so much, Jelly."

"Then you have to ask yourself if what he's offering is worth more than what you'd be giving up." Jelly stacked folded clothes into the empty laundry basket. "Take it from someone who fought her feelings for her man for way too long—the kind of love that twists you up in knots, no pun intended, doesn't fade with time or distance." She hefted the basket with two hands. "You see the plane waiting for you as Ian controlling you, but it's the opposite. He's put the decision in your hands, Lex. Does he want you? Yes. He's waiting for you to decide if you want him. I'm aware that my opinion doesn't matter, but here it is anyway. You better make up your mind soon or you might lose him forever."

Lexie was still contemplating Jelly's words long after her friend had left to put away the folded laundry. She nearly jumped out of her skin when her phone vibrated in her pocket with an incoming call. Pulling it out, she read the name on the screen and almost didn't answer, but she'd never been that kind of boss. If her former assistant was calling, she'd answer.

"Emma. What's up?"

"Oh, I'm so glad you answered." The young woman sounded frazzled. "I wasn't sure you would."

"I'd like to think you and I were friends, not just co-workers, so, of course, I'd answer."

"Thank you." Emma sounded relieved. "I thought the same, but when you were taken off the production, and they put me in your place, I thought your feelings might have changed."

"No. Not at all. Everything that happened was my fault. You didn't do anything wrong, and it was only natural that you'd take my place when I left."

"Well…that's good, because I need a favor."

"What kind of favor?"

"The season is going to air next week, and you know what that means. It's time to tape the tell-all finale."

"I don't…"

"You have to be there, Lexie. The fans of the show are going to want to see you and hear your side of the story."

Lexie scoffed. "Most of them won't even realize I was there. I was supposed to be edited out as much as possible."

"That's just it…you weren't. The final cut has you front and center as one of the prime candidates for Ian's heart. They even taped an interview with him where he explained why he didn't give you one of the final two charms, and how it broke his heart to let you go. He had everyone on the set convinced that he's in love with you."

"What?" She couldn't have heard that right.

"So, you see, you have to be here. You know every season concludes with at least a happy for now if not a happy every after. If you aren't here, this season will end with a heartbroken bachelor. Single women live for this stuff. We'll lose our entire audience, and they'll cancel the show."

"Do the suits in the office know about this?"

"Yes, and no. They've approved the final cuts and are advertising the ending as a first of its kind. That's true, but our demographic is going to shit bricks if we don't have some kind of match at the end. I need you to come back for the finale. Sort of a big surprise for Ian, and hopefully a happy for now at least for both of you."

"Does Ian know what you're planning to do?"

"No. And I hope I'm not overstepping my bounds, but I thought you were really into him, and if he was telling the truth, he loves you. We could play up the sob story—Ian, the white knight let you go to save your career—then we reveal you waiting on the charm ceremony set. It's you asking Ian if he'll accept your charm."

Silence stretched out as Lexie processed everything she'd been told. "He didn't give either of the last two women a charm?"

"No. He flat-out refused. Said he wouldn't lie to them about his feelings. I can send you a copy of the taping. You can see for yourself."

"What about the final interview?"

"Ian's? I can send you that, too."

"Thanks, Em. I promise to watch them ASAP and get back to you. How soon do you need to know?"

"Yesterday?" The woman's nervous laughter reminded Lexie why she had disliked her job so much. The pressure to produce a rating's topper every single time got to you. Emma was only doing her job.

"How about later tonight? Will that be okay?" Whatever was in those tapes, she'd decide quickly. If not for Emma's sake, for her own. Angellica was right about one thing. If Lexie wanted Ian, she'd better claim him soon, or she'd lose him forever.

"That would be great. I'll send the files over as soon as we hang up." She sighed. "And Lexie? I support your decision, no matter what you decide. But in my opinion, you'd be nuts to turn down a man like Ian Nightingale."

Lexie pulled the phone away from her ear and stared at the home screen. Emma had ended the call before Lexie could respond to her unsolicited opinion. One ping after another signaled incoming text messages. Her former assistant hadn't wasted any time sending the files. With her heart racing, Lexie went up to her room where she could view the videos in private.

INTERVIEW – IAN NIGHTINGALE

Host – "Ian, you surprised everyone when you refused to hand out a charm to one of the two beauties who made the final cut. Can you tell us why?"

Ian – "It's simple, Steve. I'm in love with someone else."

Host – "One of the other contestants?"

Ian – "Yes."

Host – "Why wasn't she one of the final two, then?"

Ian – "She asked me not to give her a charm. I had to honor her request, even though it meant breaking my own heart."

Host – "She wasn't in love with you?"

Ian – "She is, but there are lots of obstacles to overcome and she thought it best to end things before we went public with our feelings. I'd do anything for her, so I did what she wanted. I let her go."

Host – "You sacrificed your own happiness. That's very noble of you."

Ian – "It's not noble. It's love. True love is endless."

CHAPTER FORTY-SEVEN

Ian cursed as he read the email for the third, or was it the fourth time? He'd thought he was through being the Charmed Bachelor, but apparently not. According to the email from the network, he had one more duty to fulfill. He had to appear at what they called the after-party. All the female contestants would be back for the tell-all formatted show that would air following the final episode of the season. He'd go in a heartbeat if Alexa was going to be there, but she wouldn't. The network execs had probably edited her out of as many episodes as they could and wouldn't want to remind viewers of her existence.

The last thing he wanted to do was listen to all the rejected women catalog his faults and commiserate about how they'd dodged a bullet when he'd failed to give them a charm. He'd done his best to be civil with each of them, but his heart had never been in it. There'd only ever been one woman for him, and pretending otherwise tested his limited acting skills. Nevertheless, Ian arranged to take one of his few remaining vacation days in order to fulfill his contractual obligations to the show.

"What are you doing here?" Wade looked up as Ian slid into the opposite side of his booth at Dott's Diner. "Don't you have a show to tape today?"

"They don't need me until this afternoon." Dott herself stopped at their table with a coffee carafe in hand. She refilled Wade's mug and when Ian turned his upright, she filled it too. He ordered his usual, then turned his attention back to his oldest brother. "What about you? Don't you have a winery to run?"

Wade lifted a heavy white ceramic mug to his lips. "The smell of coffee makes Serenity nauseous these days, so I came here to get my fix."

Ian raised an eyebrow. "And she let you leave?"

"I promised to bring her one of Dott's cinnamon rolls. I'm waiting on one fresh from the oven. Dott said they'd be done soon."

"Maybe I'll get one to go after I finish my breakfast. Comfort food sounds good right now."

"Is Lexie going to be at the taping today?"

Ian shrugged. "Don't know. I doubt it, though. She was never supposed to be one of the contestants, and I'm sure they've edited her out as much as possible. Is the plane still in Temecula?"

Wade nodded. "It was still there about an hour ago when I checked."

"Then I guess she's not coming. With the three-hour time difference, she'd need to be in the air by now to make it on time." Ian stared at the steam rising from his coffee mug and seemingly taking his appetite with it. "I fucked it up, didn't I?"

"I don't know. Maybe. Maybe not. If the network execs don't want her here for the tell-all, then there's no reason for her to fly in today. Don't let this get to you, baby brother." He sipped from his mug. "If there's one thing I know about women, it's that you can't predict their behavior. It's like their minds exist in a parallel universe or something."

Dott arrived with Ian's breakfast and Wade's to-go order of cinnamon rolls. Ian shoved a slice of bacon in his mouth and washed it down with coffee. Wade finished his coffee and scooted out of the booth. "See you later?" Wade paused to toss a couple of bills on the table.

Ian chuffed. "Yeah. I'll be there in a few. Tell Serenity I said hello?"

"Sure thing." He placed a solid hand on Ian's shoulder. "Don't worry. I'm sure she'll come around. She'd be crazy not to."

Ian wished he had Wade's confidence regarding what

Lexie would do. He hadn't heard a thing from her since the day she'd called and asked him if he wanted kids. He'd lived on the hope that call had inspired, but when she didn't hop on the plane or even call again, hope had waned. There was a crack in his heart that widened every day he didn't hear from Lexie. Today, with the prospect of facing eleven women he'd rejected looming over him, he felt a wedge widening the crack even more.

Facing them would be so much easier with Lexie by my side.

It would be obvious to everyone why he'd turned the others down. Facing them alone made him look like a player, and he was as far from that as a man could be.

Knowing he'd need his strength to get through the next several hours, Ian forced himself to finish his meal. After a second cup of coffee, he grabbed the ticket Dott had left on the table and approached the register.

Dott took his ticket, and without even glancing at it, punched the amount into the register. "That'll be $9.97. Heard those production people were back in town."

Ian dug a twenty out of his wallet and handed it over. "Yeah. Taping the final something or other today." He waved off his change. "You keep it. Have a good day." He hustled out the door before Dott could ask more questions he didn't want to answer.

They'd only rebuilt the living room set inside the event center building, which left room for pared-down versions of Wardrobe and Makeup. Emma, who'd taken over for Lexie when she'd been pulled off the production, met him at the door. "It's about time you got here!" Taking him by the elbow, she tugged him forward. "Wardrobe first." She shoved him past a set of curtains hung from cables and into a warren of clothing racks. "This way." He followed her to a single rack in the back with three suits hanging from it. "Pick one and put it on. Stat!"

Of the three, the navy blue was the least offensive so he grabbed it along with a white shirt and a navy tie with subtle red diagonal stripes. Since all the garments were meant for him, they fit perfectly, as did the shoes Emma shoved at him when he exited the curtained-off changing room. She eyed him up and down, and apparently finding no fault with his attire, took him by the arm again and led him back through the clothing racks and into the makeup area.

"Fix him up, and do what you can with his hair. It looks like he combed it with a rake a week ago, then forgot about it. You can leave the scruff," she said, pointing to his jaw. "The viewing audience will eat it up."

Since he hadn't shaved in a while and couldn't recall the last time he'd combed his hair with anything other than his fingers, he let the comments slide. After Lexie left, he hadn't seen the point in extensive grooming. He showered daily, so at the very least, he didn't stink.

Ian settled into the salon-style chair and loosened the tie he'd knotted a few minutes ago. The makeup artist, a woman he hadn't met began stuffing tissues between his collar and his skin then she draped a cape over him and snapped it tight around his neck. Scissors and comb in hand, she'd just begun work on his hair when Emma's phone buzzed with an incoming text. "Shit. I've got to go. Do the best you can, but when you're done, don't let him leave here." Her gaze met Ian's in the mirror. "Stay here. I'll be back for you soon."

"I was going to go over to see Wade."

She pointed a finger at the mirror. "Do. Not. Leave. This. Room. Not for any reason. Do you understand?"

Ian raised both his hands in surrender. "Okay. But is it okay if Wade comes over here?"

"No." She shook her head so hard she dislodged the headset she wore and had to readjust it. "No visitors, either. This is a closed set today. Understand?"

Ian wasn't up on the Hollywood lingo, but he got the gist of *closed set*. "Got it."

Emma's firm nod and tight-lipped expression reminded him of the time Grandma Nightingale had caught him yanking clothes off her clothesline. She'd made him hang them all up again under her watchful and scolding eye, all the while lecturing him on the fine points of right and wrong. He'd taken the lesson to heart and, much to his brother's dismay, spent his youth trying to keep all of them out of trouble. Now that he thought of it, that day had probably set him on course for a career in law enforcement.

Emma checked the time on her phone. "Damnit. Gotta go."

She was out of there in a flash. Hollywood types were efficient people. Time is money was the rule of the day, so, in a few short minutes, Ian's hair had been tamed and his makeup applied. Their work done, the staff began packing up their equipment, leaving Ian sitting in a chair staring at himself in the mirror. The makeup artist knew his business. His expert work disguised the dark circles under his eyes and the frown lines on his forehead, but there was nothing he could do about the loneliness and failure lurking in his eyes.

Unable to sit still another minute, Ian bolted out of the chair.

CHAPTER FORTY-EIGHT

Ian didn't stop running until he was deep in the vineyard, well away from prying eyes. Gulping in air sweetened with the scent of ripening fruit, he dropped his head back and closed his eyes, letting the peace seep into his pores. Waning sunlight warmed his face, and a soft breeze ruffled his perfectly coiffed hair.

She's not coming back.

It was a reality he hadn't let himself contemplate, but the writing was on the wall. He'd given her time, distance, and every ounce of patience he had in hopes she would change her mind and come back to him.

She's not coming back.

He'd lost her.

Did I misjudge her? Did I push her too far, too fast?

No. He'd spent his entire adult life learning to read people, and he'd spent an equal amount of time learning how to channel his dominant nature for a woman's pleasure. He'd never been wrong about a submissive, and he wasn't wrong about Alexa.

"Why can't she see it?" He shouted his frustration into the universe.

He'd wanted lots of things in his life, but none the way he wanted Alexa Hanson. He'd been with countless women, but none set his body and mind on fire like Alexa. None had ever tempted him to give up his life's goals to be with her. Only Alexa.

Ian dropped to a crouch, his elbows on his knees, his fingers destroying the hair stylist's work. Eyes clenched shut, he tugged on his scalp until the pain brought tears to his eyes and wrenched a feral scream from the depths of his soul.

He'd never wished to be anyone but who he was, but he'd give it all up. The money, his job, his family, his dominance…everything…if it would bring Alexa back to him.

But there was no guarantee she'd want him, even if he could change who he was. And if he changed for her, what kind of life would that be for him? Or her? He'd be a shell of a man, always looking back at what he'd given up. He'd come to resent her. He'd make her life as miserable as his would be. Neither one of them deserved that.

Slowly rising, he looked out at the lush foliage surrounding him. This land. The vines. The family legacy. They were as much a part of him as the physical traits he'd inherited from his ancestors. He'd chosen not to work in the family business, but the thought of walking away from it—for any reason—made the wine pulsing through his body run cold. He'd grown up playing in the vineyard, following his brothers and Serenity around like a loyal puppy, and his children, should he be fortunate enough to have them, would grow up here, too.

He didn't need to work, but his job was fulfilling in a way he couldn't explain. The idea of walking away from it was unfathomable.

Heedless of the makeup artist's excellent work, Ian scrubbed his hands over his tear-ravaged face. All the other things in his life aside, the one thing he couldn't change even if he wanted to was the one Alexa found the most fault with. His dominant nature.

It's who I am.

Above all else, I'm dominant, and I can't change that.

Ian filled his lungs with fragrant air, held it as long as possible before blowing it slowly out. *I'm a lot of things. But one thing I'm not. I'm not a quitter.* He strode purposely toward the winery where he'd left his car. On the way, he pulled out his phone and dialed his oldest brother.

Wade answered on the first ring. "Where the hell are you?

That Emma chick is about to call the police to report you missing!"

"I'm here. Never left. I just needed space to think."

"Are you coming back to finish this thing?"

"On my way. Can you do something for me?"

"Anything."

"Either get the plane back or book me a flight to Temecula ASAP. The red eye tonight will do."

"I can fly you in the Mooney." Wade piloted his own private plane for fun. "It's not as fast as commercial or our jet, but you'll get there."

"No offense, but I'm kind of in a hurry."

"No offense taken. I'll get you situated while you finish this production shit. I'm ready for things to get back to normal around here."

Emma met him at the front door. She took one look at him and started making calls. Minutes later, his hair and makeup were deemed acceptable, and his shoes were dust-free.

"Your eyes are still bloodshot." She handed him the bottle of eyedrops. He dutifully plunked a couple of drops into each eye, blinking until the world came back into sharp focus. "Better." She took him by the arm and led him onto the renovated set.

"Sit there."

Ian sat carefully on the Victorian loveseat indicated. As Emma barked orders, he took in the changes they'd made. They'd removed the temporary walls to make room for theater-style seating for a studio audience. He vaguely recalled something about a contest where fans could win tickets to the tell-all viewing party. Every seat was taken, but strategic lighting made it impossible to discern any details about the occupants. Directly opposite him, in the center of the set, six women sat on one long sofa. Behind them, five more perched on tall stools. Ian's gaze landed on the empty stool at the end. Alexa's seat. Why couldn't he have fallen for a pliable submissive? One who wouldn't fight her own instincts at every turn? Hell, all the women facing him were beautiful. Most men would give their left nut for the opportunity to choose from that lineup.

Not me.

Alexa was stubborn, willful, bossy, and too smart for her own good. But she was his, and he was going to prove it to her as soon as he finished this business once and for all.

It was all he could do to sit through the next few hours. One by one, the women sat beside him on the loveseat while they rehashed every minute they'd spent with him. Some were kind. Others felt scorned and told him so.

He heard all about the drama that went on between the women while being sequestered at the B&B between events. It was all news to him, and he wondered how much of it had been stirred up on purpose for the sake of ratings. Most of it, he surmised, as women who had appeared to be enemies during the taping now professed to be best friends. The more he heard, the more he was convinced the fight at the pool party had been staged. Lexie hadn't had a choice. She'd intervened, and doing so cost her her job.

Perhaps his actions had played a part in her firing, too. If he'd known…no. No use going there. No matter what he did or didn't know was going to happen, he still would have marked her. Maybe not on her ass, but he would have marked her. There were any number of places on her delectable body he could have put his mark that no one other than him would have seen.

Ian zoned out as the host summed up the season in a few sentences.

"Ian."

"Ian." The man's voice broke through the haze of disinterest clouding his brain.

"Sorry, Steve. What were you saying?"

His too-bright smile said the man wasn't at all pleased with Ian's behavior, but like the professional he was, he soldiered on. "We've heard from all the contestants but one. When we first reached out to Alexa about being on tonight's show, she declined, but this morning we were informed she'd changed her mind." With what appeared to be a genuine smile, the host faced off-stage. "Everyone, please give a warm welcome to our final contestant, Alexa Hanson!"

What? Ian jumped to his feet. His heart raced as he squinted into the stage lights for a glimpse of Alexa. It seemed like forever, but it couldn't have been more than a few seconds before she materialized on set. Shoulders back, head high, she crossed the sound stage like she owned it. Ian's dick reacted instantly. This was the woman he'd fallen in love with on the set in Malibu all those months ago. She wore her confidence like a crown.

Her gaze remained fixed on the host. Ian couldn't take his

eyes off her as the two exchanged air kisses and greetings. A million thoughts ran through his brain, not the least of which was…*Why is she here?*

The other women had been extremely candid about their interactions with him, but there'd been nothing really to tell. He'd held a few hands and kissed a few cheeks. But Alexa? She had the ammunition to ruin him if she wanted to.

She wouldn't do that.
But why won't she look at me?

CHAPTER FORTY-NINE

Alexa took her place on the loveseat, and robotically, Ian sat beside her. She had so much to say to him, most of which wasn't suitable for a prime-time show. She didn't dare look at him or she'd never get through this. His laser-sharp gaze seemed to undress her, as if she didn't feel exposed enough in front of everyone.

"Folks." Steve quieted the audience. "If you don't recognize our guest, this is our final contestant, Alexa. She originally declined to return for tonight's episode but changed her mind at the last minute." He turned to Lexie. "You started out as a producer on the show. Is that correct?"

"Yes, that's correct. The twelfth contestant eloped with her boyfriend a few hours before we were scheduled to tape the first episode. It was too late to cast a replacement, so I stepped in. I explained this to the other women before we began taping. My plan was to remain on the periphery of every scene and to edit myself out of as many scenes as possible. Ian agreed to eliminate me as a contestant at the first charm ceremony."

"But…he gave you a charm anyway?"

"Yes."

"How did you feel about that?"

"I was furious, as you can imagine. We'd gone out of our way to facilitate Ian's schedule. Agreeing to move the production all the way across the country stretched our budget to the limit. To stay on budget, we condensed the taping schedule down to three weeks. There wasn't a minute to lose, and having me do double duty for more than a few days was very stressful for me."

"Can you explain what happened on the traffic stop? You and Ian were gone a long time."

"Yes, well…Ian wanted to speak with me and wouldn't take no for an answer. Since his cooperation was necessary to keep the production on track, I allowed him the extra time."

"What did he want to talk about?"

Lexie shrugged. "Nothing much. I think he really just wanted a break from all the craziness. I mean…who wouldn't?"

"Then there was the infamous pool party…"

"Let me stop you right there. I'd accidentally backed into the corner of a table and didn't know the incident had left a bruise. If I had, I would have worn a different swimsuit. That whole thing was blown out of proportion and cost me my job." A chorus of gasps rose from the audience. "I'm pretty sure the fight was staged, too."

"You were in charge. Who else could have done something like that?"

"My assistant. Shows like this one exist only as long as the ratings remain high. Nothing drives ratings more than drama."

Steve turned to the two women involved in the pool fight. "Is what she's saying true? Did someone tell you to brawl at the pool party?"

The two women glanced at each other then another woman spoke up. "We were all asked to do it." Another gasp rose from the crowd. "Those two had already determined they weren't interested in Ian, so they agreed."

"Is that true?" Every single one of the women nodded. "Who asked you to do that?"

The one who'd spilled the wine pointed off set. "It was her. The assistant. She said the suits back in California wanted to see more drama." Another collective gasp came from the audience.

Lexie nodded. "That's what I thought, but at the time, I was dealing with my own drama. Someone leaked the scene, and it had gone viral. I'd become the laughingstock of the internet and was busy trying to keep my job. Admittedly, I'd lost control of the production if things like that were happening, but I was still committed to bringing the production in on time and on budget. My stress level was off the charts."

"You left the set with Ian that day, right before taping was to begin on the final charm ceremony. Where did you go?"

"Someplace quiet. I never would have left like that on my own, but Ian saw what the stress was doing to me and got me out of there. I didn't want to go, but it was the right thing to do."

"How do you mean?"

"We talked about what was happening, and I was able to convince him not to give me one of the two final charms."

"He was going to give you one?"

"Yes. That was his plan."

"Ian? What do you have to say about that?"

"Everything she said is true. I was going to give her a charm that night."

"How did she convince you not to?"

"She told me she couldn't see us together in the future. Since her feelings didn't match mine, I had no choice but to let her go."

He shifted his gaze to Lexie. "Any regrets?"

"A million. Every moment of every day."

Ian's battered heart kicked like he'd been hooked up to a defibrillator. He reached out, his hand landing lightly on her forearm. She turned her soft gaze landing on him for the first time since she'd stepped on the set. "You have regrets?"

"Yes. More than I can tell you."

"What are you saying?"

"I should have let you give me a charm." She shifted to face him fully. "I was scared, and stupid. You aren't like anyone I've ever known, and that scared me. Being with you meant leaving my job and my life in California behind. I wasn't ready to do that. Didn't think I could. My job was everything to me." Tears spilled down her cheeks. "Then my best friend reminded me of the things I'd always said I wanted, and I realized they were the same things you wanted to give me."

Ian clasped her trembling hands in his and squeezed, letting her know he was there for her. "Why are you here?"

"Am I too late? Did I miss my chance to be yours?"

Ian let her carefully worded questions flow over and through him as he gazed into the depth of her eyes. "Meet me in the gazebo in half an hour and find out."

Her breath hitched on a sob that almost broke him, but then a tiny smile broke across her face, and she mouthed, "Yes, Sir."

CHAPTER FIFTY

Lexie held Serenity's hand like it was the only thing keeping her from plummeting off the roof of a skyscraper. "How many more minutes?"

"Two less than the last time you asked." As soon as Ian walked off set, Serenity rushed to Lexie's side and had been there ever since. A rock. An anchor to keep her from crashing to Earth. "Breathe, Lexie. Everything's going to be okay."

"You don't know that."

"Yes, I do. Ian's in love with you. He won't do anything to embarrass you, and he'd never hurt you."

"I hurt him, Sen. He offered me everything, and I turned him down. How could he ever forgive me?"

"You came back. You apologized in front of practically the whole world. Besides, he blames himself, not you."

"Why would he do that?"

"He told Wade he scared you off. I'm not sure I understand what he meant by that, but you told everyone here that you were scared, so I guess it makes sense."

Lexie couldn't explain why she'd been afraid without saying more about Ian than anyone needed to know, so she kept the details to herself. It had taken her a while to wrap her head around the idea of submission, but the benefits were clear to her now. She'd never felt as free to express her innermost feelings as she did when Ian physically restrained her. And she'd never let herself experience the kind of pleasure he gave her when she handed control over to him. He'd tried to tell her that his kind of bondage equaled freedom, but she'd been unable to grasp the concept. Until he'd let her go. Then his meaning had been all too clear. "Let's just say I'm a control freak, and I don't know how to let go of the reins—personally and professionally. Ian showed me how to let go, and it scared me. I'm not good with change, especially when it's me who needs to change."

"I get it. I think. I can be pretty stubborn myself. I was in deep financial trouble when Wade came back into my life. All he wanted to do was help, and I fought him every step of the way. Lucky for me, he hung in there, and I eventually saw what should have been obvious from the beginning. Trust me, Lexie. Ian didn't give up on you."

"How do you know?"

"He called Wade earlier today and asked him to book him a flight to Temecula. He was going after you as soon as he finished taping this episode."

Hope, sweeter than any wine, surged through her system. "Are you sure?"

"Positive. You'd already left Temecula when Wade got the call. He wasn't sure if he should have told Ian you were on the way or not, so he asked me. I told him Ian deserved to suffer a little longer for whatever it was he did. Wade agreed, so we didn't say anything to anyone."

"Thanks for telling me. I sort of figured Wade would tell his brother that I was coming." She took a deep breath and let it out. "That explains the look on Ian's face when he first saw me. I wasn't sure if it was shock or what. It had me second-guessing my plan to apologize in front of the whole world."

"Well, it looks like your apology worked. I didn't think Ian had a romantic cell in his entire body, but it looks like I was wrong."

"What…oh!" Wade stood in the doorway holding a giant bouquet of red roses tied together with a beautiful white ribbon. "Are those for me?"

"From Ian."

When Wade handed them over, Lexie noticed a metallic clink. She turned the bouquet over in her lap.

"Handcuffs?" Serenity screeched. "What in the world?"

Wade addressed Lexie. "Ian said you'd know what they meant, and to bring the bouquet with you to the gazebo." He fished a small envelope out of his pocket. "He also sent you this."

Lexie took the envelope. Her name was printed on the front in Ian's bold handwriting. "Thank you." She glanced nervously between them. "Could I have a moment alone? I promise I won't bolt."

Wade's gaze met hers, holding for a brief second before he extended his hand to Serenity. "Come on. I don't know about you, but I could use a drink."

Serenity looked at her phone. "Ten minutes until go time. I'll be back in seven?"

"Seven sounds good. I'll be here."

As soon as they were gone, Lexie broke the seal on the envelope. Inside was a rectangle of heavy cardstock with the Nightingale Vineyard logo embossed in gold at the top. Below it, Ian had written:

If we were going to be alone, I'd have you come to me naked with your hands cuffed behind your back. But we won't be alone, so this will have to do. Take off everything but your dress. No shoes. No jewelry. Fasten the free handcuff to your right wrist and hold the flowers in the crook of your elbow. No one will know but you and me.

I need you to do this, Alexa. For me.

Don't be late.

Yours forever,

Ian

"Holy shit!" she whispered. Lexie's hand shook as she read the missive again to make sure she hadn't misunderstood. She should have known he'd demand her submission in some way. But this? She fingered the handcuffs, recalling how safe she'd felt wearing them. How she'd known Ian wouldn't hurt her. How the cuffs and gag had kept her from being her own worst enemy. Memories of the pleasure he'd given her melted her core.

Her heart pounded at the idea of appearing on camera wearing nothing but a cocktail dress. It looked fabulous on her, but the hem hit her at mid-thigh. If she bent the wrong way, everyone would see…her. There was no way Ian would know she hadn't taken her panties and bra off. Not at first, anyway. But once they were alone, he'd discover her disobedience and be pissed.

That's no way to start a relationship. I need to be honest with him and with myself. I came here to get him back, knowing full well the kind of things he'd demand of me.

Lexie lifted the free cuff with her index finger. The cold steel sent a bolt of need and desire straight to her pussy. No man had ever made her want the way Ian did. No man had ever been able to read her body and mind the way Ian did. It was disconcerting but exhilarating at the same time.

You've come this far, Lex. Don't chicken out now.

The panties came off first. She looked around for a place to stash them, then gave up and tied them around the chain linking the two cuffs. Seeing the scrap of black lace would drive Ian insane. Smiling at her cleverness, she undid the zipper on the dress and shimmied out of her bra. Hastily zipping up, she once again glanced around for a place to stash the undergarment until she could come back and get it. A flash of pink on the floor next to the chair Serenity had been sitting in caught her attention. Heart beating wildly, she stuffed the bra inside Serenity's purse moments before the woman walked back in carrying a glass of white wine. "I thought you might need this."

"Liquid courage?" Lexie took the offered glass, then tipped it to her lips, downing most of it in one gulp. "Nervous?"

"You could say that." She bent to pick up the bouquet and then self-consciously tugged at the hem of her dress. "Uhm. Could you help me with something?"

"Sure. Anything. I'm your girl Friday today."

Lexie held the bouquet aloft, doing her best to obscure her panties from view. "Would you help me fasten this on my wrist?"

"This isn't what that note was about, was it?"

Lexie grimaced. "Sort of. It's kind of an inside joke. From you know…the traffic stop. He sort of cuffed me that day." She chuckled, trying to sell the partial lie. "I guess you'd have to have been there, but it was funny at the time."

"What if someone sees?"

"They won't." *I hope.*

"Okay." Serenity placed her wineglass on a nearby table. "I'll help, but one of these days you're going to have to tell me the whole story. Promise?"

Lexie crossed her fingers on her left hand while offering her right to Serenity. "Promise."

It was crazy, but as soon as the metal cuff closed around her wrist, a sense of peace washed over her. The nerves she'd had earlier faded away.

"Where are your shoes?" Serenity scanned the room for the shoes Lexie had kicked beneath a chair.

"Not wearing them." Suddenly, she remembered her bracelet and earrings. "Shit. Can you help me with these?" She held her left wrist out. "Help me get my bracelet and earrings off, please?"

"Okay, but are you sure?" Serenity asked, even as she worked the clasp on Lexie's bracelet.

"Positive." She turned her head so her left ear faced her friend. "Earrings, please."

"What do you want me to do with these?"

"Keep them for me? I won't need them anytime soon." She had a feeling she wouldn't be needing anything for several days.

"Okay, but you've got a lot of explaining to do." Serenity opened her purse and let out a gasp. "What is your bra doing in my purse?"

"Shh! I didn't know where else to put it. Please, Sen. Don't tell anyone."

Serenity fixed her with a sly smile. "Only if you promise on…on your godson's life to tell me *everything*. Soon."

"I promise. Come on. I'm going to be late." She'd kept Ian waiting for weeks. Months, really, if she was being truthful. Another minute or two wouldn't be the end of the world, but it might earn her a punishment. If Ian punished her the way he had before, that might not be the worst thing. Smiling, she slowed to a moderate pace.

CHAPTER FIFTY-ONE

"Quiet on the set!"

Ian shot Emma a quelling look. The last thing he needed was a reminder that this, probably the most important moment of his life, was being witnessed by dozens of people and would be broadcast to millions more around the world. He wasn't nervous. He was terrified. What if she didn't show up? What if she said no?

Sending her the handcuffs and that note seemed like a good idea at the time, but standing there like an idiot, waiting for her to arrive, said otherwise. But she had to know what she was saying yes to. He thought she knew, but it was a chance he wasn't willing to take. They'd both be miserable in a relationship that didn't fulfill their basic needs. He loved Alexa too much to do that to her. So, yeah, the handcuffs and demands had been necessary. If she didn't show, he'd bear the humiliation and try to move on.

There'd never be anyone like Alexa, but he'd had a few satisfactory relationships before, and he suspected he could again. But he'd never love anyone the way he loved Alexa. She filled all the empty spaces in his soul and more than fulfilled his sexual needs. He'd been lucky to find her, and he'd be even luckier to spend the rest of his life with her. But only if she felt the same.

Off-set, people fidgeted, adding to his own agitation. He

imagined the studio audience watching via the monitors inside, taking bets on whether Alexa would show or not. And they didn't even know about the demands he'd placed on her. If they did, they'd know better than to bet on her showing.

Steve checked his watch. He raised his eyebrows in question. Ian wiped away a drop of sweat on his temple before it slid down his cheek. She was late. The question was, on purpose, or had she decided not to show at all?

She'll be here.

If only to tell him no.

Alexa wouldn't leave him hanging. If she was saying no, she'd say it to his face.

Ian glanced at the platinum band on his right pinky finger. The diamond he'd picked out for her cut into his palm as he clenched his fist. He'd done a lot of stupid things in his career. He'd run toward gun battles. Had run into burning buildings and toward cars engulfed in flames. He'd faced off with knife-wielding druggies and chased down armed assailants. Waiting for a petite dynamo of a woman, not knowing if she was his or not, was by far the most frightening thing he'd ever experienced.

A commotion off-set had him looking up. His breath caught as he locked gazes with Alexa. She was a vision in the same short cocktail dress she'd worn earlier. As he'd demanded, she carried the roses in the crook of her right arm, and her feet were bare. Imagining where else she would be bare if she'd followed his instructions sent a rush of blood south. Dear god, she was going to be the death of him. But what a way to go.

Get a grip.

She hasn't said yes yet.

When she came to a stop before him, he took a second to search her eyes for answers to all the questions swirling through his brain, but found only questions in her gaze.

"Ian."

His name sounded like a prayer on her lips, and he couldn't take another second of waiting and wondering and hoping. He took her left hand in his right and dropped to one knee. The move startled a gasp from her. She started to raise her right hand to her face but stopped when the cuffs jiggled. The sound drew Ian's gaze to the band of silver metal around her right wrist. It took his brain a fraction of a second to register the scrap of black lace tied around the chain linking the cuffs, but once it did, a potent mixture of emotions flooded his system. Hope. Lust. Possessiveness. Gratitude. And love. So much love that there was no room for fear or his lungs in his chest cavity. Tears blurred his vision, and he sniffed them back, bringing a tender smile to Alexa's lips.

"Ian?"

"Alexa," he sniffed. Forcing air into his lungs, he gazed into the eyes of the woman he loved beyond all reason. "You are the most beautiful person I've ever known, inside and out. You are fierce and brave, loyal, caring, and selfless. I knew the first moment I saw you that you would change my life, and I wasn't wrong. You are everything I ever wanted in a woman, a life partner, and everything I never knew I needed. I want you to be mine in every sense of the word, and more than that, I want to be yours."

He released her hand long enough to remove the ring from his pinky. Then, taking her hand in his again, he held the ring aloft. "Alexa Hanson, will you marry me?"

***

"Yes. Oh, God, yes!"

Lexie's whole body trembled as Ian slid the stunning diamond onto her ring finger. The moment it settled into place, he lifted his gaze to hers and mouthed, thank you. His gaze flicked to her shackled wrist, then to her face. An unholy fire blazed in the depth of his eyes as he rose to his feet and took her face between his palms. His lips brushed hers once, twice. Trailed kisses over both cheekbones. His warm breath fanned her ear. His voice, low and gravely, sent a shiver down her spine. "You were late." Then he crushed his mouth over hers in a kiss that spoke of passion and wicked promises. The roses forgotten, Lexie melted against him, taking all that he gave and returning it with equal fervor. God, she'd missed him and couldn't wait until they were alone so she could tell him all the things she should have said weeks ago.

He ended the kiss, his eyes promising to make it up to her, and more, soon. Grasping her left hand in his, he created a path for them through the throngs of support personnel and past his parents, who called out congratulations as Ian and Lexie sped by. She didn't know where they were going. Didn't care as long as there were no cameras and no audience. They came to a stop next to Ian's personal vehicle where he pressed her up against the passenger side door and kissed her senseless.

"Are you sure?" he asked when they finally came up for air.

Wanting to give him all the words in private, she nodded. Wrapping her free hand around his nape, she brought him down for another kiss she hoped conveyed everything he wanted to hear. When his hands roamed beneath the hem of her dress, she broke the kiss. "Take me home. Please?"

Ian wrenched the car door open and lifted her onto the seat. After securing her seatbelt, he closed the door and rounded to the driver's side. The drive to his condo on the other side of town seemed to take forever, but couldn't have been more than a few minutes. Ian alternated between watching the road and watching her, but remained silent. Lexie spent the time rehearsing the speech she planned to deliver. Ian had seemed okay with her head nod, but he deserved all the words. And, truth be told, she needed to speak them out loud. To him. She'd heard them a million times in her own mind, but spoken words held more power than thoughts. And actions said even more.

The moment they were safely inside Ian's home, he flipped the bouquet over, released the cuff holding the stems together, and tossed the blooms onto the coffee table. He fingered the lace panties then allowed her shackled wrist to drop to her side. "I think I'll leave the panties right where they are." Lexie stood still as he moved behind her and lowered the zipper on her dress. A gentle nudge sent the sequined piece to the floor, where it pooled around her ankles. Ian pulled her wrists to the small of her back and fastened her left wrist, so she stood naked and bound before him.

His gaze met hers. "On your knees, Alexa."

"Sir. Please? May I speak?"

"If this is about your punishment, Alexa, save your breath. You were late. When I said not to be late, it was a warning and a promise."

"It's not about my punishment, sir. I knew what would happen if I was late, so I made sure I was." His eyebrows rose, but he remained silent, so Lexie went on. "I wanted to say these things to you in the gazebo, but they're for your ears only, sir."

"Go on."

"I'm sorry, Ian. So very sorry. I never should have left. In my defense, I needed time to think, and it's almost impossible to do when you look at me the way you do. And I can't think at all when you touch me. I was scared. Not of you. I know you'd never harm me, but of my own feelings. No one has ever made me feel the way you make me feel. With you, I feel loved, cherished, and empowered.

"You told me I'd find freedom in being bound, and I thought you were nuts. Until you showed me what freedom looked like. I thought I knew what pleasure was, but I didn't. Not until you forced me to give you control over my body. That last day, when you gagged me? My thoughts were trapped in my head. I couldn't argue with you. I couldn't tell you what I wanted or needed. I couldn't beg you to make me come. All I could do was accept the pleasure you gave me. Your touch made me forget everything. I think I might have forgotten my own name for a while. I came so hard, Ian. So hard I thought I might die from how wonderful it felt."

"I needed you inside me so bad, but you held back, wanting everything. I was hurting, Ian. What I did in the bathroom was inexcusable. I know that now. I should have told you what I needed then, but I was so scared to give you everything. The look of betrayal on your face when you found me…it gutted me. I realized what I'd done immediately, but the damage was done. I'd hurt you, and for that I'm so very sorry.

"I thought distance would make me forget the things you'd taught me. I was wrong. I couldn't stop thinking about you. I convinced myself I didn't need you, that I could do those things to myself. I blindfolded myself and used a pair of socks for a gag. I made myself come, imagining it was your hands on me, and not my own.

"I hated every minute of those times, Ian. I cried myself to sleep and then dreamed of you. I fought myself until I couldn't fight it anymore. I love you, Ian. And I need you."

Lexie sank to her knees. Thighs spread open, she dipped her chin to her chest. "I'm yours, Sir. Everything I am, body, heart, and soul, is yours if you'll have me."

Ian crouched in front of her. With one finger beneath her chin, he commanded her attention. Their gazes met, hers watery, his a soft caress. "You were mine the day we met, Alexa." He leaned in and placed a gentle kiss on her trembling lips. "Here are the things I wanted to say to you in the gazebo, but were for your ears only. I love you. More than life itself. I'll never hold you back, but I will hold onto you. I'll bind you, and I'll set you free. Your pleasure is my pleasure, and I want nothing more than to touch you every day. To worship your body, mind, and soul. I want to make love to you and build a life and a family with you. I meant it when I said I'm yours. Body, heart, and soul. If you'll have me."

"Ian. Please. I need you."

CHAPTER FIFTY-TWO

His name on her lips felt like an affirmation of everything he was. A lot of words had passed between them, but actions often spoke more eloquently. Ian had always considered himself a man of action. He helped Lexie to her feet, then with a hand wrapped around the chain linking her wrists, he urged her toward the bedroom.

He positioned her at the foot of the bed. "Stand right here." Facing her with the width of the mattress between them, he toed off his shoes, stuffed his socks inside them, and kicked them beneath the bed. Straightening, he eyed her with appreciation. "You're the most beautiful woman I've ever seen." His suit coat was next, carelessly tossed onto an overstuffed chair in a corner of the room. "I'm not telling you anything you don't know. You have a mirror. You see how men look at you. I'm not blind. I see it, too. But you have an inner beauty that shines through, and that's what makes you truly beautiful." He unfastened the buttons on his shirt cuffs and then yanked on the tie knotted at his throat. He pulled the length of silk free and wrapped it into a coil around his fist. Her eyes tracked his every movement. Was she thinking of the last time they were together when he'd used a necktie to blindfold her? Sensory deprivation was an excellent way to focus a submissive's attention, but today, he wanted all her attention focused on him. Watching her closely, he tossed the coiled tie on top of his suit coat. Her gaze followed its trajectory, then biting her lower lip, she rubbed her thighs together.

"Feet apart, Alexa." Her gaze met his. "Have you already forgotten who your orgasms belong to?"

"No, sir." She inched her feet apart.

"More."

When her feet were shoulder-width apart, he rewarded her. "Good girl." Her shoulders lifted with pride. Ian made a mental note to praise her often. "Are you wet for me, Alexa?" She stood her ground as he approached, stopping when they were almost toe to toe. Leaning in so his starched shirt abraded her nipples, he whispered in her ear. "Don't move. Don't make a sound, sweetheart."

He thrust a hand between her legs, cupping her sex hard. Lexie pressed her lips tight and clamped her eyes shut. "Look at me, Alexa. Know it's me doing this to you." He let his fingers explore her folds and tease at her opening. "You made me wait at the gazebo, and before that, I waited weeks for you to realize what I've always known. You're mine. Your pussy is mine." He flicked his thumb over her clit. "It's your turn to wait."

Ian jerked his hand from the cradle of her thighs and stepped back. He held his wet hand up for her to see. "You're swollen and wet. Ready to be fucked. But guess what? I'm not going to fuck you today."

Her eyes pleaded with him, just as he hoped they would. She expected punishment for her behavior, and she was going to get it. It just wasn't going to be the spanking she no doubt anticipated. There were other ways to get his point across, and he'd chosen a mind fuck instead of a physical one.

Ian returned to his spot out of arm's reach. Punishment was often uncomfortable for both parties involved, and this one was no exception. He didn't trust himself to be close to her and not touch her. Not make love to her. At least not until she realized the consequences of her actions. Just thinking about Alexa trying to recreate the pleasure he'd given her invoked a maelstrom of emotions. Rage that she'd taken matters into her own hands. Pain that she'd needed him and couldn't bring herself to admit it. Jealousy that he hadn't been there to see it. As he slowly unbuttoned his shirt, he vowed to make her repeat the performance sometime. He'd jack off watching her and come all over her hand while her pussy clenched around her own fingers.

He tugged his shirttails free, shrugged the garment off, and tossed it on top of his jacket and tie. He wasn't vain, but he knew what he had, and it never failed to impress. "Want to see what you're missing? What would be fucking you right now if you hadn't made me wait?" At her slight nod, he released his belt buckle and then slid the leather free of the belt loops. Doubling it over, he slapped it against his hand. He smiled at the satisfying sound of leather against his palm, then tossed the belt onto the end of the bed as if he planned to use it on her later. He had no such intentions, but she didn't know that.

Eyes on hers, he unbuttoned and unzipped his slacks. Hooking his thumbs in the waistband, he shoved his trousers and boxers to his knees. A leg shake sent them the rest of the way to the floor. He kicked them aside, then hands on his hips, he let her see what she'd been missing. What he'd kept only for her since the day they'd met. His cock stood tall and proud, more than eager to be inside her. To officially claim what was his.

"Ian."

His name on her lips, weak and trembling, was exactly what he'd wanted to hear. He closed the distance between them. Taking her face in the palm of his hands, he brought his lips down on hers, and kissed her with all the tenderness he felt for her. She kissed him back with a hunger he felt down to his toes. Breaking the kiss, he clasped his hand around the handcuff chain and steered her to the end of the bed. He nudged a knee into the back of one of hers. "Up on the bed. Lie face down."

After helping her into position on the bed, he checked the drawer in his bedside table then climbed on the bed to straddle her thighs. With one hand pressed into the center of her back, he explored every inch of her back and buttocks with the other before reaching for the belt he'd tossed onto the bed. The buckle rattled, startling a gasp from Lexie. Ian dragged the belt across her ass cheeks, letting her feel the smooth leather against her skin. She deserved a spanking for her behavior, but letting her believe he was going to use the belt on her was enough to get his point across. She'd think twice from now on before defying him or suffer the consequences.

Ian tossed the belt aside, and leaning forward, he whispered in her ear. "Good girl. You took your punishment very well. Now, for your reward."

He retrieved the key to the cuffs from the nightstand drawer and released her wrists from their prison. After massaging her arms, he rose to his knees and flipped her over to her back. Ian braced himself over her on one arm. With his free hand, he wiped her tear-stained cheeks. "Shh, sweetheart. Your punishment is over. We won't speak of the things you did ever again." He kissed her softly on the lips. "Spread your legs for me, Alexa. Let me in."

"But…you said…"

Ian smiled at her inability to string words together. "I said I wouldn't fuck you, and I'm not going to." Lowering himself to his forearms on either side of her head, it was all he could do to form sentences of his own. Her body beneath his felt like Heaven. "Open for me, Alexa. I'm going to love you all night long and for the rest of my life."

EPILOGUE

Lexie couldn't stop the tears from forming even as Ian settled between her obediently spread legs. Why she'd run from this man, she didn't know. He looked at her like she was a goddess, and his touch took her breath away. She was more than ready to give herself to him. Bringing her knees up, she offered herself to him.

The head of his cock nudged at her entrance. Lexie groaned and flexed her hips, trying to coax him inside, but Ian pulled away, leaving her sobbing in frustration.

"Shh, sweetheart." He stroked her damp cheeks with his thumbs. "I'm going to make you mine in a moment. I promise. But first, tell me. Are you on birth control?"

Her prescription had lapsed during her hiatus back home, and since she hadn't planned on having sex with Ian or anyone else, she'd forgotten all about it. Lexie shook her head. "No."

"Good," was all he said as he entered her with one powerful thrust that rocked her world and had her reaching for his broad shoulders to anchor her.

When he didn't move, just held perfectly still. Their bodies joined in the most intimate way possible, Lexie forced her eyes open. Ian's face hovered above hers, his jaw tense, his eyes blazing.

"Do you feel it, Alexa? The way we fit together? We were made for each other."

"Yes." She clasped her ankles at the small of his back, loving the feel of his cock inside her and his body pressing hers into the mattress. "Don't leave me. Please. You feel too good."

"I'm not going anywhere, sweetheart." He lowered his lips to hers, and when his tongue begged for entrance, she parted her lips and let him in. Then, ever so slowly, he began to move, easing almost all the way out of her and then entering her in increments so reverent she thought she might die for wanting more. Lexie raised her hips in encouragement, but once again, he held himself still. His smile was tender as he studied her face like she was a priceless work of art. "Always in such a hurry, sweet girl. Don't make me restrain you. Not tonight. I want to feel your hands on me. Claim me, baby, just as I intend to claim you." He rocked his hips, out and in again, so deep Lexie saw stars. "I don't want anything between us tonight. Nothing." Another rock of his hips, and she felt his balls slap her ass. "Let me love you, Alexa."

Ian arched his back, bending to take her breast in his hand and squeeze. "You're so beautiful, sweetheart." He dipped his head and took her nipple in his mouth. Lexie cried out and grabbed fistfuls of his hair, holding him to her breast as waves of pleasure pulled at her womb. He released her nipple with an audible *pop*, then shifted to give the other one the same attention. Delirious with need, she rocked her hips once more.

"None of that, baby, or it's going to be over too soon." Bracing on one forearm above her, he placed his free hand on her hip, pinning her to the bed. "Next time, I promise you can move all you want, but this first time, I want you to feel everything. I want you to feel me inside you, stretching you, filling you, giving you my very soul."

Lexie's heart seemed to beat in time with his thrusts. In. Beat. Out. Beat. On repeat as their gazes locked and held. She'd never felt anything like this before. Frustration slowly waned to be replaced by desire. Desire gave way to need, and need ebbed into a sense of belonging so deep she couldn't stop the orgasm that exploded through her body.

"That's it, baby. Come for me." Lexie heard his voice through the sweet violence racking her body. Then he collapsed on top of her, and with both arms wrapped around her, he tunneled deep into her core and, with a guttural cry, gave her his soul.

Ian rolled off of Alexa, taking her with him so they lay facing each other, his still hard cock nestled in the warmth of her body. Hardly believing she was finally his, he let his hand wander from her hip, along the slope of her ribcage, to test the resilience of her breast. "Are you okay?" he asked. "I probably should have asked if you were okay with that before I loved you without protection."

"It was perfect, Ian." She brushed a fresh wave of tears from her eyes. "It was beautiful, and more than I ever imagined love could be." She shrugged. "I don't want there to be anything between us, ever. I know you can't stay inside me forever, but I like knowing you left a part of you behind. I'd be good with you doing that every morning, so no matter where we go or what we do, I'll always have part of you with me."

"And if the part of me I gave you today grows into something more?"

She smiled as she cupped his cheek in the palm of her hand. "I'll love you even more than I do now."

This had to be a dream, but no dream ever felt as good as her body wrapped around his cock. And he'd never woken from a dream feeling as complete as he did right that minute. Alexa was his, and he'd given her all that he was. Together, they'd build a life together. A family. He caressed her face, mirroring her tender touch. "I don't think it's possible to love you more than I do right now, but we've got until the end of time to find out."

"How much do you love me?"

Ian rolled her to her back and covered her. "Let me show you."

ABOUT THE AUTHOR

USA Today Best-Selling author Roz Lee is the author of over thirty romances. The first, The Lust Boat, was born of an idea acquired while on a Caribbean cruise with her family and soon blossomed into a five-book series originally published by Red Sage. Following her love of baseball, she turned her attention to sexy athletes in tight pants, writing the critically acclaimed Mustangs Baseball series.

Roz has been married to her best friend and high school sweetheart for over four decades. Roz and her husband have two grown daughters and are the proud grandparents to three adorable grandkids. Roz and her husband live in the wilds of New Jersey with their Labrador Retriever, Bud which is code for Big Unruly Dog.

Even though Roz has lived on both coasts, her heart lies in between, in Texas. A Texan by birth, she can trace her family back to the Republic of Texas. With roots that deep, she says, "You can't ever really leave."

When Roz isn't writing, she's reading or traipsing around the country on one adventure or another. No trip is too small, no tourist trap too cheesy, and no road unworthy of travel.

Learn more at www.RozLee.net